THE CRIMSON CHASE

Also by Cap Daniels

The Chase Fulton Novels Series
Book One: *The Opening Chase*
Book Two: *The Broken Chase*
Book Three: *The Stronger Chase*
Book Four: *The Unending Chase*
Book Five: *The Distant Chase*
Book Six: *The Entangled Chase*
Book Seven: *The Devil's Chase*
Book Eight: *The Angel's Chase*
Book Nine: *The Forgotten Chase*
Book Ten: *The Emerald Chase*
Book Eleven: *The Polar Chase*
Book Twelve: *The Burning Chase*
Book Thirteen: *The Poison Chase*
Book Fourteen: *The Bitter Chase*
Book Fifteen: *The Blind Chase*
Book Sixteen: *The Smuggler's Chase*
Book Seventeen: *The Hollow Chase*
Book Eighteen: *The Sunken Chase*
Book Nineteen: *The Darker Chase*
Book Twenty: *The Abandoned Chase*
Book Twenty-One: *The Gambler's Chase*
Book Twenty-Two: *The Arctic Chase*
Book Twenty-Three: *The Diamond Chase*
Book Twenty-Four: *The Phantom Chase*
Book Twenty-Five: *The Crimson Chase*
Book Twenty-Six: *The Silent Chase*

THE CRIMSON CHASE

CHASE FULTON NOVEL #25

CAP DANIELS

ANCHOR WATCH
PUBLISHING
** USA **

The Crimson Chase
Chase Fulton Novel #25
Cap Daniels

This is a work of fiction. Names, characters, places, historical events, and incidents are the product of the author's imagination or have been used fictitiously. Although many locations such as marinas, airports, hotels, restaurants, etc. used in this work actually exist, they are used fictitiously and may have been relocated, exaggerated, or otherwise modified by creative license for the purpose of this work. Although many characters are based on personalities, physical attributes, skills, or intellect of actual individuals, all the characters in this work are products of the author's imagination.

Published by:

ANCHOR WATCH
—— PUBLISHING ——
** USA **

13-Digit ISBN: 978-1-951021-55-9
Library of Congress Control Number: 2024931433

Cover Design: German Creative

Printed in the United States of America

The Crimson Chase

CAP DANIELS

Chapter 1
My Best Russian

Spring 2011

I grabbed a handful of the man's filthy hair and yanked his head so far back that his Adam's apple protruded like a badly broken joint. With my face only inches from his, I growled in the angriest Russian I could muster. "*Ty otvetish' na moi voprosy ili umresh' ochen' medlenno.*"

My victim writhed and twisted in desperate attempts to escape my wrath, but I continued undaunted. I hadn't been the one to tie his hands behind his back with the rough, sinewy rope that was cutting into his flesh every time he fought against the restraint. The man who'd bound our victim's hands was a hardened warrior with a lifetime of unthinkable horrors dancing in his head. He was a man in whom I had boundless faith, and for whom I had unmeasurable respect. Clark Johnson, former Green Beret, waited only an arm's length away with the tools necessary to break the will of our prisoner.

Everyone broke. It was merely a matter of keeping them alive long enough and inflicting enough fear.

It was the fear, not the pain that drew weakness from the depths of a man's soul. It was the knowledge that the torture would never end and the agony would never cease, dismantling even the strongest resolve and leaving a man with no other option than to become a traitor of his own country, of his own people, of his own broken will.

Clark and I would destroy the man's belief that he could and would survive the coming hours, days, or weeks, if that's what it took. We would eat, sleep, and laugh, but our prey would know no such luxury. He would know only fear, exhaustion, pain, and the separation of his self-confidence from his primal need to remain alive at all costs.

In my best Russian-accented English, I spoke barely loud enough to be heard over the pain I was inflicting. "I know you understand Russian, but I will play with you game of pretend. Tell to me what I want to hear, and maybe I will kill you quickly."

To my delight, the man spat in my face and cursed every ancestor in my family tree. I couldn't have been more pleased with his defiance, but he would never see the side of me that wanted him to resist to the point of imminent death.

Still pretending to be a devoted Muscovite, I said, "You may not talk for me, but you will talk for my friend who takes great pleasure in his work. For you, though, it will be opposite of pleasure. It will be *predel'naya agoniya*."

With a length of the same burly rope that bound the man's hands, Clark wrapped the victim's ankles with several rounds and tossed the other end across a pipe suspended several feet above our heads, inside the ramshackle barn deep in the forest where the man never imagined he would die. We hoisted together, and the man collapsed to the dirt floor with his feet rising with every heave.

When we stopped hauling, he was upside down with his head a few feet above the ground. Clark grinned in the man's inverted face, but he didn't say a word. His Spanish wasn't bad, but Clark's

Russian was abysmal. Fortunately, the language he was about to speak didn't require words.

My partner pulled a dirty towel from a canvas bag and wrapped it around the man's head, tucking in the end so it would remain in place for the coming terror he was about to unleash. It started with one quart of muddy, rancid water. The towel absorbed most of it, but some of the water found its way back to the ground under our feet. The portion that made its way through the towel and up the man's nose was his first taste of what Clark Johnson called "tactical baptism."

The man bucked and snorted in wasted resistance, but we were a long way from being finished. The next application of water was far more generous than the first. It came from a water hose connected to a cistern on the roof. The only benefit of the new source of water for our upside-down friend was the cleanliness of the captured rainwater. Everything else was a new layer of Hell for him. He choked, gagged, and contorted his body in directions no one should ever experience.

After two minutes that must've felt like eons for him, I unwrapped the towel and hissed, "You will now tell to me what I want to know."

I had predicted he wouldn't last more than an hour, but Clark disagreed. Before we captured the man, he'd said, "The kid's got the goods, College Boy. I don't think he'll break until we starve him nearly to death."

Instead of breaking down and submitting to my will, he did the last thing I could've expected. He took a long, full breath of dry air and bucked like an enraged mustang, landing a forehead shot to my nose and sending blood in every direction. Clark reacted before I could. He shoved the hose into the man's open mouth and wrapped the towel back around his head. The technique wouldn't drown an upside-down victim, but it would certainly make him believe he'd found himself twenty thousand leagues under the sea.

Covered by the man's furious retching, Clark tried to hide his amusement, but he found it almost impossible. Through fits of laughter, he said, "Let me take a look at that pretty nose of yours."

I shoved him away and cursed under my breath as I pawed at my face and tried not to let the man hear my groans of pain. I wasn't angry. I was proud. I'd like to think I would've done the same thing if our roles had been reversed. I'd gotten careless and put myself in a position I shouldn't have. It was my fault. Not his. If you kick a hornet's nest, you'd better be prepared to get stung, and our bee of the day had made his first sting.

I made no effort to clean the blood from my nose. Instead, I rubbed my palms in the muddy earth beneath my adversary and smeared the filth on my face. When Clark yanked the soaked towel from the man's head, I was back, precisely where I'd been when he stung me the first time, but I wasn't so careless the second time.

I drew and pressed my knife against his cheek. "Try that again, Amerikanets."

He spat bloody water from his mouth and snorted. "I hope it hurt, you commie bastard. Cut me down, and I'll show you what this Amerikanets can do. I'll shove that knife right up your—"

Clark drove a fist into the man's gut before he could finish his foolish threat. The towel went back in place, and the waterboarding continued until I believed the man was on the verge of intentionally drowning himself to end the torture.

"Cut him down," I ordered in my ridiculous accent, and Clark complied.

He fell, landing with a thud in the puddle of water, blood, and spittle. We jerked him to his feet, tied another piece of rope around his wrists, and tossed the rope across the same pipe. It took only a few pulls to hoist his hands beyond the limit of his comfort, but we didn't stop there. We pulled another few inches until he rose onto his toes with his arms hoisted painfully behind his back.

I took a knee in front of him. "You are brave, Amerikanets, but you are foolish. You have proven you are not broken by short applications of pain, so we will now try endurance."

We left him hanging and in agony while we stepped from the barn.

As I washed my face, I said, "I guess you were right. He's not gonna be easy."

Clark shrugged. "I've been at this game a long time. I can always tell who'll crumble in the first hour and who'll be a pain in my butt. This guy definitely falls into the second category. Now, let me take a look at that nose." He examined my face. "Yep, it's broke. There ain't no doubt about that. You're going to be even uglier than you were when you woke up this morning, and that's an accomplishment."

I shoved him away. "What are we going to do next?"

"I say we put him in the coffin, but try not to let him kick your butt again."

We let him hang around for almost an hour to ensure his arms cramped to the point of unbearable pain before we cut him down. He wasn't as feisty as he'd been, but he was still a handful, and it took both of us to shove his six-foot frame into the five-foot vertical coffin in the corner of the barn. The box was two feet square and five feet tall and specifically designed to make it impossible to stand upright. He would have to flex his knees, forcing his kneecaps into the front of the box, and contort his neck into a position that would leave his spine tingling for days. A small hole in the top of the coffin allowed us to insert the water hose in a humanitarian gesture to give him an occasional drink and wake him up every fifteen minutes should he find the wherewithal to settle his brain long enough to catch a nap.

Two days later, after every enhanced interrogation technique we could think of, it finally happened. It was maple syrup and a few hundred hungry ants that sent him over the edge.

He shook his head with what little strength remained in his body. "Okay, I'm done. I quit."

Clark's water hose returned, and the ants were gone.

I cut his arms free and stuck a Gatorade in his hand. "There's no need to quit. You passed two days ago. Everything after that was just an exercise to prove to you just how far you can be taken without breaking."

He collapsed to the ground, devoured the Gatorade, and growled. "I hate you, him, everything about you, everything about him, and I hope your nose throbs the rest of your life and never stops bleeding."

I tossed him a protein bar. "You've got to work on your Russian. Eastern European chicks dig Amerikanets who speak their language."

He showed me a finger, and Clark said, "Hey, that's not nice. After all the kindness and love we showed you over the last few days, I expected a little appreciation."

He rubbed his wrists. "I've got one for you, too, old timer."

Clark pulled another Gatorade from the cooler and started to toss it to the trainee, but he stopped himself. "I think this old timer will just keep this one and stick you with an IV or another garden hose."

He shook his head and crawled toward the cooler. "How long did you two last when you went through this?"

Clark gave me a wink. "I love it when they ask that question." He turned back to the recruit and kicked the cooler a little farther away. "When I went through SERE school—before you were born —it was serious. Nothing like this touchy-feely crap we do now, but it was a walk in the park compared to the real thing."

That froze him in his tracks. "The real thing? You've been interrogated?"

Clark said, "Grow up, kid. Your turn is coming, and you'll do all right for a little while. We all do. I've never been through an interrogation I thought I'd survive. You knew we wouldn't kill you, and you still broke."

He eyed my partner for a long moment. "That's where you're wrong. I did start to think you were going to kill me, and I'd reached my limit."

"No, you hadn't," I said. "There is no limit when you're hanging upside down in a barn in Siberia and your team's out there in the snow killing bad guys. Trust me. You'd rather die than give them up."

"Come on," he said. "You guys are dinosaurs. We're not at war with Russia anymore. That was old-school Cold War stuff. If you were still in the game, you'd be fighting the fight and not teaching the Survival, Evasion, Resistance, and Escape course here at The Ranch."

I cocked my head at my partner. "Do you want to take this one, or should I?"

"Go ahead, College Boy. If you leave anything out, I'll be glad to fill in the details."

I took a seat beside the battered, beaten, potential clandestine operator lying on the ground and pointed at Clark. "He's here because six months ago he was shot down by an RPG fired by a Mexican drug cartel while he was at the controls of a Huey. In case you don't know what a Huey is, it's an old-school Cold War–era helicopter that's still in use today, all over the world, by all kinds of forces."

He said, "Of course I know what a—"

I placed the heel of my right boot on his shoulder and rolled him over. "I'm still talking. I'll let you know when it's your turn.

He not only survived the crash, but he also maneuvered what was left of the chopper away from the rest of our team on the ground, resulting in no injuries other than his own. That was less than six months ago. He's here to teach the things he's learned in thirty years on the battlefield to you, a guy who, so far, has zero days on the battlefield."

The recruit turned to face Clark. "I didn't know. I'm sorry."

My partner huffed. "Did he tell you it was your turn to talk?"

"No, sir."

"Then don't talk. I'll take it from here." The recruit sat up, and Clark pointed at me. "Don't look at me. Look at him. He was exactly where you are fifteen years ago. He was a cocky little snotnosed hotshot who thought he knew it all. And just like you, he was wrong." He motioned toward my boot. "Show the kid your leg, College Boy."

I pulled up my pants to reveal the prosthetic, and Clark continued his story.

"See that, kid? That dude you just called a dinosaur has been kicking bad guys' butts for three years with a fake foot. But that ain't all . . . You see those hearing aids behind his ears? He got those because he got blown up by a pair of Russian MiGs . . . and survived. If all that's not enough to make you swallow your disrespect, that man is here teaching this course because he's taking time off the battlefield to take care of his wife who just had a liver transplant. Oh, and I almost forgot the most important part. The donor liver came from the gut of that man's former girlfriend, who used to be a Russian SVR assassin. So, just in case your momma didn't teach you to respect your elders, I'm telling you right now, you better learn to respect the men who've been there and done that, and especially the ones who are still doing it."

Chapter 2
Postgraduate Education

A training officer collected our most recent graduate from the Clark and Chase School of Performing Arts and whisked him off to some unknown place for the next phase of his training, leaving Clark and me drinking Gatorade and replaying memories of our days of ignorance and arrogance.

"Were we ever really that green?"

Clark crushed and capped his bottle. "I wasn't, but you were. I can't believe you survived that first mission of yours. You do know you screwed that one up, don't you?"

"What are you talking about? I eliminated my target. In fact, I eliminated all three of my targets."

He held up a finger. "That's not entirely true. Anya got one of them."

"Okay, but she wouldn't have gotten him if I hadn't been involved."

"Believe what you want, College Boy. The fact remains that your real purpose on that mission was to draw Suslik out so the real gunners— like me—could take him out."

I finished my bottle. "If that's what I had been instructed to do, that's what I would've done. I was ordered to kill the bucktoothed psychopath, and that's what I did. If you're going to wind me up and point me toward a target, I'm going to bring you back a shopping bag full of body parts."

He laughed. "Yeah, maybe, but you're lucky I came along when I did."

I tossed a piece of gravel at him. "I hope you're not expecting me to get all sentimental, 'cause that ain't gonna happen. I am glad you came along, though. It's been quite a ride, hasn't it?"

He played with his toothpick. "What do you mean *has been*? We're not off the crazy train yet." He motioned in the direction that our most recent student departed. "Do you think that guy's ready to replace us?"

I laughed. "That guy's not ready to tie his own shoes."

He chuckled. "You know what they say. The proof is in the pot the kettled called black."

"What?"

"You know what I mean. They're going to cut that kid loose pretty soon and send him on some meaningless mission where he can't get killed, and he's going to fail."

"What makes you think he'll fail?" I asked.

"They all fail on their first attempt. If they're lucky enough to stay alive, though, they just might learn something and do it a little better the second time. We've both been through it. You know the game."

"When I finished here at The Ranch, they sent me out on my own with a new car, a briefcase full of money, and a sailboat to live on. Will he go to a team?"

"Who knows?" he said. "That decision is above our pay grade. We'll probably never know. I've been doing this a long time, and I don't know ten percent of the operators who do what we do in this outfit."

"How many of us are there?"

He shrugged. "I've got no idea. I'm responsible for you. You're responsible for your team. It's compartmentalization at its finest."

"I thought you had another team who you handled, too."

He contorted his face and looked away. "No. I used to have another one, but they took it away."

"Why?"

"That doesn't matter. Let's get something to eat."

"Wait a minute," I said. "Did I have anything to do with you losing the other team?"

"I told you it doesn't matter, College Boy. It's just the way things go."

"No, hang on. I'm serious. What happened?"

"It wasn't you, okay?"

"Then what was it? We've been through too much to keep secrets."

"It was me, okay? I was supposed to sit in my nice, cushy, air-conditioned office in Miami and point you toward the fight, but I'm not that kind of dog."

I furrowed my brow. "What does that mean? You're not *what* kind of dog?"

"A pointer or a setter, College Boy. Don't you know anything about dogs? I'm a pit bull."

"You do slobber a lot and fall asleep everywhere you get comfortable."

The piece of gravel I'd tossed at him came back at me, and I swatted it out of the air. "You were never cut out to be a handler. You're a shooter like the rest of us, and I, for one, am glad they took the other team from you. I'm not good at sharing."

We walked down a path that felt entirely different than it had fifteen years before.

I said, "You know, I think this is the first time I've ever walked on this trail."

He stopped in his tracks. "What are you talking about? This is the most used strip of dirt in this whole place. How could you have never been on this trail?"

"I didn't say I'd never been on the trail. I said I'd never walked on it. If I was on this piece of dirt while I was in training, I was running. If anybody caught me walking, I was about to have a bad day."

The chow hall at The Ranch was nothing special, but the food was some of the best in Virginia, and the portions were Mongo-sized. Every trainee who'd ever come through The Ranch needed five thousand calories a day to stay alive. Even Clark couldn't finish the massive pile of food they put on his plate.

Just as we were about to deliver our plates back to the window, an old familiar voice echoed through the chow hall. "There you are. I've been looking all over for you two."

I turned to see the most terrifying training officer who's ever lived, and I leapt to my feet. "It's good to see you, Gunny. I didn't know you were still around this place."

"Semi-retired is what they call it. I've got another word for it. They keep me around just enough to prevent this place from going soft. How'd our boy do in SERE?"

"He did all right," I said. "It took us three and a half days to break him."

Gunny turned to Clark. "Did you baptize him?"

"You know it. That was day one. He broke Chase's nose while I was doing it."

"I've got high hopes for that kid. He reminds me a lot of you, Chase. He was a football player from somewhere in Ohio or Kansas. One of those places like that."

"How'd he end up here?" I asked.

"It's a long story, but the short version is, he was home from college during his junior year, and some coked-up gang of thugs thought they'd have a little fun with a home invasion. They picked the wrong home. The thugs killed that boy's mom and dad, but the boy made them pay. He killed two of them with a fireplace poker, broke one guy's back, and beat the fourth guy so bad that he'll never eat solid food again."

Clark lowered his gaze. "That kid? Are you sure?"

Gunny said, "Oh, I'm sure. I saw the pictures myself. The judge in that Podunk county was my platoon leader in Vietnam. He called me up and said he had a kid who needed a place to let off a little steam for a few decades, so we brought him here."

"Can he shoot?" I asked.

Gunny pointed at our plates. "Just leave those right there. Somebody else will get them. I want you two to come with me."

We followed the old warrior through the concrete block building that had likely been on that site since World War II. He led us down the stairs to his cramped, damp, tiny office that I remembered all too well. The metal filing cabinet with a hole in one side reminded me of the day when Gunny stuck his K-Bar through the sleeve of my shirt and pinned me to that cabinet while I thought I was winning the fight. It didn't take long for me to realize the fight was already over, and I had lost the instant it began.

Gunny caught me staring at the slit in the cabinet and groaned. "You know, you did a lot better than I expected you to back then, Mr. Fulton."

I laughed. "I don't remember doing very well that particular day, Gunny."

"Well, maybe not that day, but overall, you did all right."

I pulled up one of the old metal folding chairs and took a seat. "What did you bring us down here to see?"

Gunny dropped himself onto his chair and pulled a file from a drawer. He rubbed the file between his thumb and fingers for a moment before sliding it across the desk. I reached for the file, and he planted his fist on it. His face said he was having second thoughts about what he was doing, but he didn't resist enough to keep me from sliding the file from beneath his knuckles. My eyes never left his as I laid the folder on my lap and he looked away first.

He said, "Ah, what are they going to do? Fire me? Go on. Open it."

Paper-clipped to the inside of the front page was a black-and-white picture of the boy who'd endured three and a half days with Clark and me doing our best to break him without killing him. I studied the picture in the file against the picture burned into my mind. The determination, the anger, and the fire were all there in both pictures, but they'd somehow been honed into spear tips by the men and women who took the boy in that black-and-white picture and turned him into a weapon. Would he be a surgeon like me, or a freight train like Clark?

Two dozen pages remained in the folder, but I didn't need to see them. It didn't matter what his name was or when he was born. It didn't matter if he got caught smoking pot in high school or stealing street signs when the sun went down in whatever nowhere place that had been his home. Behind those defiant eyes, and behind the forehead that had broken my nose when I got careless, was the mind of a dangerous animal on the precipice of becoming a predator.

I closed the file and tossed it back onto Gunny's desk. "I don't need to read it. I don't care what it says. I want him."

Gunny recoiled. "You want him? What does that mean?"

"I want him on my team. He's raw and green, but there's something there. He's got that thing—that intangible thing that the three of us have."

Gunny shoved the file back into the drawer. "I wasn't trying to sell him to you. I wanted you to psychoanalyze him and tell me if we created a warrior or a monster."

I pointed through his desk. "There's nothing in that stack of paperwork that'll answer that question. You've created both. It's up to the rest of us to figure out how to control him."

Gunny propped up his feet, lit a cigar, and tossed the lighter onto the desk. "And you think you can do that?"

"Since Dr. Richter's not an option anymore, can you think of anybody else you'd rather have poking around in that boy's head . . . other than me?"

He studied his cigar as a stream of white smoke trailed toward the ceiling. "Do you know why we sent Clark to Jekyll Island after your first mission?"

My mind flashed back to the day I met the man who'd become not only my training officer, but a brother in every sense of the word. "Yeah, I know why you sent him. He was going to put a bullet in my skull if Anya had flipped me."

Gunny said, "That's one way to put it. I need to know if you can do the same if that kid turns into a Tasmanian devil."

I swallowed hard. "I don't know if I can do that or not, but if there's anybody in the world who can predict whether or not that kid's going to go off the deep end, I'm that guy. Give him to me, Gunny. We'll turn him into the sharpest tool in the shed."

"And if you can't, what then?"

"If we can't, we'll make sure he never hurts anybody."

Gunny pointed his cigar at Clark. "And what's your take on this idea?"

"That boy called me a dinosaur, Gunny. I can't wait to take him out behind the woodpile and teach him a little respect for his elders. We might be dinosaurs, but if we are, we're T-Rexs."

Clark and I stood, and Gunny said, "Do you want his file?"

I stuck out a hand. "Sure, I'll take it."

He retrieved it from the drawer and handed it over.

I plucked the cigar lighter from his desk and lit the edge of the file, then I turned it several times to ensure every sheet of paper inside was well lit. When it was too hot to hold, I tossed it onto the floor beside the hole in Gunny's cabinet. "By the way," I said. "You're not fooling anybody, you old spook. You got exactly what you wanted."

I pulled a Cohiba from my shirt pocket and rolled it across his desk. "One more thing . . . Get rid of those stinking, rotten Dominicans, and smoke a Cuban like a civilized human being."

Chapter 3
Mostly

Back in the Suburban, Clark said, "You've developed quite the knack for picking up strays. What are you going to do with that boy?"

"Wrong pronoun," I said.

Clark lowered his chin. "Oh, he's still a boy all right."

"No, you ignorant wretch. *Boy* isn't a pronoun. The question is, what are *we* going to do with that boy?"

"Ignorant wretch? That's just hurtful."

"So is listening to you try to speak English. *We* are going to teach that boy the same things you taught me, and *we* are going to turn him into a warfighter."

Clark huffed. "I'm not sure who the other half of your *we* is, but the *I* of *we* is finished teaching Introduction to Espionage."

"Okay, then. You can sit back and point when I screw him up. Isn't that what we determined you're so good at? Sitting and pointing?"

"Sometimes, College Boy, you really get under my skin. When do you think they'll let us have him?"

My phone chirped. "Hello, this is Chase."

"Sir, this is Clint. Uh, I was told to call you."

"Clint who?"

"Uh . . . your SERE student."

I pointed toward the phone, raised an eyebrow, and whispered, "It's our boy."

Clark slapped his forehead. "No, that's *your* boy. What kind of name is Clint anyway?"

I ignored my handler. "Hello, Clint. You're not a SERE student anymore. You're a SERE graduate. What can I do for you?"

"Well, they told me you'd be giving me a ride to wherever I'm going, and I guess I'm ready to go."

"You're finished with the course?"

"Yes, sir. They tell me I am. I guess there ain't no real graduation around here."

That made me chuckle. "No, not really. Where are you?"

"I'm at the pay phone outside building number six."

"Is all your gear packed, Clint?"

"Yes, sir. I've just got two bags. They're right here at my feet."

"We'll be there in five minutes, and we're in a black Suburban."

He said, "Of course you are."

I hung up and turned to Clark. "They want us to take him now."

"Now? There's no way he met all the requirements already. How long has he been here?"

"How should I know? I burned his file."

"Why did you do that, by the way?"

"Haven't you seen those commercials for buying precious metals? 'Past performance is not indicative of future results.'"

"You're not indicative of future results."

"I guess we've got a new stray to take home. Should we have him neutered?"

That got a laugh from Clark. "I think we already did that over the last three days."

"I guess you're right. Aren't they giving away cars to graduates anymore?"

"That's never been the rule. New cars are the exception for new operators who show particular promise. I can't explain why you got one."

Clint was still standing beside the pay phone when we pulled up. Clark rolled down the window and pointed at his bags. "Is that really all you've got?"

"What else do I need, sir?"

"Get in."

Clint threw his two bags across the back seat and buckled up. "Thanks for picking me up. Where am I going?"

Clark pulled down the sun visor and eyed Clint in the small mirror. "If you think this place was bad, you're going to hate the next two years of your life."

Clint didn't say a word and stared down at his boots.

"What's wrong?" I asked.

He shrugged. "I just thought maybe I might be headed somewhere to do some real work. I didn't know there was more training."

"There's always more training," I said. "We've been at this a long time, and we still train almost every day."

"Yeah, but you get to run ops, too."

"You're right, and we get to stay alive on those ops because we train so hard."

I let him stew for a few minutes on the drive to the airport, and then I said, "Clark's just pulling your chain. You *are* headed for more training . . . a lot more. But you'll be doing it with our team down in Georgia."

His eyes lit up. "A team? Like an A-Team?"

"Yeah, kid. Exactly like an A-team. I'm team lead, and my name is Chase Fulton. The crusty old guy in front of you is our handler, Clark Johnson."

"I've got a lot of questions," Clint said. "I don't even know where to start."

"I had the same questions when they sent me packing from The Ranch. We'll answer all of them—probably before you ask—and you'll have a thousand more before the week is over."

"Speaking of the week . . . What day is it?"

"Friday," I said.

"No, I mean like what date? I've been in the dark for a while, and I guess I kinda lost track of things."

"It's Friday, March fourth, two thousand eleven."

He cocked his head. "Really?"

I double-checked my watch. "Yep, why?"

"I guess I've been there longer than I realized. They dropped me in a nasty lake in a beat-up pickup truck on December seventh of two thousand eight."

Clark shoved his visor back up. "POWs usually find a way to scratch out a day count or a crude calendar so they don't lose track of real time."

"I guess I didn't know I was a POW."

"Sometimes it's hard to tell," I said. "Are you hungry?"

"No, sir. They fed me well."

Clark pulled the visor back down. "Can you shoot, kid?"

"Yes, sir, I can."

"What's your favorite weapon?"

Clint met Clark's eyes in the mirror. "One that's bigger than the one the bad guy's got."

My handler tried not to laugh, but he couldn't pull it off.

We pulled into the airport, through the gate, and onto the tarmac. I brought the Suburban to a stop beside the airstairs to the *Grey Ghost*, our Gulfstream IV business jet that had been converted into a multi-role tactical transport. That day, though, she was dressed up in her finery as a luxury business jet. The cargo rollers for transport pallets were well hidden beneath the plush carpet and leather captain's chairs.

We stepped from the SUV, and Clint stared up at the grey jet. "You guys chartered a jet to go to Georgia?"

"Not exactly," Clark said. "Get your gear. We're not your valets."

He pulled his pair of bags from the Suburban, and as he headed up the airstairs, I asked, "Did they teach you to fly?"

"Some, but it wasn't really my thing."

"Did you get a license?"

"I got a private, single-engine land ticket and an instrument rating, but that's it. I enjoyed it, but I wasn't very good."

"We'll work on that when we get home," I said. "We've got a couple old planes and a few instructors hanging around."

Out of the blue, he said, "I don't have a gun."

"What made you say that?" I asked.

"I don't know. This is the first day I've not carried a gun in two years. It just feels strange . . . like I'm naked or something."

"We'll work on that, too. Pick a seat, and we'll be on the ground in about an hour. You're not going to need that sweatshirt when we get home. It's in the mid-eighties today."

He shucked off the K-State sweatshirt and slid onto the first seat.

As we climbed away from Northern Virginia, through the complex airspace of the nation's capital, I asked, "What do you think his first real question will be?"

Clark said, "I think it'll be, 'Is all this yours'?"

"I don't want to overwhelm him on his first day out of the POW camp," I said. "Maybe we should give him a few days off to go do whatever twenty-four-year-old guys do when they've been in captivity for two years."

"There's only one thing on that boy's mind right now, and it has nothing to do with training or flying or chasing bad guys. He's thinking about chasing something else entirely."

"I guess you're right. Maybe we should find him a Russian sparrow."

He gave me a shot to the arm. "Oh, yeah. That worked out real well for you, didn't it?"

"Not so much. Maybe we'll give him a hundred bucks and Dr. Richter's VW Microbus for the weekend."

"Yeah, I don't think a van is a great idea. We don't need our new project locked up in the drunk tank in Jacksonville or Savannah on his first weekend out of prison."

"Maybe we could chaperone."

We touched down at what had been the St. Marys, Georgia, municipal airport before it floundered and the city sold it to Clark and me. I shut down the turbines, and the three of us descended the stairs to find a man pulling up on a tug.

I threw up a hand. "Hey, Don. How's it going?"

"Not bad. How was the flight?"

"Excellent," I said. "Don, meet Clint. He's going to be spending some time with us for a while. You'll probably see him around."

Don wiped off his hand and took Clint's. "Nice to meet you. I'm Don Maynard. I look after things here at the airport."

Clint made eye contact, shook like a man, and said, "It's nice to meet you, sir."

Maybe we were making progress already.

Don said, "The fuel truck is acting up. If you don't mind, I'll put the *Ghost* away for the night and fuel her up when Earl's finished with the truck."

"That's fine," I said. "I think I'll introduce our new arrival to our diesel mechanic."

Don laughed. "Oh, that ought to be good."

Clint looked between us with uncertainty painted all over his face. Little did he know that would be the least confused look he'd wear for the next fifteen minutes.

We led Clint into the maintenance hangar, where our fuel truck seemed to be in a thousand pieces on the floor. Sticking out from under the truck was a pair of filthy-socked feet on a creeper.

"Hey, Earl. Come out here a minute. We've got somebody who wants to meet you."

She yelled back. "Whoever it is, he better be six feet tall and gorgeous with a pizza in his hands."

Earl dug her socked heels into the concrete floor and pulled herself from beneath the truck. She stood to her full five feet in height and stared up at Clint. "Well, he's got everything except the pizza. Reminds me of you fifteen years ago, Stud Muffin."

Clint's expression was priceless as he stuck out a hand.

Earl slapped it away and waddled into his arms. "What's wrong with you, boy? We ain't shakers 'round here. We're huggers. Give Momma some lovin'."

Clint pleaded with his eyes for help, but he was on his own.

She squeezed him until I was afraid his head was going to pop off. "Name's Earline, but everybody calls me Earl at the End. It's a long story, but Stud Muffin there can fill you in on it. Are you one of them double-naught spies like them two?"

His panic grew, and we left him hanging. If he couldn't handle Earl, how could he be expected to handle real life in our world?

When she'd apparently doled out all the squeezing she had in her, she stepped back and studied Clint. "You sure are a fine-looking specimen of a man, but don't you get no ideas. You hear me? I've got me a man, and he's as jealous as . . . well, something that's real jealous. You can look at Momma, but you keep them hands to yourself. You can't handle this much woman." She leaned closer and gave him a wink. "You can dream about it though, Sugar Muffin."

We rescued Clint and headed for the main hangar.

He spent half of the walk looking over his shoulder. "What *was* that back there?"

"That was Earl at the End, Sugar Muffin. She's the finest mechanic on Earth. Just ask her."

"But she is a woman . . . right?"

Clark said, "Mostly."

Chapter 4
A New Name

"Welcome to Bonaventure Plantation," I said as we pulled into the drive. "This place has been in my family longer than we've been a country, and for now, it's your home, too."

Clint leaned forward and stared at what appeared to be a two-story colonial brick house nestled on the banks of the North River, but was, in fact, a three-story structure with a hidden state-of-the-art operations center on the top floor and a massive, water-tight weapons armory for a basement.

He said, "A plantation? Like with cotton?"

I said, "Cotton, yes, but mostly pecans. And it's pronounced pee-cans, not puh-kahns. When you can think of an English word in which c-a-n is pronounced kahn, I'll change my mind, but until then, they're pee-cans.

"I don't think I've ever met anyone so passionate about the name of a nut," he said.

"Welcome to the South."

"I can't wait to see the inside."

"That'll have to wait. First, we're headed around back to the best part."

We led him around the house to the backyard sloping to the North River, where my favorite place on the planet waited patiently. "Welcome to the gazebo, Clint. I'll make introductions, and yes, there will be a test later. A lot of tests, in fact."

He pulled off his cap and stepped into the gazebo. The gathered team caught his eye, but just like most first-time visitors, he couldn't pull his attention from the centerpiece.

I said, "That's a seventeenth-century naval cannon. It came off a British man-o'-war that sank a few miles from here during the War of Eighteen-Twelve. Are you ready for some names?"

As I introduced them, each member of the team stood and welcomed Clint to the family.

I said, "That ugly little guy there is Hunter, former Air Force combat controller and current bad guy killing machine."

I could see Clint's wheels turning as he chiseled each name into his brain.

"That gentleman is Singer, the finest and deadliest sniper you'll ever meet, but that's not his specialty. We call him Singer because he tends to unconsciously sing old Southern Baptist hymns while he's killing people. It's weird, but he makes it work. Without him, we'd all be on the road to Hell."

That seemed to fascinate Clint even more than the cannon. "Hmm. A gospel sniper?"

Singer nodded. "I do a little shooting, a little preaching, and a lot of singing."

Clint took his hand. "That's the only thing I excelled at while I was . . ." He turned to me as if asking permission.

I said, "You can say it. We've all been, and we all have clearances."

He motioned toward Skipper and Penny. "Even them?"

"Yes, they have clearances, too."

His eyes gleamed when they fell on Skipper, and she not so subtly slipped her hand into Tony's. "I'm Elizabeth, the analyst, but none of these knuckle-draggers are smart enough to remember my real name. Everybody calls me Skipper, and this is my husband,

Tony. He's a former Coast Guard rescue swimmer turned historic nautical warship painter."

"You paint ships?"

That got a laugh, and Tony said, "It's not that hard, really. They're all haze gray, and I've got a big brush."

I continued. "The bearded wonder is Kodiak, former Green Beret, and most recently called Bear Boy, but that's a long story. The guy who looks like the professor from *Gilligan's Island* is Disco. He's our chief pilot and a retired A-Ten driver. And finally, the oversized teddy bear in the big-boy chair is Mongo."

He shook hands and said, "Nobody's got a real name. I feel like the odd man out."

"Don't worry," I said. "You won't get to keep your name. You'll get a new one as soon as you do something dumb enough to earn one."

I motioned toward my favorite resident of Bonaventure. "She's got a real name. Clint, meet Penny Fulton, screenwriter extraordinaire and my wife."

He blurted out. "Is she the one with the Russian liver?"

That drew a glare from my beautiful wife, but she brushed it off long enough to say, "It's nice to meet you, Clint. Welcome to Bonaventure. Chase used to live here until he started telling stories about his beloved Russian and what used to be her liver."

I threw up my hands. "It wasn't me! Clark told him. I swear!"

Penny continued glaring. "Nice try, but Clark knows better."

I changed the subject. "Did you get them all?"

He said, "I think so. Tony, Hunter, Mongo, Singer, Kodiak, Disco, Skipper, Penny, Clark, and Chase. Oh, and Don and Earl at the airport."

"Not bad. How does everyone feel about a night on the town? Clint's been living off the grid for a couple of years, and I think he's earned a Chatham Artillery punch."

Singer said, "I'll pass on the punch, but I'm always up for a trip to Savannah."

Penny asked Clint, "Have you ever been to Savannah?"

"No, ma'am, but I heard they turn the river green for Saint Patrick's Day."

"They do," she said. "And if you hit the Artillery punch a little too hard, it hits back, and you'll turn green as well."

"I haven't had a drink in over two years, and to be honest, I don't really miss it."

Singer raised his glass of sweet tea. "Now you're talking. I like the new guy already."

Kodiak slapped the arm of his Adirondack chair. "Hey! That means I'm not the new guy anymore."

Clark said, "No, you're still the new guy until the *new* new guy proves he can cut it. Then you'll be the old new guy, and the new new guy will be the new guy."

I shot Clark a look. "That made sense inside your head, didn't it?" He nodded, and I said, "I wish it had stayed there."

Clark growled. "Wish in one hand, spit in the other, then see which hand is on the other foot."

I shook my head. "I'm sure that means something deeply philosophical that I'm not smart enough to understand, so I'll just ignore it. While I'm doing that, now would be a great time for everybody to get ready for a road trip. I'll bring the short bus around."

The gazebo emptied, except for the new new guy and me.

He said, "I've got four pairs of cargo pants, two blue jeans, six T-shirts, socks, filthy running shoes, and two pairs of boots."

I threw an arm around him. "I hope there's some underwear in that mix. Skipper and Penny can take you shopping when we get to Savannah."

He looked around as if landing in a world he never imagined could exist. "Is this really what team life is about?"

"No, this is what real life is about. Team life comes when we have to shoot back, but don't worry. You'll get plenty of that before you know it."

"Speaking of shooting back . . . I still don't have a piece."

"That's right. Come with me. We'll get you fixed up. Are you a Glock man?"

He followed me from the gazebo. "Not an off-the-shelf Glock. We had nice ones at The Ranch with a good trigger job and red dots and lights. I liked those."

I made it through the authentication required to open the door to the subterranean armory beneath our house.

When the lights came on, Clint looked like a kid at Christmas. "You've got to be kidding. This place is a shooter's dream come true. Are those M-Two-Four-Nines?"

I said, "The first six are, but the other four are FN Minimis. That's what the Two-Four-Nine design is based on, and frankly, I prefer the Belgian version."

He strolled through the armory as if it were a modern firearms museum, and perhaps it was.

"What's your favorite?" he asked.

I wrote it off as a question of youthful ignorance. "That's like asking which wrench is my favorite for driving a nail. I don't have a favorite. They're all the right tools when dictated by the job. If I need to shoot a bad guy twelve hundred yards away, I'm not going to pull something from the pistol rack."

"That was the wrong question," he said. "I meant, what do you carry when you're not operating?"

I lifted my shirttail, revealing my concealed carry holster inside my waistband. "Most of the time, it's the Glock Nineteen, always with a light, and always with a red dot. There are times when the Twenty-Six is more appropriate, depending on how I'm dressed. But it comes down to personal preference."

He stopped in front of the pistol rack. "This is like a Glock showroom. You've got 'em all."

"Pick a couple of your early favorites, and we'll dig out holsters to fit. You'll probably change your selection over time, so don't get hung up on what everybody else carries."

"What about on a mission?"

"That's the exception. When we're downrange, we carry Seventeens and Nineteens. The Seventeen magazines fit the Nineteen, but it sticks out a little. If you get dead, I want to grab your magazines and keep gunning. That's not an option if you're running a Sig and Mongo's running a Smith. Downrange, it's all about compatibility."

He frowned. "Does Mongo really carry a Smith?"

I chuckled. "No. The only oddball is Clark. He sometimes carries a Nineteen-Eleven because he's old, but on a mission, it's all Glocks all the time."

"All right, then, I'll take a Seventeen and a Nineteen."

"Excellent choices. Find some holsters you like. They're in the blue cabinet and organized by model number."

He found what he liked, loaded four magazines for each pistol, and tucked them away.

"Now, for a rifle," I said. "We're an M-Four team, as you can see, but you're welcome to customize it any way you want. Optics, slings, lights, lasers, IR, ambidextrous controls, whatever. We run night vision, of course, so you'll want an IR light and laser. The rest is really up to you. We'll do enough drills for you to learn exactly what you like, and the rest of the guys will tell you their preferences. Both Hunter and Mongo are excellent gunsmiths, so they can do any work you want. I encourage you to learn that skill set as well. I like my operators to know why their weapon fails when it does. And sooner or later, everything mechanical fails."

"We can save that for another day," he said.

"Of course. No hurry. We always have at least four rifles in every vehicle. You never know when you're going to run into trouble and need to start stacking bodies. Do you have a good knife?"

"Not a good one," he said as he drew his pocketknife and held it out for me to see.

I motioned toward a second cabinet. "Pick out a Benchmade you like, and keep it nice and sharp."

With our shopping trip complete, we climbed from the armory and rounded the back of the house.

Clint pointed toward the river. "What's that?"

I followed his finger. "Surely you've seen an alligator before."

"Not up close. This may be the best day of my life."

He trotted toward the riverbank, and that left only one thing for me to do. I thumbed my phone, and Penny answered on the first ring. I said, "Get out here, and bring everybody. Clint is experiencing his first alligator."

Soon, the back gallery was full of anxious spectators, and the new guy was in his first dance with a live gator on the banks of the North River. I should've warned him that the pointy end is almost as dangerous as the end with teeth, but lessons learned the hard way tend to make a lasting impression. The more they danced, the braver each became. With every lunge of the gator, Clint proved his sidestep game was strong. He even dared to slap the gator's snout a couple of times.

Penny leaned over the gallery rail. "Chase, you've got to do something. He's going to get hurt."

"The gator has to learn, sweetheart. I can't help it if Clint hurts him."

"You're terrible," she said. "Clint! Get away from that thing! They're dangerous."

He ignored my wife, and that's rarely a great plan. As the dance continued, the gator turned and swept Clint's feet with his tail, sending the new guy to the ground with a mighty thud."

Singer drew his pistol and bounced down the stairs. "I won't let the kid get hurt."

I made no effort to stop our sniper, but even he wasn't going to intervene unless it became an unwinnable fight.

Singer took up a position beside the gazebo and continued watching as Clint leapt onto the gator's back, shoved his mouth closed, and clamped his snout in a death grip. The gator reacted as most four-hundred-pound animals with a brain the size of a pea. He thrashed about, trying to shed the burden on his back, but Clint was determined.

Hunter said, "What do you think he'll do next?"

"Clint or the gator?" I asked.

"Both."

Clint glanced across his shoulder at the gathered audience and yelled, "Somebody come tape his mouth!"

No one moved except the gator. Obviously convinced he couldn't win the fight on the muddy bank, the creature headed for a playground, where he was king of the hill.

Down the bank they slid until the gator and Steve Irwin were both underwater and thrashing like crazy.

"That's not good," I said in a trot to the river's edge.

Singer wasn't the only one with his pistol drawn. Soon, the whole team was amassed on the riverbank with eyes wide and weapons at the ready.

Penny yelled, "Do something, Chase!"

"What do you want me to do?"

"I don't know! Something!"

I emptied my pockets in preparation to join the water aerobics, but my plan was even worse than Clint's.

Penny stopped me. "No! Don't go in there. Do something else."
Hunter rolled his eyes. "I'll get him."

His boots came off first, followed by his shirt. Two strides before Hunter hit the water, Clint emerged, gasping for breath and
pawing for the shoreline. He crawled up the muddy bank with all
of his limbs still attached, but victory wasn't the look he was wearing. Exhaustion, coupled with thanks to be alive, was a more accurate description.

We holstered our pistols, and Singer said, "It was nice of you to
let him go. Now, get in the house and get cleaned up, Gator."

Chapter 5
Savannah Smiles

Having grown accustomed to doing everything quickly, Gator didn't drag his feet. He was showered, dressed, and out the door in ten minutes. The short bus Earl converted from an abandoned school bus made the perfect limousine for our drive to Savannah.

There was no question that somebody was going to bring it up. Clark just happened to be the first to ask. "What were you thinking, Gator?"

He stretched his arms above his head as if working out a kink. "I figured I'd try out some of that jiujitsu they taught me at The Ranch on something other than one of you old guys. You know, I didn't want to hurt you, so I picked the alligator."

Hunter jumped in. "I, for one, approve. That was some gutsy stuff. I was leaning toward calling you Crock, but we all agree that Gator is a much better call sign."

"I'll take it."

I said, "You taking it is not a requirement. You're Gator, regardless of your vote. By the way, did you clean your weapon after your little dip in the river?"

"Yes, sir. You know it."

Singer shot a thumb at the new kid. "He gets one more point in my book."

Gator turned to our sniper. "Thank you, sir. We didn't get to talk much earlier, but I started to tell you that shooting was the only thing I was really good at up at The Ranch. I did all right with everything else, but gunning was definitely my thing. Do you think you and I could maybe do some long-range stuff? You know . . . if you have time."

"I think we can work that into the schedule. Can you sing?"

"No, sir, but if I drink a couple of those Artillery punches they keep talking about, I might."

Singer said, "Maybe you ought to think about sticking with that two-year dry spell you've been on."

Gator said, "Maybe so. I've never tried sweet tea. That might be my new jam."

Our first stop was a shopping trip for Gator and the girls, and to my surprise, it was quick. They were back aboard the bus in less than half an hour with four shopping bags and the new kid in much snazzier duds than he'd worn into the store.

We parked and walked up to the Pirates' House restaurant.

Gator asked, "What is this place?"

Penny became the tour guide and historian. "This is the Pirates' House, an old Savannah tradition built around an inn and tavern from the mid-seventeen hundreds. Over the years, it was neglected until the local gas company bought the property with plans to demolish the whole block. A lady named Mary Hillyer fell in love with the property and began the long process of having it restored. And now, it's the Pirates' House restaurant, and their sweet tea is divine."

That earned her a golf clap from the team, and we were soon seated around a long rustic table with drinks flowing and appetizers arriving.

When the waitress made her way around to Gator, he looked up and said, "I'm a little out of my element. I'm from Kansas, so I'm not sure what most of this stuff is."

She laid a gentle hand on his shoulder. "You ain't allergic to nothin', are you, Sugar?"

"No, ma'am, but I've recently learned I don't like alligators."

"Then no alligator for you. Don't you worry none. I'll bring you a mess of food like you ain't never seen. How 'bout a Chatham Artillery punch to get you going?"

Gator eyed Singer, and the sniper shrugged.

"No, thank you, ma'am. I'll stick with sweet tea."

She pinched his ear. "You're cute. You know that? How do all y'all know each other? You act like family, but you don't look much like one."

We apparently decided as a group to let the new guy field that one, and he did fine. "They all work together, and I'm interviewing for a position with them."

She leaned down and whispered, "If they don't hire you, just give me a call. I've got some work you can do."

She gave him a hip bump to the shoulder as she walked away, and Clark raised an eyebrow. "I'm not sure I like what's happening here. I'm supposed to be the pretty one that waitresses can't resist. Now Gator's horning in on my territory."

Penny pulled out her phone. "Let's see . . . Yes, here's Maebelle's number. I think I'll give her a call."

Clark threw up a hand. "It won't be necessary to call my wife. I was just messing with the new guy. If you think that gator was a handful this afternoon, you couldn't handle the kind of manual labor that girl's got on her mind for you, Mr. Kansas."

To no one's surprise, Gator's plate came out first, and the waitress made a show of describing what she'd put together for him. "Now, this is shrimp and grits. Once you taste that, your whole world is gonna change. Come to think of it, I'm a lot like shrimp and grits in that respect."

She went on, and Gator grew more and more red with every flirtatious advance from the twenty-something Savannah native.

We ate for over an hour, and Gator slowly began to meld with the family. He had a long way to go, but from early indications, I'd picked up a stray who had the makings of a loyal member of the pack.

I paid the bill, and Gator accepted the slip of paper from the waitress that, I assumed, held her name and number.

Penny noticed the exchange and leaned toward the young woman. "*A ty govorish' po Russki*?"

Both the waitress and Gator stared up at my wife, and Penny nodded. "It's okay. I just wanted to make sure you didn't speak Russian."

The waitress furrowed her brow. "That's an odd thing to say, but you've got nothing to worry about with me. What little English I speak qualifies as Southernese."

We piled back into the short bus limo for the hop down Bay Street.

"Where are we headed?" Gator asked.

I said, "It's just a boring little piano bar. You won't have any fun. I promise."

"Piano bar? That sounds classy."

When we walked through the door at Savannah Smiles and got our hands stamped, it was immediately obvious to our stray that *boring* and *classy* would not be the words he'd later use to describe what I'd called a piano bar. On the stage were two grand pianos, a drummer, a guy playing an electronic keyboard that looked like a guitar hanging around his neck, and nine members of a bachelorette party singing "Sweet Home Alabama."

To my surprise, we got a table. Well, it was actually three tables shoved together with almost enough chairs for everyone. A dreadlocked waiter materialized, memorized our drink orders without writing them down, and took my credit card.

The high-energy environment held everyone's attention, and the involvement of the packed crowd made it even more exciting. A bidding war broke out between some Tennessee fans who were trying to scrape together enough cash to get the band to play "Rocky Top," but Clark apparently negotiated an agreement to double the Volunteers' tip if the band agreed to not play the song he despised. It was an expensive night for him, but Clark never heard the first note of "Rocky Top."

At some point in the evening, Gator admitted that he could play guitar, and that was all the news Hunter needed to volunteer our boy for a guest star appearance on the Savannah Smiles stage.

One of the piano players held up a note and cleared his throat. "Okay, okay. Calm down and listen up. I hear we've got a guitar player in the house who just graduated from . . . I can't make it out. But anyway, he just graduated from something, and he wants to do some Aerosmith. Get up here, Gator!"

Gator stood and shook his finger at Hunter. "I'll get you for this."

He bounded to the stage, and someone handed him an electric guitar. After a few twists of the tuning pegs, he leaned toward the piano player. "Do you know 'Living on a Prayer'?"

The piano man rolled his eyes. "What key?"

Not only did the band know every Bon Jovi song ever recorded, but apparently, Gator did, too. After a short set, he handed back the guitar and returned triumphantly to the table.

Singer leaned in. "I thought you said you couldn't sing."

Gator demolished a bottle of water. "No, I said I *don't* sing, but I guess that was a lie, too."

We danced, drank, bought our favorite songs, and Gator did another set with the band. It was the Black Crowes and Hank

Williams Jr., but it got the same roaring ovation as Bon Jovi. He finally surrendered the guitar and microphone, and we called it a night.

A stroll down the cobblestones and bricks of River Street along the famed Savannah River capped off our night. Near the famous Waving Girl statue, Mongo, our resident giant, grabbed Gator and raised him over his head.

The new guy yelled, "What are you doing?"

Mongo laughed. "I thought you might like to see if you can find another reptile friend in this river."

To my surprise, Gator twisted in Mongo's massive arms until he had both legs wrapped tightly around the big man's neck. "If I go, you're coming with me."

Mongo relented and placed the new guy back on the ground. "Nice move, kid."

Gator straightened his new clothes. "Everything's a test, isn't it?"

Mongo grinned. "You betcha."

The drive south found Gator sound asleep before we were twenty miles out of Savannah.

Our sniper fired a warning shot across his bow to make sure he wasn't faking sleep, but the rhythmic rise and fall of his chest and gentle snore told the story. "The kid can sing a little."

I said, "Yeah, but something tells me he doesn't know any good old gospel hymns. You may have to teach him "The Old Rugged Cross.""

"I think I can handle that. What do you think about his desire to learn to snipe?"

"I plan to put him through a pretty tough day on Monday. I want to see him shoot, dive, fly, and fight. We'll find his weaknesses and focus on those at first, but I think it would be a great idea to get him qualified to sneak around and shoot from a mile away."

"That's what I thought you'd say. I'll stay out of the way and watch while you put him through your paces."

Back at Bonaventure, we went our separate ways and sent Gator to the first real bed he'd seen in years. My plan was to let him sleep as long as his body wanted, but he was clearly still in the mindset of proving himself. Coffee was made by 6:00 a.m., and I found him in the gazebo with a steaming mug of his own.

"Good morning. Are you gator hunting already?"

He raised his mug. "Good morning. No, sir. I'm done with those things."

"Wise decision."

After several minutes of silence as the world awoke around us, he asked, "Are the horses yours?"

"No! They're Penny's, and I have nothing but contempt for them. Are you a horse guy?"

"I don't know. They're kind of like gators for me. Until yesterday, I'd never ridden either one. Now I guess I'm halfway there."

"Penny will be more than happy to teach you everything you want to know about those beasts, but don't expect my involvement."

"It sounds like there's a story in there somewhere."

"Oh, there is, but I don't know you well enough to tell it yet."

"I'll be looking forward to that day." We watched a pair of pelicans diving for their breakfast, and he said, "This is quite a place. Your family must've done well."

"My family worked hard and devoted their lives to service to others. Aside from this property, they never accumulated any significant wealth. Instead, they sacrificed for others, and I'm proud to continue that tradition. To answer your poorly veiled question, what material wealth I have is less than a decade old. Most of the equipment you'll see in the next few days belongs to the team. The real estate is mine and Penny's, but the airplanes, boats, and tools of our trade are community property."

"Even the sailboat?"

"That's an exception. The boat was sort of a gift from Clark's father, who was my original handler. We call her *Aegis*, and she's a personal asset."

"I've never been on a sailboat."

I checked my watch. "The wind will pick up around ten, and we'll change that. There's some great sailing around here. The Atlantic is ten miles that way, and from there, we can be anywhere in the world that touches salt water without burning a drop of diesel fuel."

"What's in the boathouse?"

"We'll save that one for Monday."

He checked over his shoulder for prying ears.

I said, "It's just the two of us."

He ground his toe into the deck of the gazebo. "I'm not trying to cross any lines, but I get the feeling the Russian organ donor thing is a sore subject."

"That's a long story, too. When I was fresh off The Ranch, like you, I got caught in what we call a Russian honey trap. They're very good at those."

"I've heard the term."

"Her name was Anya Burinkova, and she was almost the ruin of me. Since then, she defected, and she's doing a little work for the government. Occasionally, we'll bring her in as a consultant or fighter when we're down a man. She's quite capable. She donated part of her liver when Penny had her car wreck last year. It saved Penny's life, but there will always be a little bad blood between those two. You'll understand when you meet her."

"I won't bring it up again," he said. "What's on the agenda for the weekend?"

"I thought we'd take it easy. As I said, we'll do some sailing if you're up for it, but you're welcome to do whatever you'd like. We'll hit the ground running on Monday."

Chapter 6

Through the Paces

When the sun came up on Monday morning, we were on the range and putting Gator's shooting claims to the test.

Clark said, "On the buzzer, draw, put two in the high A-zone and one in the T-box in less than two seconds. Do you understand the course of fire?"

"Yes, sir."

"Shooter ready . . . Stand by."

The timer emitted its shrill tone. Gator drew, put three rounds exactly where they were supposed to be, and Clark checked the timer.

"Not bad, kid. Change magazines, and do it again."

Clark started the same drill the same way, and the timer buzzed. The first two rounds were dead center in the high A-zone on the target's chest, but on the third press of the trigger, the weapon clicked. Gator didn't miss a beat. He tapped the magazine to ensure it was well seated, racked the slide, and put shot number three right between the guy's eyes.

Clark ignored the timer. "Nice job. Continue with the same magazine. Put six rounds in the A-zone in less than five seconds."

Gator looked up. "Are you serious?"

Clark scoffed. "What? You can't do it?"

He said, "Anybody can do that. That's leisure shooting. Push me, sir."

Clark repeated. "Six rounds in the A-zone in less than five seconds. Shooter ready . . . Stand by."

Two rounds came in perfect form, and the slide locked to the rear. Without flinching, Gator dropped the empty mag, slammed a new one into the mag well, dropped the slide, and put four more shots on target well within the allotted time.

Room-clearing drills went much the same as the flat-range work. After adapting to our speed of movement and violence of action, Gator demonstrated full mastery of close-quarters battle skills.

I pulled Singer aside. "What did you see?"

"I see a shooter. The only thing I'd change is his shoulder position on the rifle. I'll fix that, but it'll take him some time to break the habit."

"There's nobody better to fix a rifle issue than you."

He said, "If he can do a little math and learn to move silently, I think I can turn him into a sniper."

"I have no doubt," I said. "Let's see if he can breathe underwater."

We cleaned weapons and tidied up the range before cramming some calories down our throats.

"How did you do in dive training?" I asked.

Gator shrugged. "Not bad. I didn't have any scuba training before The Ranch, so it was a drastic introduction. I enjoyed it, though, and I think I'd like to do some recreational diving if I ever have time."

"There will be plenty of time for that. The diving around here isn't very good, but it's less than an hour to the Keys in the Gulfstream. Did you dive banded doubles or singles at The Ranch?"

"Both, but mostly doubles."

I hopped to my feet. "All right, then. Let's get wet and see if you can swim as well as you can shoot."

Hunter watched carefully as Gator assembled his gear and checked every piece as if his life depended on it. And it did. We shouldered our gear and headed for the boathouse.

"Are we diving from *Aegis*?" Gator asked.

"No, we've got a little powerboat we like to dive from."

Mongo unlocked the boathouse and flipped on the lights. The massive electric door rose, exposing the stern of our dive boat to the North River.

Gator stood in awe of the massive 80-foot patrol boat. "That's a Mark Five. I thought only the SEALs had these."

"We do like our toys around here," Hunter said. "Climb aboard. You're gonna enjoy this."

I backed the Mark V out of the boathouse and pointed her downstream. "She's all yours. Just follow the river until it opens up. We'll bear left and run up behind Cumberland Island."

Gator took the controls and learned quickly. Skippering a boat the size of the Mark V isn't an experience most people are ready to do, but I was pleased by how quickly he caught on.

Cumberland Sound isn't particularly deep, but it's definitely challenging for novice divers. Low visibility and shifting tidal currents make everything underwater more challenging than it should be.

I stepped behind the wheel. "I have the controls. Get your mask, snorkel, and fins on."

He abandoned the helm and did exactly as I instructed.

With the transmissions out of gear and the engines at idle, I said, "We're in twenty feet of water. Go find your gear and come back to the boat with it in place."

He looked at me in sheer confusion until he heard the splash of his buoyancy compensator and tanks hitting the water behind the boat. Hunter had been in the water for several minutes by the time Gator stepped from the Mark V. I didn't envy the coming battle Gator was on the verge of facing. If he thought the alligator was a handful, he'd really hate Hunter pretty soon.

I let the current pull us southward, away from the spot Gator would expect the boat to be if he surfaced alone.

Five minutes passed, and Mongo said, "He's either dead or wrestling with Hunter. If it's the latter, I suspect he wishes for the former. I know I wouldn't want to tangle with Hunter in the water."

Minutes later, a head popped above the water, and a broken dive mask landed on the deck. "Somebody throw me another mask. The kid broke mine."

I leaned over the gunwale. "How's he doing?"

"He broke my mask. How do you think he's doing?"

I tossed a fresh mask overboard.

Hunter caught it and said, "Meet us at the Dungeness dock. I'm gonna find out if he can read a compass."

"Are you okay?" I asked. "You look winded."

He pulled on the mask. "He's twenty-three years old and fresh off The Ranch. You'd be winded, too. I'm starting to feel a little like that alligator he wrangled."

Without another word, Hunter was gone, and I took the opportunity to get a little stick time with the Mark V. It would take Gator an hour to find the dock to Dungeness, the nineteenth-century ruined mansion on Cumberland Island that had been owned by several notable Americans, from James Oglethorpe to the Carnegies.

The boat reminded me how much I'd missed having my hands on her. For her size, she was the nimblest vessel imaginable. Massively overpowered, thanks to Earl, the Mark V danced through turns, accelerated like a sports car, and stopped on a dime. It would be impossible to ask more of the workhorse.

We'd been tied alongside the dock for ten minutes when a pair of heads emerged from the water.

Hunter was first aboard, and Clark threw him a towel. "How'd he do?"

"Better than I expected. We'll work on some rebreather training, and he'll be good to go."

Gator hopped aboard as if he'd been out for a pleasure swim. "Well, that was fun. Are you okay, Mr. Hunter?"

"It's just Hunter, and I'm fine. Get yourself dried off, and clear that mud off your gear."

Hunter's tone told me that Gator had likely gotten the best of him on the bottom.

We cast off and headed out the Pass and into the North Atlantic.

When we reached the spot I wanted, I brought the Mark V to a hover and stepped into my wetsuit. "You said you wanted to do some recreational diving, so let's go. Nobody's going to try to kill you on this one."

"What's down there?" Gator asked.

"It's an old shipwreck. It's not much, but there's some pretty good sea life on it, and we'll probably see a shark or two."

Gator changed his tanks and followed me into the water. I led him to the bow of the sunken tugboat in about ninety feet of water, and we explored the wreck for thirty minutes or so. A pair of blacktip reef sharks patrolled by several times, and Gator seemed to be mesmerized by the predators. We found a goliath grouper that was bigger than Mongo, and even a sea turtle lounging on the deck. Everything in the environment seemed to fascinate our new hire, and I quickly came to believe Gator absolutely belonged in the water.

We swam through the pilothouse and a few of the tighter spaces inside the sunken ship so I could see how he handled confinement. He moved slowly but efficiently, and he made an obvious effort to avoid stirring up the silt and sand inside the passages. All in all, I was impressed and pleased with Clint's performance.

Our long, slow ascent allowed plenty of time for the nitrogen in our bodies to dissipate, but we still conducted a safety stop at fifteen feet to keep ourselves on the safer side of the bends.

Back on the boat, Gator said, "That was amazing! Did you see those sharks?"

"I did. They're pretty common around here, and I've never seen them show any aggression. Nice job inside the ship, by the way. You were cautious, and you didn't stir anything up. The fastest way to turn a relaxing dive into chaos is to kick up the silt inside a confined space. Suddenly, you're lost, blind, scared, and confused. None of which is good in the water."

We peeled off our wetsuits, stowed our gear, and I said, "Take us home, Gator."

Everything was indeed a test, and he passed with flying colors.

I wasn't ready to risk tearing the side out of the boathouse, so I took the controls when we reached the Bonaventure dock. With everything shut down, tied down, and locked up, it was time for one more test.

I asked Gator, "How do you feel about doing a little flying? I'd like to get a feel for your skills in the cockpit."

He froze in place. "Flying? We can't go flying after spending almost two hours at depth. We'll get the bends for sure."

I threw an arm around his shoulders. "I told these guys you were smarter than you looked. That's the perfect answer. I got blown out of the water by an explosive charge under the Bridge of the Americas in Panama several years ago, and I got bent badly. It took several hours in a recompression chamber, but it worked out, and I was okay. I'll tell you this, though. You never want the bends."

Singer said, "If you're finished puffing up the kid's ego, I'd like to take him shooting."

Gator turned to me with that Daddy-can-I-go look, and I said, "Have fun."

The rest of us assembled around the kitchen table for sandwiches and an after-action review.

"So, what do you think?"

Hunter was first. "He's sharp. I've got no problems with him yet. I'm sure he's going to be bad at something, but he's doing fine so far."

Clark nodded. "I agree. If he's right about flying not being his thing, that may be his weakness, and I'm okay with that. We've got enough fliers in the family. Right now, a gunner is more valuable, and the kid can shoot."

I took a bite and replayed the morning in my head. "Anybody can shoot a paper target. How's he going to do when they start shooting back?"

Mongo said, "Let's rough him up a little after Singer gets finished melting his brain. I'd like to see how he fights."

"That's my plan," I said. "He's stout and nimble. I'm not sure I want to tangle up with him."

Mongo said, "I don't mind rolling him around a little, but Tatiana is home, and she brought her fourth-degree Brazilian jiujitsu black belt boyfriend with her."

Tatiana was Mongo's stepdaughter, but he'd likely rip anyone in half who dared call her anything other than his daughter. She would graduate from Juilliard in less than a month and would no doubt become the prima ballerina with a major company soon thereafter. Her boyfriend, Grayson Knox, would be right behind her with his shiny new diploma and piano prowess. Penny had already put Grayson to work writing the score for a small picture her studio was producing, and he was in love with the movie business.

Grayson's small frame and boyish look made him the least threatening physical presence in almost any room, but one second into the fight, any aggressor would know he'd made a terrible mistake grabbing the pianist.

"Get him over here," I said. "This'll be fun to watch."

Mongo thumbed his phone, and an hour later, Grayson, Tatiana, and Irina—Mongo's Russian wife—made their appearance.

"What's this all about?" Tatiana asked.

I said, "We're trying out a new guy for the team, and we want to know if he can fight."

Grayson's eyes lit up. "Does he know about me?"

I grinned and shook my head.

Grayson said, "I'll go change. When do you want to make this happen?"

"Let's do it just before dinner. He's shooting with Singer now, but they'll be back before dark."

Chapter 7
Piano Man

When Singer and Gator arrived back at the house, I pulled our sniper aside for a one-on-one. "How did it go?"

He said, "Not bad. He's a little noisy, but he'll learn. We're going to do some classroom ballistics together, and if you're okay with it, I'd like to keep working with him. I think he can learn to snipe."

"Did you see any red flags?"

"Just one," he said. "He's easily distracted, but I can work on that, too. He's sensitive to noise behind him and tends to check his six a lot."

"How's his soul?"

Singer sighed. "We'll work on that, too."

"I thought we'd have a little fun before dinner. I want to see Gator fight, and Tatiana brought Grayson home."

Singer grinned. "I'll make some popcorn."

The assembly happened in the gazebo, and more introductions were made.

"Gator, meet Grayson Knox. He's a classical pianist and composer."

Gator towered over the much smaller man and almost chuckled. "A composer?"

"Yeah," Grayson said. "I'm scoring a movie, and I play with a few orchestras across the country. What do you do?"

"I play guitar a little."

Grayson said, "We should jam sometime. I'm sure you're quite good."

Gator laughed. "Not orchestra good, but I like to play. My dad taught me. He was in a couple of bands . . ." His words trailed off, and a distant look came over his face. "Sorry. I was just . . . never mind. I don't really have a guitar right now. I've been in school for a while. Sort of."

I made a mental note to poke around inside Gator's head a little and get him talking about his parents. I didn't care about the new kid's past deeds, but understanding his psychology was crucial. Evaluating his physical capabilities was easy, but dissecting his mind wouldn't be.

I said, "You've had quite a day, Gator."

"It's been fun."

"It wasn't really meant to be fun, but I'm looking forward to the next event."

"Next event?"

I said, "They taught you to fight, didn't they?"

He nodded at my ham-fisted segue, and I asked, "Boxing, grappling, Krav Maga?"

Gator continued nodding.

I asked, "Are you up for a little demo?"

He cocked his head. "A demo? They didn't really teach me to do demonstrations. I just learned to fight."

"Pick one of us," I said. "We'll spar with you."

"One of you guys?" he asked, clearly unsure what was about to happen.

"Sure. Any of us. Mongo might not be a great choice, but anybody else will be fine."

Grayson came in right on cue. "What about me?"

Gator couldn't contain his laughter. "Maybe that's not a great idea. I've got eight inches and a hundred pounds on you, and I've actually been trained to fight."

Grayson wiggled his fingers wildly. "I don't know. I've been working these fingers on piano keys for twenty years. I might be a handful."

Gator continued chuckling and threw an arm around Grayson's shoulders. "Thanks for volunteering, but I think I'll—"

Before Gator could finish, Grayson swept his legs, spun him around, and sent the much larger man to the ground. Gator reacted, but not fast enough. His widely thrown elbow missed Grayson by more than a foot, allowing the pianist to slip a hand beneath his neck. In the next second, Grayson had his right arm snaked around Gator's neck and beneath his chin. He grabbed the bicep of his left arm with his right hand and layered his left behind the crown of Gator's head. Grayson smiled, arched his back, and locked the rear naked choke in place.

Gator tapped Grayson's arm as if he were on the verge of death.

Hunter said, "Does tapping out ever work in a real fight?"

Gator resorted to more desperate means and grabbed a handful of Grayson's hair, but with the circulation to his brain cut off, he lacked the strength to continue the fight. His arms fell limp, and Grayson released the choke and laid his opponent's head gently on the ground.

"I guess he wasn't expecting me to do that."

When Gator rejoined the land of the living, most of us were still laughing. He shook off the stars circling his head. "Hey! I wasn't ready."

"Yeah, we noticed," Mongo said. "That might be something you want to work on . . . being ready."

Grayson offered a hand, but Gator slapped it away and climbed back to his feet under his own power. "You guys clearly set me up for that one, but it won't happen again."

Irina laughed, and that seemed to wound Gator's ego far more than our jeers. At Irina's size—much like Grayson—no one would ever consider her to be a physical threat, but most people would never know about her training under the Russian FSB.

In her beautiful and disarming Russian accent, she said, "I can teach to you how to break choke hold with only one thumb. You would like for me to show you this, yes?"

Gator scoffed. "Nobody can break that hold with one thumb when it's locked in correctly."

"I can show to you this. Is very easy."

Gator said, "Sure, let's see it."

The tiny Russian stepped in front of him and turned around. "Do to me this same choke and tell me when you are ready. I will break free in less than one second."

"Not possible," he said again as he looked up at Mongo. "Are you sure this is okay?"

Mongo said, "You're the only one who's been unconscious in the past few minutes. You make the call."

Gator said, "I won't hurt you. I promise."

"Is okay," Irina said. "Do to me just as you would with man who was trying to kill you. I do not want to win because you let me. I want to win because I am smarter."

He glanced back at Mongo, and the giant said, "Go for it."

He laced an arm beneath Irina's chin and locked in the hold. "Okay, let's see you break it with one thumb."

Irina held up her thumb, lowered it to the striker wheel of a cigarette lighter, and raised the small orange flame beneath the flesh of Gator's elbow. He shoved her away and pawed at his scorched flesh.

Mongo roared with laughter. "I tried to warn you, kid, but you wouldn't listen."

Gator turned to me as if I was supposed to be a sympathetic ear, and I asked, "Have you ever heard the phrase 'all's fair in love and war'?"

He shook his head. "I think I want to go shoot some more."

I said, "Okay, we've had enough fun. Let's get serious for a minute. The whole point of this exercise was to show our new hire just how different the real world is from the training environment he's been in. I think we made our point, don't you?"

Gator nodded. "Yes, sir."

"Now, let's dance a little. I'll spar with you. No strikes to the face or groin, no broken bones, and no biting. Are you good with those rules?"

He nodded, and we circled like a pair of predators sizing up an opponent. He threw a few pretty good punches that I managed to deflect, but I missed the knee shot he sent to my ribs, and that got my attention. Once we went to the ground, things got interesting. He was a pretty good grappler, but I'd spent half my life studying and training to survive fights. When it was over, I won, but I'd be the one who groaned a little too loud getting out of bed the next morning.

I helped him up. "Not bad, but we'll pair you up with Clark for a few days to work on a few things. Don't let the old man fool you. He's got the goods."

Gator straightened his shirt and brushed his hair back. "I'll take Clark all day, but I don't want any more of piano man."

A phone chirped, and everyone reached for their pockets. Clark came out with his cell and pressed it to his ear. A few seconds later, he trotted away from the gazebo and up the back steps to the house.

We watched him go, and Penny sighed. "I'll order pizzas."

Skipper hopped from her chair. "I'll meet you guys upstairs."

Everyone was on their feet and migrating toward the house.

Gator asked, "Uh, what's happening?"

I said, "That's the batphone, kid. When that phone rings, life is about to change."

His confused expression didn't change. "Can I come?"

"It's not a matter of can you come," I said. "You're coming, and you may be only hours away from your first real mission."

The elevator at Bonaventure didn't get much use unless one of us was recuperating from a war wound, and that evening was no exception. We jogged up the stairs to the third floor and through the door to Skipper's lair, the Bonaventure ops center. I stepped through the door immediately behind Gator, and he locked up in his tracks, his eyes absorbing every inch of the room.

I put a hand between his shoulder blades. "Keep moving, or we'll get run over."

He stepped aside, and Skipper spun in her chair. She pointed to one of our high-back chairs sitting in a far corner of the room. "You sit there, new guy. And don't speak."

Gator followed her finger and planted himself in the assigned chair. The rest of us gathered around the conference table in our typical arrangement and waited for Clark to arrive.

He wasn't far behind, and when he came through the door, he closed and locked it behind him. "Where's Gator?" Skipper pointed to the corner, and Clark said, "Perfect. Stay there, and don't speak."

The new guy nodded his agreement, and Clark slid onto his chair. "We've got an assignment, and it's sensitive."

"Aren't they all?" Hunter asked.

"Not as sensitive as this one. The potential exists for this to turn into an international incident with far-reaching ramifications." He instantly had everyone's attention. "Another team—obviously not as good as us—has gotten itself into trouble. It was supposed to be a relatively simple snatch-and-grab of three guys who were each carrying a piece of a terror plot. The team apparently made the snatch, but the whole thing went south shortly thereafter."

Clark paused as if looking for something, and Skipper tossed a bottle of water toward him. He plucked it from the air and swallowed half of it. "Thank you. Now, back to the snatch-and-grab. They hit the targets in Maracaibo, Venezuela, Colón, Panama, and Barranquilla, Colombia. Can you get us a graphic, Skipper?"

In seconds, a map of the Western Caribbean filled the overhead monitor with the three cities highlighted.

Clark asked, "Would anybody care to guess what these three cities have in common?"

"Large commercial ports on the Atlantic side of Central and South America," I said.

Clark rang an imaginary bell. "Ding! We have ourselves a winner. We don't know for sure what their objective was, but based on the geography, that big ditch running right through the country of Panama looks like a pretty convenient target."

"Who were they working for?" Mongo asked.

"We'll get to that," Clark said. "But first, I need to tell you about the botched op."

I bounced a pencil off my notepad. "I thought you said they pulled off the snatch."

"They apparently pulled it off, but soon thereafter, things went downhill. A blue badger was quasi-running the op, and he was in way over his head. There were too many moving parts and not enough knuckle-draggers."

Clark uncapped and finished his water. "It was a twelve-man team, so it would make sense that each S-and-G team would've been made up of four men. They all reported clean and exfilling with the packages. That alone was a pretty big feat. They hit their marks within minutes of each other and had the bad guys rolled up before anyone could sound the alarm."

I leaned back in my chair. "Let me guess. They never made it to Guantanamo."

Clark snapped his fingers. "You're on a roll, College Boy."

"How were they moving?" I asked.

"I don't have that detail confirmed, but it was likely an airlift operation. They made it to San Andrés International Airport on the archipelago of San Andrés, Colombia. For those of you, like me, who have no idea where that is, it's a hundred twenty miles off the coast of Nicaragua."

"That's a long way from Colombia." I glanced up to see that Skipper had located the island for us, and I said, "How did I not know that island existed?"

"You don't know everything, College Boy. Would you let me finish?" I pretended to be sorry for interrupting, and Clark continued. "So, they apparently made it to this island, but they haven't been heard from since they checked in with feet dry."

I asked, "Has anybody looked for them at the airport?"

Clark closed his notebook. "Not yet. We're the first call the Board made, so there's a lot more to this than we know. My job is to pitch it to you. If you want to get involved, we'll get a full briefing."

I leaned in. "Off the record, what do you think?"

Clark chewed on his pencil for a moment. "I think the Agency dropped the ball. I told you the op was being run by a blue badger." He paused and turned to Gator. "Do you know what a blue badger is?"

Obeying his mandate not to speak, Gator shook his head, so Clark said, "When a CIA case officer is running an op with civilian contractors, the Agency guy wears a blue badge. That means he thinks he's in charge. The contractors wear green badges. That means they get shot first. Got it?"

Gator nodded his appreciation for the explanation, and Clark turned back to the table. "Off the record, I suspect the blue badger screwed up and he's trying to push the blame off on the contractors. If we get involved, we're volunteering to assume the mess the CIA guy poured out on the other team."

"Was the team run by the Board?" Mongo asked.

"Unclear," Clark said. "That doesn't really matter, though. Apparently, the Board is running the game now, so whoever goes, it'll be one of our teams."

I asked, "I know we're compartmentalized for a reason, but do you know of another team as capable as ours in this kind of op?"

Clark shook his head. "No. We've got the ship, the plane, and the experience. Those tools alone make us unique. We're not the first call the Board makes when there's a tragedy on the top of a mountain, but if there's salt water involved, my phone tends to ring first."

I dropped my pencil onto my pad. "I say we take the briefing and make an informed decision."

Chapter 8
Tower of Blood

I spun my chair to face Gator. "Everybody else has heard this speech a hundred times, but this is your first, so listen up. We're not a democracy. We don't vote on courses of action, especially not when bullets are in the air. I'm team lead. I make the calls. When I'm wrong—and that happens sometimes—I'm open to listening for alternate ideas, but when it comes to accepting or turning down a mission, that decision is made right here in this room. I listen, I ask, and I consider opinions, but ultimately, I make the call."

Gator nodded as I continued the explanation. "When I say yes to a mission, that doesn't mean you're required to go. No one is ever required to go, and if you step off the field, no one will ever beat you up for not going."

The new guy held up a finger, and I said, "Go ahead."

"I know you told me to shut up, but I'd like to know how often that happens."

"How often what happens?"

"Somebody decides not to go."

Snickers and muffled laughter arose from the table. "So far, it's never happened. We've turned down missions, but we've never had anybody step aside while the rest of us stormed the beach."

"That's what I thought," he said.

"There's something you need to understand. If we got dispatched to a job in Kansas to pick corn or whatever you guys do out there, we'd ask your opinion, but until you get a little experience under your belt, your input isn't going to be encouraged. What will be encouraged, though, are your questions. If you don't understand something, ask. Always ask. I'd much rather take the time to explain something in this room when nobody's shooting at us than when we're huddled behind a rock with bullets bouncing off everything. There's nothing wrong with not knowing, but there's a ton wrong with not asking."

I stopped to let that sink in, and Hunter took the floor. "Don't get Chase wrong, kid. We're going to laugh at you when you ask stupid questions, but we asked them, too. And not so long ago. Take the ribbing and learn, but like Chase said, do not hesitate to ask."

Gator said, "This isn't how I expected it to be."

"I know the feeling," I said. "And it wasn't like this when I got started. I took my first mission briefing on the deck of a sailboat in Jewfish Creek of Key Largo from two guys who showed up in a motorboat. We've come a long way since then, and this is how we do it now."

"The boat thing is pretty much what I expected."

"Do a lot of listening and not a lot of talking over the next few days, and you'll learn more in a couple of weeks than you learned in a couple of years at The Ranch." I turned back to the table. "Is anybody opposed to taking the briefing from the Board?"

Heads shook, and Skipper typed furiously while Clark made the call. Every overhead monitor came to life with maps and charts of various parts of Central and South America.

When Clark disconnected the call, he said, "They're assembling, and they'll be ready to brief in half an hour."

I knocked on the table. "Okay, folks. If you need to hit the head or the galley, now's the time. Gator, any questions?"

"About a million, but I'll watch and listen before I ask."

"We're going to keep you out of the picture," I said. "The Board knows you're here, but we're not going to throw you in their faces for this one. We run independently, but it's none of their business how we introduce a new man to the team. You're going to feel left out for a while, but you'll get to sit at the grown-ups' table soon enough."

"It's cool," he said. "I understand, and I'm happy to stay right here in the corner."

As Clark headed out the door for a refrigerator run, he almost tackled Penny.

"Whoa, big fella. Where are you going in such a hurry?"

He hopped back and reached for the stack of pizza boxes in her arms. "Nowhere now. You saved me a trip."

"Can I come in?" she asked.

He stepped aside. "Of course. We're still half an hour from the briefing."

She passed out pizzas and bottles of water until she came to me. It wasn't a smile, but the look on her face said she understood. She whispered, "You're going, aren't you?"

I took her hand. "Probably."

She leaned down, kissed me on the cheek, and whispered, "I love you."

We ate pizza like animals and discussed what we expected from the coming briefing. With fifteen minutes left before the call, Skipper's notifications chimed, and soon, some of the charts she'd posted on the overheads were replaced with pictures of people.

She said, "Look at monitor number one. That's the team of contractors. I've got a list of names if you want them."

Kodiak pointed at the monitor. "Hey, I know some of those guys."

Mongo said, "I suspect we all know some of those guys. The question is, do you have any doubts about any of those guys?"

In my mind, that was an excellent question. If we could identify a weak link that may have led to the team vanishing, we might have a solid place to start.

Kodiak said, "Everybody I know in that shot is a solid dude."

Having never been in the military, Gator and I were at a disadvantage. I recognized a couple faces, but I'd never worked with any of them. I was certain Gator had never seen any of the operators.

Penny closed the door when she left the ops center, and the communication system came to life.

"Good evening, gentlemen and lady. We understand you have a new recruit."

Clark typically managed the conversation with the Board, but I stepped up. "That's correct, but he's not operational yet."

"We have faith in you, Chase. You'll have him up and running in no time. Do you need anything from us on that front?"

"No, sir. We've got that covered. Let's hear about the missing team."

Skipper brought up a single headshot of a man in his forties with a full beard and the need for a shower.

The briefer said, "This is Kennedy. Some of you may recognize him. You may have even worked with him in the past. He's the team lead on the operation we named Crimson Spire." He paused, apparently to let the name sink in before continuing. "Sixteen weeks ago, we picked up signal intelligence about a group calling themselves Burj Aldam. If you don't already know, that's Arabic and translates to Tower of Blood."

I didn't like anything about the sound of that, but I held my tongue for the moment.

"It became clear through further SIGINT, and human intelligence as well, that Burj Aldam wasn't an outlying splinter group. They are hardline Al Qaeda and run by a man named Hamza al Kassis. Kassis was radicalized from boyhood to despise Western decadence, Jews, and everything that didn't further the cause of Islam. He's extremely devout and follows most of the tenets of his religion. His one indulgence appears to be women. He has at least eleven wives and thirty children. Although he may not be the mastermind behind this attack, he is certainly in the upper echelons of Al Qaeda hierarchy."

The man took a breath, and I asked, "Do we know the details of the planned attack?"

He said, "We do not, but we have every reason to believe it's not on the scale of 9/11. Apparently, whatever the target is, it's designed to strike fear instead of killing thousands of Westerners, and the intel community has several theories on why Burj Aldam chose that particular style of attack."

I said, "My guess would be to keep more troops out of the Middle East. If they killed thousands of Americans, the country might rise up like we did after 9/11 and support massive troop deployment. I doubt any element of Al Qaeda wants half a million more American boots on the sand."

"You're quite right, Chase. That is the prevailing theory, but in spite of that, we still don't know the exact target. What we do know is that three men who've likely never heard of each other, and who've certainly never met, were dispatched with one piece of either the plan or the actual attack. We got ahead of them and laid three traps in Central America, using Kennedy's team to abduct each of the three messengers. The plan was to capture and transport the three men to Guantanamo, where they would be interrogated and imprisoned until we gathered enough information to dismantle the organization. Obviously, that did not happen."

"I understand the CIA was overseeing the op," I said.

"Yes, that's correct, but that scenario was less than ideal. Any time the federal government is involved in anything, everything about it becomes exponentially more complex and less efficient. Thankfully, the Agency has backed away and disavowed any knowledge of this operation, so they're out of the picture."

"Is the blue badger missing as well?" I asked.

"Yes, and the Agency is already circling the wagons and preparing a statement about their officer going rogue. That's part of the reason you and your team are in the picture. You have the ability to work around the bureaucratic nonsense and achieve results in days instead of weeks or months. Chase, we want you on this mission. We want you to find the missing contractors, as well as the CIA case officer, but most importantly, we want you to find, detain, and deliver the three messengers alive for interrogation. A dossier on each of the terrorists and as many of the team members as possible is included with the electronic package we delivered to you moments ago."

"What about air and naval support?" I asked.

He didn't hesitate. "None."

"None? This sounds exactly like the kind of mission the SEALs would undertake. Why can't we expect at least a little backup?"

"The official position of the administration is that Burj Aldam is a peaceful organization with no history of violence against Westerners. As you might imagine, our stance is quite different."

"Is the destination still Guantanamo?"

"No. The destination is now the Research Vessel *Lori Danielle*. We'll supply a team of interrogators, if necessary, but the questioning will happen at sea, in international waters, for obvious reasons. Are you capable of conducting this operation?"

"We are. And we will. Send everything you have, and we'll be wheels-up in less than thirty-six hours."

"There's one more thing, Chase."

"There always is."

"There's no chance that these three messengers were capable of dismantling Kennedy's team. It's our initial theory that operators of Burj Aldam may have intercepted the team in San Andrés. If we are correct, the organization may be much larger than we initially believed."

"Thank you. We'll take all of the information and your theories into consideration. Now, on the issue of funding—"

He interrupted me. "The mission is fully funded, and a deposit into the operating account for the *Lori Danielle* will be made within the hour. Any more questions?"

"Not at the moment," I said. "We'll report directly to Clark, and I'm certain he'll keep you well informed."

The line went dead, and the mood of the ops center changed in an instant. The carefree family we'd been only moments before was now a team of some of the hardest-hitting civilian operators on the planet.

Chapter 9
Where's Our Ship?

Our tablets came alive when Skipper sent the mass distribution, and each of us buried our faces in the screens. Some of us were, no doubt, looking for old comrades, but I was looking for weakness. What I found left a bitter taste in my throat.

I rolled beside Skipper at her console and held up my tablet. "Did the Board send you these dossiers on the team, or did you snatch them from somewhere?"

"I know what you're thinking, and I agree. I don't like the idea of the Board throwing our dossiers around. Yes, we need to know who we're looking for, but these things are complete files."

I scrolled through Kennedy's information. "Do they keep files like this on us?"

She said, "I don't know. I suspect they do. If we ever drop off the face of the planet, it's nice to know somebody will know who they're looking for when they come after us, but I'd like to know what kind of safeguards are being taken to protect our info."

"I agree. I guess it's out of our hands, but at least we know the information is out there, regardless of how little we like it."

She said, "I've got an idea. I'll pretend that I don't know us, and I'll see if I can piece together dossiers on each of us through my sources. That'll give us a pretty good idea of who knows what about our team." She glanced over her shoulder. "Are you taking Gator?"

I spun in my seat and motioned for him to join Skipper and me at the console.

He leapt from his chair, and Skipper rolled her eyes. "Bring your chair, dummy."

He pulled his seat with him and settled in beside us. I tried to keep the conversation quiet enough to avoid disturbing the rest of the team, who were reading dossiers and studying pictures.

"We've obviously got a mission," I said. "We'll run it from our ship."

"The Mark Five?" he asked.

Skipper brought up a picture, and I pointed toward the screen. "No, not the Mark Five. Our ship is the Research Vessel *Lori Danielle*. She's five hundred eighty feet long and can do things your brain could never imagine."

He stared, mesmerized at the vessel filling the screen in front of Skipper. "What's next? A spaceship?"

I thought of *Penny's Secret*, my North American P-51D Mustang. "We've got one of those, too."

"Why am I not surprised?"

I said, "We typically run ops from here, with Skipper and Tony sharing analyst responsibilities."

Skipper cut in. "Actually, we don't share. He answers the phone while I get a couple of hours of sleep every two days."

"That's more accurate. Anyway, when we're operating from the *Lori Danielle*, we have an ops center on board called a combat information center or CIC. Do you know anything about ships?"

He shook his head.

"That's okay. We'll teach you. We'll run this op from the ship. That means we'll deploy the whole team, and we'll live aboard until the mission is complete. I can't promise you we'll put you in the field, but I want you on the boat with us, at least. Are you good with that?"

He huffed. "Am I good with that? Yeah, of course. I'm good with whatever you want me to do, except wrestling alligators or piano players."

The stern look on my face said the time for jokes was over, and he said, "Sorry."

"Don't be sorry. Just learn the difference between on and off duty."

"Yes, sir."

I said, "Hook him up with a tablet, and get him up to speed."

Skipper pulled a pair of boxes from the storage locker and issued Gator his new tablet and cell phone. She said, "Both of these are preprogrammed with the team's contact information. That alone makes them classified, but there's going to be a lot more information on those devices than just names and numbers. Guard both of these with your life. Nobody else touches or even smells them. Got it?"

"Got it."

She continued. "Everything is encrypted to protect the data, but a good hacker like me can get through the encryption with enough time. Let's set up your passwords and biometrics."

She spent several minutes scanning Gator's fingerprints and retinas into the devices. She taught him how to access stored information and even how to destroy the devices if things went south.

While Skipper was playing tech wizard with Gator, I rolled back to the table. "Is anything jumping out at you?"

Clark rubbed his eyes. "Not yet. It all looks clean. They just vanished."

"People don't just vanish. How did they get to San Andrés?"

Mongo scrolled through his notes. "From Maracaibo and Barranquilla, they took an Agency seaplane to Colón. From there, they put them on a go-fast boat for the two-hundred-fifty-mile run to San Andrés."

"Wait a minute," I said. "They had a seaplane, but they made the last leg of the trip in a boat? That doesn't make any sense."

"Maybe they were heavy," Mongo said.

"Maybe, but think about it. If we were running the op, wouldn't you leave part of the team in Colón to make use of the seaplane for the two-hundred-fifty-mile run across open water?"

Disco chimed in. "Why not split up and take half in the boat and half in the plane?"

"Where's the plane now?" I asked.

Fingers scrolled wildly on tablets, but no one came up with an answer.

"How about the boat?" I asked. "Where is it?"

I got the same absence of an answer, so I asked, "Skipper, is there a dossier on Kennedy's analyst?"

"Give me a second," she said, and dived into her computer.

Two minutes later, she said, "There's nothing on the analyst, but they had to have one. You can't run an op that big without an analyst. There's too much to coordinate."

"Who was the blue badger?" I asked.

She said, "Oh, that's funny. You think they're going to divulge the name of the CIA case officer? No chance."

"So, maybe the Agency was operating as their analyst."

Skipper clicked her tongue against her teeth. "It's possible, but I've never heard of an Agency analyst running a contractor's op."

"It wasn't the contractor's op. It was the CIA's op. Their blue badger was in charge."

"You're right, but it's still weird. I don't even know if that ever happens, but I know who to ask." In seconds, Skipper had Ginger on speaker. "Hey, girl. How's it going in Virginia?"

Ginger said, "You never call this number when you just want to talk. What's up?"

Skipper adjusted herself in the chair. "Since you're my mentor, I tend to believe you know everything."

"That's a good assumption."

"Yeah, I thought so. Anyway, we just inherited an op that fell apart in the Caribbean. It was a civilian contract team, but they were working for the Agency under a blue badger."

"None of that is rare," Ginger said. "Especially the part about their op falling apart. Any time you mix feds and real fighters, things go bad."

"I know. The problem with this one is a sketchy trail of bread-crumbs from unlikely sources."

"Keep talking," the seasoned analyst said.

"We're on a secure line, right?"

Ginger said, "Oh, yeah. Of course. Go ahead."

"Okay, here's the deal. A twelve-man team of operators hit three targets scattered across Central America and rolled them up. They joined up in Colón, Panama, before heading for an island called San Andrés off the coast of Nicaragua."

"Yeah, I know the place."

Skipper said. "We believe they used an Agency seaplane to hook up in Colón, but then it appears they may have used a boat to get to San Andrés. That's two hundred and fifty miles."

Ginger said, "Let me guess. You can't find the boat or the plane."

"You're good at this game."

"It's the only game in town, baby. When did this happen?"

Skipper checked her clock. "Within the past twelve hours."

Ginger said, "Ooh, this one's getting cold. Twelve hours is a long time in Central America. Send me what you know about the plane and boat."

Skipper sent the electronic packet, and Ginger said, "Give me three minutes."

"Do you want to call me back?"

Ginger huffed. "No. Just hang on."

Two minutes later, Ginger's voice came back on the line. "Girl, what have you gotten yourself into this time?"

Skipper eyed me. "What? What did you find?"

Ginger said, "If this is what I think it is, it's got counterterrorist task force written all over it, and you don't want to be caught up in that net."

"I'm over my head here. Help a sister out."

"Let's put it this way," Ginger said. "Whoever briefed you left out the part about the FBI being involved, didn't they?"

I took the bait. "What do you mean, FBI? The Board briefed us. If the FBI was involved, they would've known."

"Not necessarily. From what I'm seeing, everybody's crawfishing away from this one. Nobody wants to touch it. Twelve dead contractors, one dead Agency case officer, and cell leaders from Syria, Saudi, and Iraq. That's one hot potato."

Skipper said, "I didn't say anything about anybody being dead."

"Sorry, I just assumed. If any of them were still alive, don't you think they would've found a way to call for help?"

Skipper sighed. "See? I told you I was in over my head."

"Are your boys going?"

Skipper turned to me, and I gave her a nod.

She said, "Yep, they're going."

Ginger said, "Then you'd better pat them on the butt and kick them out the door. This thing is going to be ice-cold in a matter of hours. If there's any evidence left on the ground, you can bet your cute little tush the Agency will have somebody clean it up before you get there."

"This is starting to sound like a conspiracy," Skipper said.

THE CRIMSON CHASE · 81

"Everything is a conspiracy when the government gets caught with its pants down."

I grabbed my phone and dialed Don Maynard.

"Hey, Chase."

"Don, is the fuel truck up and running?"

"Yeah, Earl finished it up on Saturday. The *Grey Ghost* is topped off and ready to go."

"That's great news. I need you to pull her out and rig for one pallet of cargo and up to ten humans. How long will that take?"

He said, "Maybe an hour and a half, but I can hustle if you need me to."

"Try to cut it to an hour," I said. "We're under the gun on this one."

"That's nothing new. I'll call you when it's ready."

"No need to call," I said. "We'll be there before you're finished."

He said, "I'm on it," and the line went dead.

Almost before I tucked my cell phone away, the team was powering down their tablets and gathering their notes.

Clark said, "I guess that means it's time to make like chimpanzees and get the heck out of here."

I palmed my forehead. "That doesn't even . . . oh, never mind."

As everyone headed for the door, I caught a glimpse of Gator still nestled in his chair. "Don't just sit there. Put everything you own in a bag, and let's go."

Before I reached the door, I spun on a heel. "Uh, Skipper . . . Where's our ship?"

Chapter 10
Typical?

Our analyst giggled. "Honey, have you seen my ship? I can't seem to remember where I put it. Get back in here, you crazy old man." She pulled up a new screen. "I always know where it is, and now you can, too. I'll add the tracking software to your tablet."

"That'll come in handy. It looks like they're in the Keys."

She said, "Yep, they're doing environmental sampling in the Straits of Florida. It's contract work, but they can pull off anytime."

"See if you can get Captain Sprayberry on the phone."

Seconds later, Barry's no-nonsense voice came through the speaker over our head. "Bridge, Captain Sprayberry."

"Hello, Captain. Chase here. Are you up for a little excitement?"

"I'd rather count grains of rice than what I'm doing right now. Please put me to work."

I asked, "Have you ever been to San Andrés off Nicaragua?"

"A thousand years ago when I was a quavering midshipman, but that was a long time ago. What's going on in Nicaragua?"

"We don't know yet, but we're going to find out. Have Ronda No-H check your operating account. You should've received a deposit to cover expenses for the next month or so."

"I like it when other people put money in my account. When do you need us on site?"

"We'll be on San Andrés later today. Can you be there in twenty-four hours?"

The clicking sound coming from his mouth said he was doing the math. "We'll need to bunker fuel in Key West to run on the foils, but I think we can make twenty-four hours happen. Do you want me in port or laying off?"

"For now, lay off twelve miles or more. We may shuttle aboard if the chopper's available. I like the idea of keeping prying eyes off of our boat."

He gave a set of commands and returned to the line. "We're headed for Key West now, and we'll lay off the north end of San Andrés until we hear from you. All systems are up and running, so whatever you need done, the ship and crew are ready to make it happen."

I asked, "Do you have any researchers or outside staff on board?"

"Six of them, but I'll kick them off in Key West. I assume that's why you were asking."

"You're pretty good at this game, Captain. We'll see you tomorrow."

With that, Skipper shut down the ops center.

When our convoy of Suburbans pulled onto the tarmac at the airport, Don had just finished configuring the *Grey Ghost* for our deployment.

I rolled down the window. "It looks like you've got her ready."

"She's ready, and I staged your pallet inside hangar one."

"Thanks, Don. We'll have it packed and ready to be loaded in twenty minutes."

He said, "I'll bring the forklift around."

We backed our three SUVs within a few feet of the empty pallet and threw open every door. Gator watched with enormous interest, but he obviously had no idea how to help.

Hunter saw him standing doing nothing and couldn't resist getting involved. "Get over here, kid. You don't get to stand around while the rest of us lump gear."

Gator said, "I don't know what to do. I'm afraid I'll be in the way."

"If you get in the way, we'll let you know. Start handing me anything that looks square enough to be a base layer, and I'll teach you how to build a gear pallet."

The lesson slowed our progress, but only by a few minutes. Soon, Gator was stacking and strapping while Hunter supervised.

When the cargo net went across the pile of gear, Hunter demonstrated how to tighten the net evenly to make sure nothing fell off the pallet. He said, "The way these guys fly, we'll be lucky if the pallet stays inside the airplane. Tighten it until it can't be tightened another inch, and then tighten it two more inches."

Don loaded the pallet and sealed the cargo door on the *Ghost*.

While Disco conducted the preflight inspection, I spent a few minutes with Penny in the office inside the hangar.

"I know you don't want me to go, but—"

She pressed a finger to my lips. "Stop, Chase. I'll never *want* you to go, but I understand why you have to. It's okay. I'm almost back to full strength, and I've got a script calling my name."

"I don't foresee this one getting dangerous. It's just a hide-and-seek mission."

She planted her hands on her hips and cocked her head. "That makes me feel better. I suppose you're taking that pallet full of guns and ammo so you can do some duck-hunting while you're down there."

I took her in my arms. "Why did I have to marry a smart woman?"

She squeezed me. "Because you had the hot girl, and she wasn't enough for you."

"You *are* the hot girl."

"Speaking of the hot girl, I hope she's doing okay after the surgery. I still can't believe she gave me part of her liver. That makes me think your old Russian girlfriend is a better person than me. I'm not sure I would've volunteered an organ for her."

"I don't know what you're trying to lure me into saying, but I'm not falling for it. I wouldn't trade you for a thousand Anyas."

She glanced away. "What would you think about me calling her to thank her?"

"It's not necessary."

"I know, but I think it's the right thing to do. I don't hate her, you know. I've just always thought I couldn't really compete with her. I mean, she knows all about this stuff you do, and I just write movies about it."

I brushed the hair from her face and tucked it behind her ear. "It's not a competition. You're the one with my last name."

She rolled her eyes. "Have you seen Anya's passport?"

"Okay, maybe she's got my last name, too. I didn't give it to her, though. The government did that."

"It's always somebody else's fault, huh?"

I took her hand in mine, and we danced to music neither of us could hear.

She said, "Be careful out there . . . please."

"I'm always careful."

"No, you aren't. Remember, I'm the smart one. Just because your retirement plans have been delayed doesn't mean I don't want you home in one piece when this is over."

"I'll be careful. I promise."

We danced for the remainder of the imaginary song, and she said, "I think I'll call her. I just feel like I should."

"Do whatever you want, sweetheart. Just don't expect her to say or do anything that makes sense."

"I don't have any trouble understanding her."

"I wasn't talking about her accent. I meant—"

She cut in. "I know what you meant, and her motivation is crystal clear, so everything she does makes sense to me."

"Oh really?" I asked.

"Yep. She wants you back, and she'll do whatever she can to make that happen."

I held up a finger. "I'm not taking her side, but if that's what's going on, how do you explain why she'd give you the organ you needed to stay alive? Why wouldn't she just let you die?"

She played with my beard. "Oh, Chasechka, how naïve you are. She gave me part of her liver so you'd think about the sacrifice she made instead of the terrible things she did to you in the past. Women are snakes. Especially the ones who look like her."

"You're a mess," I said. "I'm right where I want to be, with exactly who I want to be with. Don't overdo it. You're still healing."

"I won't. Now, go. Your boys are waiting for you."

I gave her a kiss and twisted the doorknob. "I'll check in when I can. I love you."

"I love you, too, hero."

The team settled into their seats aboard the *Grey Ghost* for the three-hour flight to San Andrés, and Skipper spun to face me. "Do you have a plan?"

"I'm piecing one together," I said. "We need to know who the team's contact on San Andrés was, and we need to find him."

"I know. I'm working that, but I'm not getting anywhere."

"We also need to know if Kennedy's team was an asset of the Board, like us, or if they were freelancers."

"I know the answers to that one."

I frowned. "Answers? Plural?"

"Yes, they were both. Kennedy was a team leader like you, but he only had four men on the team. Here they are."

She turned her tablet so I could see, and I motioned for Kodiak to take a look.

I said, "Do you know any of these guys?"

He studied the screen and pointed to a guy in a backward baseball cap and wraparound shades. "I know that dude. He's a sniper, and a pretty good one. He took a round in the hip in Afghanistan and got medicalled out. I thought he was doing private security stuff, but I didn't know he was on a team."

Skipper asked, "What's his name?"

"Everybody calls him Jet, but that's not his name. Give me a minute. It'll come to me."

I asked, "Has the Board notified any next of kin yet?"

Skipper shook her head. "They don't do that."

"What?"

She said, "Yeah, they don't make notifications. If a team is lost, it's just gone."

I leaned back in my chair and let that wash over me. If the day should come when we step onto a battlefield but never step off, no one would hand Penny a folded flag. No one would knock on the door at Bonaventure with the news.

Skipper rarely missed anything around her, and my reaction wasn't going to fall through the cracks either. She said, "Think about it, Chase. I'm never on the ground with you, even when we're operating from the ship. I'm locked away in the CIC. If, God forbid, it should ever happen, I'll be the one to tell our family back home."

"I can't believe I never thought about it before."

Kodiak said, "You can't let things like that creep in, man. They'll eat you alive. We've got to keep kicking down doors and pressing through targets. There's no room for worrying about stuff we can't change."

"I get it," I said. "I've never been in the service, but it had to be at least a little reassuring knowing that if you went down while you were deployed, your family would be taken care of."

Kodiak shook his head. "Taken care of? What does that mean? If a soldier catches a round in the face, his family gets two hundred fifty K and a flag. That sounds like a lot of money to an eighteen-year-old kid from Des Moines or wherever, but by the time you pay off the two cars you financed and buy a coffin, that single mother with two little kids who don't have a daddy anymore has to find a way to feed those babies and keep the house. No, dude, it's not reassuring at all."

Hearing a career soldier explain the system from his perspective was sobering.

I said, "That's just not right. Something should be done."

"What is there to do?" Kodiak asked. "It's just the way it is. Nobody forces anybody to join up. It's an all-volunteer Army. There's just so much these kids don't know when they sign that four-hundred-page contract at the recruiter's office."

Skipper tapped on her tablet. "I know this is serious, but we're getting way off task here."

"Sorry," I said. "Where were we?"

"I was explaining to you that, as far as I know, the Board doesn't do anything when a team is lost."

"It won't be that way with this team. We're putting a policy in place to make sure everybody's family is well cared for and given all the support they need if one or more of us goes down."

"That's cool," Kodiak said. "I wonder how many more teams operate like this one."

Skipper chuckled. "I can't imagine there being another team that's anything like this one. We're not your typical anything."

Chapter 11
No Stupid Questions

As the island nation of Cuba passed seven miles beneath us, my hearing aids gave me a bit of an unfair advantage when it came to eavesdropping. Gator slid onto the seat beside Singer, and our sniper slipped into the self-appointed role of mentor for the new guy.

Gator said, "You know how you told me to always ask questions, even if I thought they were stupid?"

Singer said, "That's not what I said, but it's close enough. What's on your mind?"

Gator paused and finally said, "I know this is one of the most rookie questions I could ask, but I like knowing what's going on around me. What's going to happen when we hit the ground? I know I'm new and all, but it doesn't feel like we have much information to go on. We're not going to blast off the plane and start shooting, are we?"

Singer chuckled. "That's a great question, and it's not rookie at all. Everyone on this plane is asking himself the same thing, and the answer is simple. We don't know, but we're certainly not blasting through the door with guns blazing. We'll watch, listen, ask some locals a few questions, and listen some more. You'll be amazed at how much of our job is just listening when other people start to talk. Sometimes, what people don't say is more important than what actually comes out of their mouths. You'll learn. For now, just stay close to me, and keep your ears open and your mouth closed."

"Thanks. I really appreciate what you're doing for me."

Singer leaned close. "I'm not doing it for you. I'm doing it for three hundred million Americans who need you on that battlefield. Look around. We're getting old, and if we don't train our replacements, who's going to?"

Gator chewed his bottom lip for a moment. "What if I fail?"

"What do you mean by fail?"

"What if I can't do it? I mean, what if I freeze up out there?"

Singer said, "We can train until everything we do is second nature, but there's no way to know how a man will react when there's just as much fire incoming as there is outgoing. We learn a lot about ourselves when the situation around us becomes a matter of life and death, not only for ourselves, but for those around us. I'd gladly take a bullet for anybody on this airplane . . . including you. I know my reward is waiting for me when I cross that river."

Gator swallowed hard. "I wish I could say I'd be willing to take that bullet, too, but the truth is, I just don't know."

"We've all been where you are, Clint. We've all had our first gunfight, and we all survived it. So far, we've survived every one of them, but that doesn't mean we'll make it through the next one. You'll be a different man after it happens. If you stick around, the day will come when you can definitively say that you'd step in front of a bullet for any one of us. That's the kind of men we are, and you're well on your way to joining those ranks. Don't worry. Just do your job, listen when we teach, and shoot back when they start shooting at us."

He nodded. "That still doesn't answer my question, though."

"About freezing up? It's not going to happen, but if it does, we'll be right there with you, and if we live through it, you will, too. We'll make sure of that."

Gator said, "Cowards don't always know they're cowards until they're forced to prove otherwise."

"You're no coward. I've seen enough out of you already to know there's no yellow streak down your back. You'll do fine. When all else fails, just do whatever the rest of us are doing."

"Thanks, Singer."

"You're welcome, kid. Now, leave me alone so I can get some sleep."

Singer wasn't going to sleep. He was going to pray. But the two postures from our sniper were difficult to distinguish.

I didn't know enough about our new brother-in-arms to know if his eyes being shut meant slumber or communion.

As we began our descent into San Andrés, Skipper slid onto the seat beside me. "I found something. Well . . . someone, actually."

She had my attention. "His name is Quentin Palmer. He's a former Agency guy and current ex-pat living in Central America, and he spends a lot of time on San Andrés. He's probably not the contact, but he might be a good place to start."

"Where can we find him?"

She grimaced. "That's the tough part. He's not exactly advertising. Guys like him don't exactly hang out a sign saying 'Ex-Spook for Hire,' but I've got a few leads."

I said, "If he's not the contact, it's a pretty good bet he'll know who some of the local players are, and that should get us pointed in the right direction."

"Right. I plan to have Clark talk to the Board again when we get on the ground and see if they can dig up the local coordinator for the failed mission. The problem I see with going straight to the source is that it's possible that source was the breakdown."

"What do you mean?"

She said, "Look at it like this. The team rounded up the three bad guys and headed to San Andrés. We know they had to be meeting a local contact there to coordinate the hop to Guantanamo. If he dropped the ball or screwed up the transfer, he's likely dead or he's gone to ground. If he was an Agency guy, you know they recalled him to the States, and if he was just a contract guy, they either put a bullet in his head or he's running for his life. Either way, we're never going to put eyes on him."

I played her scenarios through my head. "So, this Palmer guy. What do we know about him?"

She opened her tablet and laid it in my hand. "Here's the dossier I put together."

I handed the tablet back. "Just give me the high points."

She said, "Naval Academy dropout. Did five years in the Marines as an enlisted intelligence analyst. Courted by the CIA and Defense Intelligence. Hopped on board with CIA and worked embassy duty in Poland, Czechoslovakia, and then the Middle East."

"Whoa. He jumped from Eastern Europe to the Middle East? Does that ever happen?"

"Apparently, in his case, it did."

"Does he have language skills?"

She said, "Unknown, but he apparently burned out in Yemen and walked away. Since then, he's been bumming around Central America, drinking too much, chasing women half his age, and picking up the odd job from time to time. Apparently, finding work for a guy like him in that part of the world isn't particularly challenging."

"What kind of work?"

"That's where it gets a little sketchy. There's some evidence that points to him being a trigger-puller."

I recoiled. "And you think he's our best back door into this whole thing? If he's a shooter, he's not likely to roll out the red carpet for an American ops team he's never heard of."

She put on a brilliant smile. "That's the best part. Palmer did eleven months in Caracas at the same time Clark's father was in the embassy down there."

I threw open my arms and hugged her as if she'd just made my greatest wish come true. After a sloppy kiss to the forehead, I said, "You're—"

But she wouldn't let me finish. "I know, I know. I'm a genius, and I deserve a raise."

"Yes, all of that is true"—I held up a finger—"but I know more money would be offensive to a brilliant mind like yours, so I won't risk offending you."

She rolled her eyes and wiped her forehead. "You're disgusting, but I love you, and I'll talk to Clark as soon as we land."

I unbuckled my seat belt. "I've got a better idea. I'll land, and you can talk to Clark now."

Before she could protest, I slipped from my seat and kicked Clark out of the cockpit. "I've got it from here. Skipper needs you."

He didn't put up an argument. Instead, he slipped past me, and I took his seat on the right side of the cockpit.

Disco gave me the briefing, ending with, "It'll be a visual approach to zero-six. The wind is zero-eight-zero at twelve. Any questions?"

"None," I said.

The tiny speck of an island came into sight and slowly morphed into San Andrés.

The runway finally appeared on the northern tip of the island, and I said, "Runway in sight."

The local air traffic controller cleared us for the visual approach to runway 06 and sent us to the tower frequency. The tower controller spit out a phrase in some combination of English and Spanish that sounded enough like "clear to land" for me to believe the runway would be empty when we touched down.

It was, and we landed without incident and taxied to the parking ramp, where two men in official-looking uniform shirts and khaki shorts waited for us to open the door.

The first man came aboard without invitation and demanded passports. We produced them, and he stamped each of our little blue booklets without inspection.

"Welcome tah San Andrés. Enjah dah island."

I turned to Disco for translation, and he laughed. "That's San Andrés–Providencia Creole. He welcomed us to dah island, mon."

"If you say so."

The second man replaced the first and stuck his head into the cockpit.

More Creole came, and Disco said "*Gracias*" and stuffed a collection of folded bills into the man's outstretched palm.

He disappeared, and a tug materialized beneath the nose of the *Ghost*. We were towed into a hangar alongside two other business jets, and the tug driver made his escape.

"Excellent service," I said.

Disco closed his checklists and slid the binder into the slot beside his leg. "American dollars speak every language. Especially this close to the equator."

The pair of SUVs Skipper arranged were waiting just inside the hangar door, and we wasted no time pulling gear from our pallet and loading each vehicle. Gator wasn't shy anymore, and he more than shouldered his share of the heavy lifting.

We pulled into the driveway of the rented house about two miles south of the airport in La Loma. The property was remote enough to provide the privacy we wanted, yet close enough to San Andrés to work our mission.

Singer took his understudy around the house and taught a master class on residential security. They positioned temporary cameras in several locations to establish an uninterrupted picture of the perimeter. Each camera overlapped with two more, making it virtually impossible for anyone to approach the house without us seeing them coming.

With room selections made, we settled into the living room in a hodgepodge collection of chairs, and I called the informal meeting to order. "Clark, have you talked to Dominic yet?"

He pulled out his phone and glanced at the screen. "I called, but he was in the middle of something he couldn't step away from. I suspect she didn't speak much English and wore too much lipstick, but he assured me he'd call back in fifteen minutes. That was twenty-two minutes ago."

Before I could encourage him to make the call again, his phone chirped, and he said, "Well, speak of the devil and dancing with people you don't know."

Chapter 12
Old Dawgs

Clark pressed the button to place his phone on speaker and slid it onto the table. "Good afternoon, Mr. Better Late Than Never."

Dominic Fontana scoffed. "Give me a break. What's a few extra minutes among friends?"

Clark said, "I hope you enjoyed *whatever* you were doing. It's time to talk business, though."

"For your information . . . oh, never mind. It's none of your business what I was doing, and I don't talk business anymore. I'm retired, remember?"

"Semi-retired," Clark said. "Listen, Dad. We need the goods on a cat named Quentin Palmer. You probably ran across him when you were in Caracas."

Dominic said, "Palmer . . . Palmer . . . Let me see. Was he an Agency guy?"

"He was, but he's out of the game now."

"Out of the game. That's funny. The CIA and the mafia share an employee handbook. There's only one way out of either organization, and if Palmer is still breathing—"

"He's still breathing," Clark said. "Or at least he was last week. What can you tell me about him?"

"Caracas, huh? That's interesting. What have you gotten yourself into this time, son?"

"Focus, Dad. We need to know about Quentin Palmer."

"Keep your pants on."

Clark groaned. "I could say the same thing to you. Give us the
goods, would you?"

"Okay, okay. Palmer was one of those guys who hit the job
hard, and it hit him back even harder. He brought a deadly piece
of baggage with him when he took the oath."

"What's that?" Clark asked.

Dominic took a drink of something that was likely older than
his lady friend lounging by the pool. "A conscience. He let it get to
him. That's why he burned out. He couldn't let go of the things
we were asked to do back then. The guy should've been a school-
teacher or something, but not a spook."

"Do you know where we can find him now?"

"I could do some digging, but to tell you the truth, I'm surprised
the guy is still alive. When I knew him, he drank too much, spent
too much time by himself, and read too many philosophy books."

"That's not much help, Dad. We could use some solid intel on
the guy. He probably plays a prominent role in this thing we're
looking into."

"I don't know if I can be much help, but if I were you, I'd start
by finding out where the local hippies hang out and smoke whatever they smoke in Caracas these days."

"We're not in Caracas," Clark said. "We're on San Andrés."

"San Andrés? Why didn't you say so? Look up a joint called
Momma Tay Tay's. If he's not there when you arrive, have a beer
and smoke a cigar. Momma's got a nice stash of exquisite Cubans
under the bar. Give him enough time, and Palmer will show up . . .
if he's still alive."

Skipper was already hard at work before Dominic finished spouting wisdom. She spun her laptop around so we could see the screen. A picture of a building that was little more than a shack stared back at us. It had a hand-painted sign propped up beside the door that read "Momma Tay-Tay's – Don't ya start none and der won' be none."

"Looks like a real classy joint," Clark said.

"Don't let the looks fool you, son. That place is a gem. Oh, and when you find Palmer, tell him he still owes me a C-note and reimbursement for that round of penicillin. He'll remember."

"We'll be sure to do that. If you think of anything else, drop a dime, will you?"

"Sure. I'll do some digging. You guys aren't working for the DEA, are you?"

"Nothing like that," Clark said. "We're just having a little vacation on a remote island a long way from home. If we happen to stumble across some more folks like us and three little pigs they rounded up, it'll just be a bonus."

"Three little pigs, you say?"

"I guess it's not polite to call them pigs since they're Muslim, but you get the picture."

"I do now," Dominic said. "I'll call you back."

The line went dead before we could say goodbye, and Clark said, "Well, that was interesting."

I said, "It sounded like he knew more than he was willing to say."

"He always sounds like that. Maybe he's got some inside track on this whole thing."

"That'd be nice, but for now, it sounds like we'd better put on our tuxedoes and make a reservation at Momma Tay-Tay's."

We opted out of the tuxedoes, but we caught Momma Tay-Tay unprepared for an onslaught of customers. We kept it simple for the cook and asked for rice, beans, and fish, family-style.

Clark slid his chair close to mine. "I'm not sure bringing the whole gang was a good idea. We're gonna be hard to forget."

"That's exactly the point," I said. "I want everybody talking about the guys who are looking for Quentin Palmer. If this guy is living the burned-out spook life, he's got enough feelers in the community to find out about us anyway. I'd rather present as a harmless group than a couple of covert operators prowling around in the dark."

"It's your show, College Boy. I can't fault the logic. It just feels weird to sniff around in a pack. You know I'm a lone-wolf kind of guy."

I dug into a pile of rice and beans as if I hadn't eaten in days. "This is fantastic. Get in there."

Clark scooped a heaping pile onto his plate and soon forgot all about being any kind of wolf other than a hungry one. "You're right. This is stupid good."

After thirty minutes of minding our own business and eating until overflowing, everyone else in the bar seemed to forget we were there. A drummer and a local singer took the stage and did a nice job of keeping the music loud enough to drown out the whir of spinning fans but soft enough for us to continue our conversation without yelling.

Gator and Singer were inseparable, and from the looks of things, the sniper was conducting a seminar in mentally cataloging every person who came through the door.

Singer said, "It's called KIM—keep in memory. It's important that we see and understand everything in our environment because any of it might have value or represent a threat in the future. I'll teach you how to store everything in your brain so you can recall it on command. It'll take a little time to master, but if you're going to be an operator, and especially a sniper, there may be no more important skill than KIM."

An hour and three rounds of drinks later, the real lone wolf on the island dragged himself through the door and parked on a stool that was obviously familiar with his butt. A beer landed in front of him almost before his body came to rest, and an ashtray slid down the bar, coming to a stop just beneath his left hand. He didn't speak, and he didn't have to. Everyone seemed to accept him as part of the environment. Our target was clearly a regular.

Clark and I watched him carefully for several minutes, and he showed all the signs of a man well on his way to tying on a solid drunk.

"Maybe we should talk to him before he gets too deep into his evening," I said.

Clark nodded. "Are you going, or am I?"

"I'll do it," I said. "You can be my wingman."

The two guys sitting to Palmer's left had been there since before we arrived and had only abandoned their stools long enough to visit the head twice.

I stuck my head and shoulders between the two men sitting beside Palmer, and they flinched. "Sorry, I didn't mean to startle you guys, but I wonder if we might buy these two seats from you."

They looked up at me, and one said, "What are you talking about?"

"I'll cover your tabs tonight if we can have these two seats."

"Are you for real, man?"

I pulled two hundreds from my pocket and laid them on the bar between the two men. "How's that for real?"

They snatched the bills from the bar and abandoned their seats. Clark and I replaced them, and Palmer glanced my way.

"How's it going?" I asked.

He ignored my question and raised a finger toward the bartender. A replacement beer and a clean ashtray arrived in seconds.

I kept pushing. "What are you drinking?"

He grumbled. "Beer."

I glanced at Clark. "The man's drinking beer."

"He's drinking beer," Clark said. "I wonder if he's ever heard of Agency Ale."

He said it loud enough for Palmer to hear, but the man didn't show any reaction.

I said, "They have that at the bar in Langley, right?"

Palmer drained his mug, slid two twenties onto the bar, and stood. Clark slid off the back of his stool and stepped between the man and the door. I took his elbow in my hand, and to my surprise, Palmer grabbed my hand and pinned me to the bar with a twist of his wrist.

Clark took a step closer. "Relax, Mr. Palmer. I think you know my dad, Dominic Fontana, from your time in Caracas."

He looked down at Clark without releasing my hand. "You guys clearly have me confused with somebody else. Get out of my face. I'm going home."

"We just want to talk."

"So, talk to each other and leave me alone," Palmer said.

I glanced back at what had been our table, and I was pleased to see it empty. I said, "Okay, I'm sorry we bothered you. Have a good night."

We watched him walk from the bar, and Clark said, "How long should we wait?"

I checked my watch. "I think it's been long enough."

I led the way through the door and into the crushed shell parking lot, where Mongo, Singer, and Gator were making a new friend.

Clark and I joined the party, and I said, "You hurt my feelings, Mr. Palmer. I just wanted to have a talk, and you got up and left."

He scowled. "Just do it. I know how these things work. There's no reason to play games. Just make it quick, would you?"

"If we were here to kill you, we wouldn't have spent two hours in a bar waiting for you to show up so everybody on the island could identify us as the last people to see you alive. That's not our style. If we wanted you dead, our sniper would've popped you from half a mile away, and nobody would've seen any of us."

Palmer seemed to consider my explanation. "So, what is it you want? I'm just an old man trying to live out his days on a little island a thousand miles away from nowhere."

"We just want to know about an operation that was supposed to pass through here a few days ago. It was a twelve-man team with three bad guys rolled up. Their reception party is still waiting up at Gitmo. Would you happen to know anybody who might have a little insider information on a gig like that?"

He stuck a hand in his pocket, and Gator leapt into action. He pinned the man's wrist against his hip bone so fast I couldn't piece together what was happening.

Palmer tried to shove him away, but the younger, stronger man wouldn't relent until the old spook said, "Would you relax, hotshot? I was just reaching for my keys. It's against the law to carry a gun on this island."

I laid a hand against Gator's shoulder. "Just relax."

The new guy took a step back, and Palmer came out of his pocket with a University of Georgia keyring. "See? It's just my keys. You sure are jumpy for a young fella."

I motioned toward his keys. "Why are you carrying a UGA keyring?"

He stared into my face and cocked his head. "Not that it's any of your business, but my daughter went to school up there. When you write a hundred-thousand-dollar tuition check, they give you a keyring."

"I don't have a keyring, but that's my alma mater, too. When was your daughter there?"

Palmer closed one eye and cocked his head. "I think she graduated in ninety-eight, if I'm not mistaken."

Clark stuck his cell phone toward Palmer, and the old spook
looked up at him. "What do you expect me to do with that?"

Clark said, "Talk to a guy you used to know."

Palmer took the phone and held it to his ear. "Yeah . . . Who's
asking?" He listened for several seconds and said, "I remember,
but I put down a quart of whiskey a day and beer backs trying to
forget."

I had no way to know what Dominic was saying on the other
end of the line, but based on Palmer's reactions, I could guess.

"Which one is your boy?" Palmer said.

Clark raised a finger, and Palmer eyed him up and down. "He
doesn't look much like I remember you looking." After several
more seconds, Palmer said, "They've got one kid who's a little
jumpy, but the rest of them are pretty calm." A minute later, he
said, "All right. I'll talk to them, but that's where it ends. You
know what they say about old Dawgs."

Chapter 13
Behind Closed Doors

Clark recovered his phone and snatched Quentin Palmer's Bulldog keyring from his hand. "How about you let us do the driving tonight?"

The man shrugged. "In for a penny . . ."

Clark drove Palmer's car back to our rented house, and we reconvened in the living room.

"Can I get you a drink?" I asked.

Palmer wiped his brow. "I thought you'd never ask."

"What'll it be?"

"Whatever you've got is fine."

I poured three fingers of Blanton's, and Clark delivered the cocktail.

Palmer took it from his hand. "So, are you really Dom's boy?"

"I really am, and that scrawny kid over there is my brother, Tony."

Palmer downed a sip. "You'll have to forgive me. It's been a long time, but I guess I didn't know Dom had any kids."

Clark crossed his legs. "He wasn't what you'd call an involved father. We didn't see much of him when we were kids."

"I get it. My daughter feels the same way about me. Other than cashing my checks, she's not interested in much of a relationship with her old man."

I let the stroll down memory lane play out. I wanted Palmer as comfortable as possible before I started pounding him with questions. Between the bourbon and family ties, I hoped he was well on his way to a condition that would give us the answers we needed.

To my surprise, he turned the conversation before me. "So, you guys are some kind of contractors. Is that right?"

"Something like that," I said. "We're not with the Agency, and we don't love them any more than you do."

He emptied his glass, and Clark took it from his hand.

Palmer said, "How'd you end up in the middle of this thing?"

I played out the coming minutes in my head and opted for the truth. "We work for an organization that isn't on anyone's balance sheet. That gives us the freedom to be a little less concerned with the consequences of our actions."

"Like kidnapping an old man from his favorite bar?"

Clark handed the refilled drink back to our guest, and I said, "We didn't kidnap you, Mr. Palmer. We invited you to come have a conversation with us. If this were a kidnapping, your wrists would bear the impressions of flex-cuffs, and you'd be sleeping off a tranquilizer."

He raised his glass. "That's what this is."

"It certainly can be," I said. "Here's the truth. We're down here to find out what happened to twelve contractors, a blue badger, and three Middle Eastern terrorists who apparently vanished into thin air."

"That sounds like some Bermuda Triangle stuff to me."

"We're a long way from Bermuda."

Palmer laughed. "We're a long way from everywhere, and that's exactly how I like it. What I don't like is Langley ramrodding an op through this place. There's no reason for it."

I wouldn't have started talking for a million dollars at that moment, and I prayed nobody else would either. When a drunk former spy started talking, listening was the only game in town.

"I'll tell you one thing for sure. They'll never do it again." He paused and searched frantically for his drink. When he located it, the remainder disappeared in seconds, and he handed the empty glass back to Clark. "Keep that stuff coming, Cowboy. It's pretty good."

Clark shortened the ice and lengthened the pour, but he didn't stop there. Instead of continuing his role as cocktail waitress, he brought the bottle with him back to the living room.

Palmer raised his glass. "Good thinking, hotshot."

Skipper thumbed her phone and slid it into the crease of Palmer's chair. *Having a recording of the coming minutes could prove to be the most valuable piece of intelligence we could possibly gather.*

He repositioned himself in the chair and cleared his throat. "That ignorant bastard, Claven, could break an anvil with a glass hammer."

My brain began a prolonged series of backflips. *Who's Claven? Why don't I know that name? Was Claven one of the operators? Was he the CIA blue badger? Did he really just say he could break an anvil with a glass hammer?*

Palmer held his glass up to the light. "What is this?"

Oh, no. I can't let him get off his soapbox. I need him to keep talking.

In a desperate attempt to keep the intel flowing, I pulled the cork from the bottle and topped off his drink. "It's Blanton's, and you're right. It's excellent bourbon. Do you know Claven?"

He glanced at the bottle. "Know him? Hell, I know a thousand Clavens. He's typical of those operations pukes at Langley who think they know how to run an op. They're a den of idiots feeding off other idiots. It's like a perpetual motion machine producing jackass after idiot after moron. It just never ends."

We sat in a jagged semicircle around a man who'd spent his life in the shadows doing things the rest of the world would never believe, and we looked like a gathering of first graders at story time.

Singer asked in his confident baritone, "Are you saying Claven got them all killed?"

Palmer frowned. "Killed? Are they all dead?"

Oh, no. Now he's asking questions.

I tried to save it. "We don't know. That's why we need you. If the terrorists are dead, that's a win, but if we lost a whole team and the terrorists are still out there, that's a real problem."

Palmer continued scowling. "You guys don't even know what you're looking for? Am I hearing this right?"

"Here's what we know," I said. "The team rolled up the three bad guys and headed for this little piece of an island nobody's ever heard of so they could rendezvous and head to Gitmo, where the hospitality committee would welcome them with open arms."

Palmer rolled his eyes. "Gitmo. That's another melting pot of intellectual dysfunction. That place is a sleeping mat and a cup of raisins away from being a daycare. Nobody with any sense would ever process these guys. You pin them to a rock and shove a rifle barrel down their throats until they puke up the intel you need. Then, you roll the rock off a cliff. Pretty soon it gets tough to recruit suicide bombers when all their buddies are tied to rocks on the bottom of the Atlantic."

I suddenly wanted a glass of the Blanton's. "That's quite a diplomatic foreign policy you've got there, Mr. Palmer."

"That ain't foreign policy, son. It's a master class on how to keep a country free. Go ahead, Sheik Ali Baba Doo Doo. Send all the suicide bombers you want. We've got plenty of rocks and no shortage of oceans."

I was afraid we'd let our retired spook dive into one too many tumblers of bourbon. "What do you think happened to the team and the terrorists?"

He emptied his glass and lay back as if I'd tucked him into bed. "Who knows? If the Agency knows, they'll never tell. If something blows up in the States in the next few days, we'll know the bad guys made it through the net. The way I figure it, something went downhill on that boat, and the operators decided to euthanize their new Arab friends. They probably figured out what was going to happen to those guys and chose to prevent having three bombers released as part of some prisoner swap thought up by some politician with his hands in the pockets of somebody's dish-dasha. If I was a betting man, I'd put money and odds on Claven's old man being the guy."

"Dishdasha?" I asked almost before realizing I'd said it out loud.

"Yeah, you know. Dishdasha . . . a thawb. That white dress all the men wear over there."

I turned to Clark and mouthed, "Claven?"

He shrugged and turned to Skipper, and she nodded and pointed toward her computer.

She said, "So, Mr. Palmer, are you sure Claven was the CIA ops officer running the capture?"

"Of course it was him. Who else would it be? His old man loves backroom deals and telling everybody how his son is saving the world."

I felt as if Clark and I were the only two people on Earth who didn't know who Claven was, but I had to press on. "If you're right and the team pulled the trigger on the terrorists, what do you think happened to them?"

Palmer took a long, deep breath and spoke with sleep clawing at his tongue. "Probably a couple of clandestine services plants took 'em out."

Eyes scanned the room, and Clark leaned in to check on Palmer. "We lost him. He's out. Maybe we'll get something more out of him when he wakes up and sobers up. Am I the only one who's lost? Who's Claven?"

Skipper spun her laptop so we could see. The picture on the screen showed two men at a graduation ceremony at Cornell University. The older man stood beside one of the graduates with his arm around his shoulders and a huge grin on his face. The caption read: "Congressman and chairman of the House Permanent Select Committee on Intelligence, Richard Claven of New York celebrates his son's graduation and pending assignment to the Central Intelligence Agency."

"That explains part of it," I said.

Skipper closed the laptop. "I did a little digging behind closed doors and off the record and discovered that Richard Andrew Claven III is currently serving as an operations officer with the Central Intelligence Agency."

"How did you get into Langley's system?"

"You know better than to ask questions like that, but in this case, I'll come clean. When a prominent politician's son wants to make the world believe he's the next best thing on the scene, he tends to let certain tidbits accidently leak to the press, and Quentin Palmer's favorite ops officer, Mr. Claven, falls squarely into that category."

Clark untied Palmer's shoes, wrestled his legs onto an ottoman, and tossed a blanket over him. "I guess we're having a sleepover."

"How much did he have to drink?" Skipper asked.

I said, "He was pretty toasted when he showed up at Momma Tay-Tay's. I don't know how many he had there, but he drank almost half a bottle of Blanton's after we got back here."

Clark said, "I've got a feeling he ends most nights of his life just like this."

Palmer began a rhythmic chorus of snores and snorts, and I said, "Now that we know who the blue badger was, what do we do with that intel?"

Skipper said, "One thing is even more certain now. Knowing who Claven is and who his daddy is means we'll never get any information out of Langley. They'll circle the wagons and roll out the powder kegs."

"What about his theory involving clandestine services officers on the op?"

Skipper tapped her laptop. "According to the dossiers the Board gave us, none of those guys was a case officer or paramilitary officer with the Agency."

I scratched my beard. "I still want to know where those dossiers came from, especially if some of the guys weren't directly tied to Board-operated teams like ours."

"I'll do some digging," Skipper said. "Maybe I can come up with some background. How would you feel about me bringing Ginger in?"

I said, "As far as I'm concerned, you have free rein to bring anybody you want on board if you think it'll help untangle this mess we've inherited."

"That's what I figured, but you're still the boss, so it's polite to ask. Oh, by the way . . . I got a note from Captain Sprayberry. They had a small maintenance issue in Key West, but it's resolved and they're steaming south. They'll be here tomorrow evening around sunset."

Chapter 14
Violence of Action

Skipper and I made breakfast as the team rolled out of their racks and our former spook slept off the night before.

"Are you sure he's alive?" Skipper asked.

"He snores every ten minutes, so if he stops doing that, I'll check for a pulse."

She plated a trio of omelets. "The info he gave us last night is nice to have, but I don't see how it gets us any closer to finding Kennedy's team and the three terrorists."

I peered over the back of Palmer's chair to see his chest rising and falling in slumberous rhythm. "I hope he's wrong about an embedded operator taking out the team."

She stopped what she was doing and wiped her hands. "I lay awake most of the night thinking about that same thing. Why would they do that?"

"I think there are only two reasons. First, things got out of hand and the terrorists escaped. To cover their butts, embedded ops officers might go off the rails and put down the team."

She cocked her head. "Come on, Chase. You read the dossiers. Even if it were six on six, do you really think they could put down the whole team?"

"I don't know. Think about Teresa Lynn on the Uzbek mission. She didn't have any trouble putting me and Kodiak down."

"She has to be an exception, though. Most operators never get to her level of skill and experience."

"Maybe," I said, "but we have to throw that possibility into the mix."

"What's the second option?"

"This is the one I really don't like. It's possible the team got flipped."

She threw down the dish towel. "Seriously, Chase? Not likely."

"Money talks. And these guys are well funded. I don't like to think about it, but we've got weak spots, and big paydays are tempting for some guys. On our team, we've been fortunate to do well enough financially to take that temptation out of play."

"That's not the only reason we're bribe-proof, though."

"No, definitely not. There's not a single member of this team who would ever consider turning his back on the rest of us for any reason."

She glanced down the hall. "Even Gator?"

"Time will tell," I said. "I don't see any warning signs yet, but if the day ever comes when he gives me the slightest indication of being unfaithful, I'll put him out the door immediately."

"I never hope for a gunfight, but I'm anxious to know how he'll do when it happens."

"There's no way to predict. He's a rock star on the range, but time will tell."

One by one, the team filtered into the kitchen and claimed plates. Palmer didn't move, and we ate like the family we were.

Hunter took a break between bites to ask, "What's on the agenda?"

I wiped my mouth and swallowed a drink of coffee. "I want to talk with the Board again. They know more than they're telling us, and I'm not okay with that. This thing is either insanely simple and they went down in the ocean, or it's incredibly complex with a thousand moving parts that all add up to treason."

Clark tossed his napkin onto his empty plate. "I suspect the reality of this whole thing is somewhere between those two possibilities, but I'm with you. We definitely need to talk with the Board again. We've got too many missing pieces to get a clear picture of the whole puzzle."

After showers and a second round of coffee, our guest of honor groaned himself from his hibernation and opened one eye at a time. "This doesn't look much like my house."

Skipper held out a steaming mug of coffee. "Good morning, Rip Van Winkle. How are you feeling?"

He took the offered mug and stared up at our analyst as if it were the first time he'd ever seen her. "Thanks. Where am I?"

Skipper smiled. "Bermuda. Don't you remember the flight?"

He took a sip and seemed to ponder the news. "Bermuda, huh? Well, all right. Have you got anything I can spike this up with?"

She motioned toward the half-empty Blanton's bottle still resting on the table beside him. "It's a little early, but there you go."

He closed one eye and uncorked the bottle. "The trick to keeping the hangover from coming is to never sober up."

Palmer situated himself on the chair that had been his bed and gave me a stare. "You're Dom's boy, right?"

I pointed to Clark. "No, I'm Chase. That's Dominic's son, Clark."

"Oh, yeah, that's right. Did you boys figure it out yet?"

"What's that?" I asked.

He took a long swallow. "The missing terrorists."

"Not yet, but we've got some feelers out," I said. "Did anything else come to your mind while you were sawing logs?"

He grumbled. "I ain't slept in forty years. I just pass out and come back every eighteen hours or so. That condition isn't conducive to quality thinking. You boys seem pretty bright, though. You'll figure it out."

"How about throwing us a bone? You're not as out of the loop as you want us to believe. Did that team ever make it to the island?"

"This island," he asked. "Bermuda?"

"You're a funny guy," I said. "Did they make it here or not?"

He studied the remaining coffee in his mug. "I don't know, but I know a guy. He's not an Agency guy, but he pretty much runs the docks. If you've got a pocketful of American folding money, this guy can find almost anything that comes or goes through the docks."

"How about an introduction?" I asked.

Palmer looked over his shoulder toward the kitchen. "Have you got any grub left? Hostages like me get hungry."

I loaded and delivered a plate, and he dived in like a hungry bear. Somewhere near the end of the feeding frenzy, he looked up. "What day is it?"

Skipper checked her watch. "Wednesday."

Palmer polished off the plate. "He'll be there. Come on. I'll introduce a couple of you. We can't show up with a football team and expect him to talk to us. Just two of you is all I can get in."

"Make it three," I said. "Skipper, Clark, and me."

He finished his coffee. "Is Skipper the chick?"

It was time to change the dynamic, so I took a step close enough to smell everything Palmer had ever poured down his throat. "No, Skipper is the best analyst in the business. Grow a little respect."

He threw up both hands. "Easy, big boy. I'm from the old school."

I didn't back up. "I'm from the school where we learned to respect women."

"Sorry, man. I didn't mean anything. I was just trying to get the picture."

"The picture is this. You're going to introduce our handler, our analyst, and the team lead to your man at the docks, and you're going to walk away."

"What makes you think you're in any position to start calling the shots, hot rod?"

I gave Skipper a nod. "Play the recording."

The next thirty seconds passed while Palmer listened to himself spouting off about the son of one of the most powerful congressmen in DC.

When Skipper paused the recording, I said, "That's why. Now, find a breath mint, and let's roll." I pulled Hunter aside. "Take Palmer's car back to his house while we're meeting this guy on the docks. We'll drop him off when we're finished."

"You got it."

* * *

We pulled into the docks, and I turned to our guide for the morning. "Is this the place?"

Palmer said, "He's in the back seat of that black Escalade. His name is Gi-Gi."

I stepped from the Suburban and opened Palmer's door. "Introduce us."

He hesitantly slid from the seat and ran his fingers through what remained of his hair. "I'll do the intro, but then I'm bugging out."

"Just be cool," I said. "We'll take you home when we're finished here."

"No, I'm good. I just need to find my car."

"Your car will be waiting at your house when we drop you off. Just make the introductions and chill out. If you want to sit through the talk with us, that's fine, but if you'd rather wait in the truck, that's good with me."

Palmer led us to the Escalade and tapped on the blacked-out window. The window lowered an inch, and a wall of white smoke rose from the space. He said, "Gi-Gi, these are some friends of mine, and they'd like to have a sit-down with you."

I found the mafia terms interesting. *Friends of mine* typically means the guy doing the introduction was vouching for the people unknown to the other guy. And *sit-down* was the term for an informal meeting to work out some differences.

The window descended a few more inches, and the mirrored shades of a black man in his forties appeared through the smoke. "What do they want?"

Palmer kept his hands noticeably visible. "They just want to know about a boat that maybe came in a couple nights ago."

"I'm a busy man, you know. My time is valuable."

I folded five bills together and laid my hand on the top of the glass still filling more than half of the space. "I won't take up much of your time, Gi-Gi. I just need to know what might have happened to some friends of mine."

With any luck, the phrase might give the man behind the shades enough to hear me out and believe I wouldn't bring anything he didn't want to his doorstep.

Gi-Gi said, "Get in." I reached for the door handle, and he said, "No. Get in the front seat. Only you. No one else."

I shot Skipper a look and tapped a finger to my jawline, and she gave me a barely perceptible nod. The transceiver designed, built, and attached to my jawbone by Dr. Mankiller would broadcast my conversation with Gi-Gi loud and clear.

When I opened the front door, it felt like a slab of concrete in my hand, so I made a small lifting motion, telling Clark his 9mm likely wouldn't penetrate the skin or the glass of the Escalade. His nod of acknowledgment was even less obvious than Skipper's.

I slid onto the front seat and twisted in an effort to see Gi-Gi, but with him nestled directly behind me, it was impossible to see him face-to-face. It was an excellent tactical position on his part.

I was left a little vulnerable, and I didn't like the feeling at all. "My name is Chase. Thanks for the sit-down."

"What do you want to know, Chase? I'm a busy man."

I caught a glimpse of movement in the mirror and tried to watch the action outside the vehicle without being obvious. The movement made me feel a little better about my position. Clark pulled the Suburban within inches of the back bumper of the Escalade, effectively pinning the car in place. He might not have been able to shoot through the doors if things got out of hand, but Gi-Gi's driver would have to destroy a seven-thousand-pound Suburban to get away.

"I need to know about a boat, or maybe as many as three boats that came through here three or four days ago."

"I told you I'm a busy man. You want me to tell you about three random boats that may or may not have come through my docks three or four days ago. Surely you understand how ridiculous this sounds."

I ignored the admonishment. "Twelve Americans. They all looked a lot like me with beards, skinned knuckles, and a whole lot of situational awareness. They would've had three Middle Eastern men with them and possibly another American who looks nothing like us. He would've looked out of place and wanted to appear to be in charge."

Gi-Gi said, "Hmm. How much is this information worth to you? These men were your friends?"

"I already paid you five hundred."

"And that got you in the door, my friend. You don't pay a cover charge and then drink for free in America, do you?"

I shucked two more bills from my fold and laid them on the center console of the Escalade.

Gi-Gi said, "I thought these men were your friends, but now you insult me with two hundred dollars. Get out." I laid three more bills on the console, and he said, "Twelve men? This is what you said, right?"

"Maybe as many as sixteen, including the Arabs and Claven."

"Claven? I know this man, and he is big trouble. Are you going to kill him?"

I didn't like anything about where the conversation was heading, but I was up to my ears in Caribbean corruption and doing my best to stay afloat. "I don't know. Maybe. Do you want him dead?"

"How much?"

"How much what?"

He took a long draw from whatever he was smoking. "How much for you to kill him for me?"

"That's not what I do."

"Then you are a coward."

"A coward? That's a serious accusation in the States."

He leaned forward. "But you are not in the States. You are on my island, at my docks, in my car. And in my world, I get what I want."

The bad turn the conversation had taken two minutes before turned into a dead end that I liked even less, so upsetting the balance of power inside the Escalade seemed like a reasonable option.

I reached for my pistol, and my plan worked flawlessly. Just as I hoped, Gi-Gi's driver drew his pistol, cocked the hammer, and pressed the muzzle to my forehead.

With speed faster than I thought I possessed, I gripped the slide of the driver's pistol and shoved it backward just far enough to force the gun out of battery, rendering it practically harmless . . . to me. With the same motion, I ripped the gun from his hand and spun it in my palm like a short club. In the same instant, I swung the gun-turned-hammer, striking the driver on the tip of his nose and sending blood in every direction. I followed up the nose strike with a blow to his right temple, sending the oversized man slumping over the steering wheel. His considerable weight pressed the horn, attracting far more attention than Gi-Gi wanted.

He reached forward, yanked his driver from the wheel, and shoved him against the window, silencing the horn. "Impressive."

I dropped the magazine from the pistol and racked the slide, ejecting the round from the chamber. It took only a second to strip the slide from the pistol and toss it across the seats to the back of the Escalade.

I spun in the seat, landing on my knees and facing Gi-Gi. I plucked his mirrored shades from his face and crushed them in my palm. "My time is valuable, too, amigo, and you're wasting it. Either you know the information I need, or you don't. We're finished playing games."

The man didn't flinch. "So, maybe I was wrong. You're not a coward. You're a fool because only a fool would threaten me on my island, in my car."

"I didn't threaten you because I'm not the kind of man who does that. I bring the required force, plus an extra measure for my own amusement. Your gorilla drew on me. I neutralized the threat. That's all that happened so far. Now, it's your turn to start talking. Were the Americans here or not?"

Gi-Gi glanced toward his driver. "Is he alive?"

I didn't take my eyes from his. "I don't care. His life—and yours—are meaningless to me. Were they here, or not?"

To Gi-Gi's surprise, the driver's door flew open, and his unconscious chauffeur tumbled to the ground. Skipper stepped over the man and positioned herself behind the wheel at the same instant Clark jerked open the back door of the luxury SUV. Before the door came closed, Clark had Gi-Gi handcuffed to the headrest, and Skipper had the car in drive.

She tapped the accelerator, and we rolled forward a few feet.

I said, "It's starting to feel like this isn't really your island at all. It feels to me like it may, in fact, be mine."

I pulled my handcuff key from my pocket and laid it on the five one-hundred-dollar bills still resting on the console. "I don't know if you can get those cuffs off before you drown, but I'm willing to give you a sporting shot."

The big SUV rolled ever closer to the docks and the twenty-feet-deep blue Caribbean, and Gi-Gi eyed the three of us in turn. "Okay. I underestimated you."

"That would appear to be the case," I said. "The next decision you make has a fifty-fifty chance of being your last, so think carefully but quickly. Were the Americans here?"

He struggled against the cuffs. "No, they weren't here, but the Arabs were. You're wrong about the count, though. There were six or seven of them."

Skipper tapped the brakes, and I asked, "When and how did they leave?"

"Two days ago in a boat. A big boat. Maybe sixteen or eighteen meters. It was white with a broad blue stripe. The name on the stern was *Lady Margarita*. There were no Americans."

I folded the cash from the console and shoved it into his shirt pocket, along with the handcuff key. "Surprise, speed of response, and violence of action. That's how we operate. We're not going to be on this island long enough to be a problem for you, nor for you to be one for us. Is that understood?"

He glared at me with the look of a man digging in his heels for revenge, and Skipper pressed the accelerator. The ocean drew ever closer, and Gi-Gi growled.

"Just a couple more questions," I said, "then you can go for a nice little swim. How did they arrive, and which way did they go when they left?"

He jerked his hands against the headrest. "You have no idea who you're playing with."

"I told you once. I don't make threats, and I don't play. I offer options, and yours are crystal clear. Tell me what you know, or place your bet on whether or not an Escalade can float."

Skipper leaned forward, pulled up the floor mat and laid it across the accelerator, sending the SUV toward the water at ten miles per hour, and then she stepped from the vehicle.

Gi-Gi's eyes flashed wildly from the empty driver's seat to the Caribbean Sea and back. "They came in a cigarette boat—black and gold. It's at the west end of the docks. They left to the west toward Nicaragua."

Clark landed a right jab in the perfect spot to send our new friend into the spirit world for a few minutes. I shoved the transmission into park, and Clark removed the handcuffs from Gi-Gi's wrists.

He retrieved my key from the man's shirt pocket and held up the five hundred bucks. "Do you want this back?"

I opened my door. "No, consider it a tip."

He shoved the cash into his pocket. "Thanks. I like to think I deliver quality service with a dazzling smile."

Chapter 15
The Camel's Gorilla

Quentin Palmer sat in the back seat of our Suburban with his face in his hands. "You have no idea what you've done."

"What we've done," I said, "is get the information we needed from a hostile source."

Palmer said, "You've burned every bridge on the island and put a target on your backs. Nobody gets away with that kind of crap with Gi-Gi. You'll be lucky to survive the day."

"If he's foolish enough to come after us, we'll make this the worst—and last—day of his life."

"Oh, he won't come after you, but his goons will. Did you kill the driver?"

"No, but he's going to have a nasty headache when he wakes up."

"What kind of rodeo clowns are you guys? You can't run around slapping bulls between the horns and stay alive down here."

"Thanks for the concern," I said, "but there's a confirmed terrorist threat in play against the U.S. We'll slap—and kill, if necessary—as many bulls as it requires to stop that threat. Small-time island thugs are minor players and little more than cockroaches. There's nothing more important than stopping whatever they're planning."

Palmer's tone grew ominous. "Well, isn't that some scout's honor, red-white-and-blue patriotic crap? How long do you plan to stick around and keep me alive? I vouched for you, remember? Well, guess what? You didn't stop when you drew a target on your head. You drew one on mine, as well, and I have to live here. That means I should put a bullet in your head and drop you at Gi-Gi's doorstep so he won't come after me."

I said, "You told me it was illegal to carry a pistol on this island, so that means you don't have a bullet to put in my head. And yes, it is some red-white-and-blue patriotic crap. That's what we do."

"You bunch of rookies. I can't believe you've stayed alive this long."

I said, "If you're really afraid that cockroach Gi-Gi will come after you, we'll do one of two things for you. We'll either take you under our wing while we're working this op so we can keep you alive, or we'll take you wherever you want to go. It's your call."

He huffed. "I'd be safer sleeping on Gi-Gi's couch than with you bunch of clowns. I'm out. You're on your own."

He pushed open the door and stepped from the Suburban.

I met Clark's gaze. "What was that?"

He said, "I don't think it was what he wanted us to think it was."

"I get the same feeling. Something's not right."

Clark unbuckled his seat belt. "Put me out behind that container. I'm gonna put eyes on him and see what he does."

I pulled behind a rusty shipping container that had probably been on the docks for decades, and Clark slipped from the vehicle. With a touch of his cell phone linked to his bone conduction device attached to his jawbone, Skipper and I could hear and talk back and forth with him seamlessly.

Pulling from behind the container, we bounced across the lot and back onto the access road, giving the appearance of us leaving the docks. It was impossible to know if we were being watched, so assuming that we were gave us the best possibility of completing our mission without interruption from Gi-Gi, Palmer, or anyone else who felt the need to flex their muscle.

Well clear of the docks, I pulled the Suburban behind a convenience store and waited for Clark's report. We didn't have to wait long.

"Guess who's helping the driver to his feet?" Clark said.

I gave Skipper a wink. "My gut told me Palmer wasn't as far out of the game as he wanted us to believe."

"And once again, College Boy, your gut was right. From the looks of things, they're as thick as thieves."

Skipper asked, "Have you got eyes on the cigarette boat Gi-Gi mentioned?"

Clark said, "Affirmative. I'd like to give it a look. Wouldn't you?"

She said, "I'd like to give it a forensic look."

"We'll wait for the sun to cross the horizon before poking around," Clark said. "Palmer just put the driver in the back seat and climbed in behind the wheel of the Escalade."

I said, "Maybe we can use that little relationship to our benefit as this thing plays out. I'd like to know how far former CIA Officer Quentin Palmer is willing to take the charade."

Clark said, "They're clear of the docks and headed out the same access road you used. Are you behind cover?"

"Affirmative. We'll watch for him to pass, then we'll pick you up."

"I'll meet you just outside the gate. I don't see any security cameras, but that doesn't mean they're not out there."

Skipper and I watched Gi-Gi's Escalade pass and pull back onto the road. Clark was back inside the Suburban two minutes later, and we were headed south toward our rented house.

"Are you surprised?" I asked.

Clark shook his head. "Nothing surprises me anymore. At this point, I expect everything to be the eight-hundred-pound gorilla that breaks the camel's back."

I let that one go because the mental picture made me laugh.

"It's time to break camp," I said the second I walked through the door.

But it was wasted breath. Gear was already packed and loaded in the second SUV, and the team was on their feet.

"How'd it go?" Hunter asked.

I said, "It took a little arm-twisting, but we got what we needed . . . I think."

"I hate I missed the arm-twisting. That's my favorite part."

I said, "Our friend Palmer turned out to be quite the social butterfly. After crying about being scared that Gi-Gi, King of the Docks, was going to kill him, he didn't waste any time climbing in the car with him when he thought no one was watching."

With every bullet and every butt in the vehicles, we headed for the west side of the island in search of a nice, quiet place to catch our magic carpet to the mother ship. We found just the spot, and I opened the newly installed tracking app on my tablet. The *Lori Danielle* was less than a hundred miles north of the island and steaming at fifty knots. It was the perfect time to make the call.

Barry answered promptly. "Bridge, Captain."

"It looks like you're making good time."

He said, "We are now. We had to dodge some commercial traffic that didn't need to see us on the foils. You know how it is. Spider-Man doesn't take off his mask in public."

I gave him the coordinates for our location and said, "Put the chopper in the air when you can. We'll send a load of gear and a couple of bodies on the first run."

"Bodies? Already?"

I chuckled. "No, sorry. That was a poor choice of words. These bodies on board still have souls. We're not stacking corpses yet."

"I'll dispatch Barbie, and she'll be airborne ASAP. Do you need anything else from me?"

"Just a ride," I said. "How are the seas?"

"We're still a hundred miles out, but it's not bad. I'd say three-to four-foot swells in twenty-knots of wind out of the southwest."

"Perfect. I'm planning a RHIB run in the witching hour."

"It should be a great night for it," he said. "They're forecasting swells less than a foot in light wind on coastal waters after sunset."

"Maybe I won't get seasick this time."

The captain said, "I'll let you know when Gun Bunny is airborne. We'll be on station in an hour forty."

"Sounds good. We'll see you soon."

We staged our gear on the edge of a secluded beach and returned the rented SUVs. Half an hour later, we were kicked back beneath a collection of palm trees, waiting to hear the buzz of the MH-6 Little Bird's rotor over the ocean.

Gun Bunny put the chopper on the ground, just beyond the trees to keep from sandblasting us, and we stacked gear in every open space we could find. I sent Disco, Hunter, and Tony on the first lift, and the Little Bird spirited them away over the open ocean.

The second lift carried the rest of us, and we touched down on the helipad at the same time Captain Sprayberry brought the ship to a hover in forty feet of water, just on the edge of the drop-off to the abyss.

Gator was first off the chopper, and the same astonished look he'd worn for days remained in place. "This is outrageous. How many more surprises do you guys have in store?"

"We're running out," I said. "But the ship may have a few secrets she'd like to whisper in your ear. I'll give you the nickel tour when we get settled in."

He said, "We never stay anywhere long enough to get settled in."

"It's not always this hectic," I told him. "Sometimes we have weeks and even months between missions. You just happened to show up at the end of one of those breaks."

I dispatched Hunter and Mongo to prep the rigid hull inflatable boat, and Gator and I began our tour.

I said, "We're heavily armored above and below the waterline, so we're not exactly bulletproof, but anything short of an anti-ship missile will bounce off. We've put her in ice that was almost thirty inches thick, and she did fine. We have hull heaters and hot-water jets at the waterline to soften the ice. If I have my way, we'll never need that cold-water capability again. I hate wintertime."

"It's not my favorite, either," he said. "But I'll work where you put me."

I continued the briefing. "We've got two main engines and three auxiliary generators. We run on Azipods in normal operations, but we have a pair of turbine water jets and a set of foils that descend from the hull for high-speed ops. Believe it or not, we can make better than fifty knots in smooth seas when we're flying on the foils."

"Astonishing," he said. "I guess that means you can outrun most threats. Is that why I'm not seeing any defensive weaponry?"

"You're not seeing it because we're very good at keeping our aces in the hole. We can fight off anything short of an air raid and maybe a determined fast-attack sub. All of the *Lori Danielle*'s weaponry is stowed below decks until we need it. When the old girl gets mad, you'll see her fangs come out."

Gator planted himself atop a heavy gray enclosure. "I gotta tell you, Chase. I never knew anything like this existed."

"The ship?"

He waved his arms. "All of it. The ship, you guys, the plane. It's all unbelievable."

I sat beside him. "I know how you feel. I was where you are not so long ago. I don't know what the Board had planned for you when you finished at The Ranch, but Clark and I handpicked you for our team."

He cocked his head. "Why?"

I thought about my answer for a moment. "You're going to make a billion decisions throughout the rest of your life, and a bunch of those decisions won't have a clear-cut reason. They'll be based on a gut feeling and not much more. It'll just *feel* like the right thing to do. I've been pretty lucky. My gut and I make more good choices than bad ones, and you're one of those decisions."

"Are the other teams like this one?" he asked.

"I don't know. Believe it or not, I don't know how many other teams there are. We're team number twenty-one, so I assume there are at least twenty more, but I can't be sure. They may not be numbered sequentially."

"Did you come to this team right out of training?"

I laughed. "Not hardly. I didn't go to a team. I was on my own. Well, sort of."

"What does that mean?"

"My first mission was a hit. Or at least I thought it was. I was tasked with killing a Russian assassin in Cuba. And get this . . . His name was Suslik."

Gator shrugged. "Is that supposed to mean something to me?"

"Didn't they teach you a language at The Ranch?"

"Arabic and Farsi. I'm pretty fluent in Arabic, but I'm still working on Farsi."

"Suslik is Russian for *beaver*. The dude I was supposed to kill had the two biggest buck teeth you've ever seen."

"Did you do it?" he asked.

The memory of the night I pulled Suslik from Dmitri Barkov's yacht and turned him into fish food in Havana Harbor played through my mind. "Yeah, I did it, but I wasn't really supposed to."

"What does that mean?"

I said, "The real mission was for me to lure Suslik out into the open so the real operatives could take him out. I was supposed to fail."

He scratched his head. "So you failed at failing?"

"That's a good way to put it. It turned out that Suslik wasn't just one guy, though. He was triplets, and we got all of them."

"We? I thought you said you were on your own."

My brain took another deep dive down memory lane. "I hooked up with a Russian SVR officer who helped."

He shook his head like a dog shedding water. "Wait a minute. A Russian SVR officer helped you find and kill three Russian assassins. Is that what you're saying?"

"I told you nothing was going to make sense for a while. Welcome to your new reality. The SVR officer was Anya Burinkova— the deadliest assassin I've ever met, and one of the most physically beautiful women on the planet. Those Russian girls are something else."

A light came on inside Gator's head. "She's the liver donor."

"Yep."

"Am I ever going to meet this Anya person?"

"If you stick around, it's unavoidable. She has a way of showing up from time to time."

"I'll bet Penny isn't a big fan of her showing up."

"I think Penny may have changed her mind a little bit after Anya gave her part of her liver. That's a pretty big deal."

He said, "Yeah, I'd say so."

I knocked on the steel panel we'd made our seat. "Just in case you were wondering, we're sitting on top of the Phalanx Close-In Weapon System."

He hopped to his feet. "The SEE-wiz?"

"Yep. Just wait 'til you see it in action. It can blast seventy-five twenty-millimeter rounds per second."

"Amazing," he said.

"It'll all become routine before you know it, but all these tools and toys aren't what keep us alive when it hits the fan. Ultimately, it all comes down to fundamentals, just like the football you played. We shoot, move, and communicate better than the bad guys. That's what keeps us fighting and winning."

He dropped his head. "What about the other team? Did they . . ."

"That's the reality of this life. If they're not dead, they've made a terrible decision. It's up to us to find the truth and stop the guys they were supposed to stop."

"Can we do that?" he asked.

I stared out over the endless ocean. "We'll either do it, or we'll die trying."

Chapter 16
Toto

Gator seemed to chew on the "die trying" portion of my attempt at assurance. "I've got one more question, and I may be out of line, but I'd like to know."

"What is it?" I asked. "Don't worry about being out of line. You're being baptized by fire, and I'm sure you've got a thousand questions. It's always okay to ask. If you feel like you can't—or don't want to—ask someone else, I'm the team leader. You can *always* come to me. Always."

"I appreciate that," he said. "I almost hate to ask, but will I get paid?"

I hopped from the CIWS cover. "Come with me."

I led Gator through the interior of the ship to the purser's office and knocked on her hatch.

"Come on in," Ronda said from inside.

We stepped through the hatch, and I made introductions. "Clint, meet Ronda No-H. She's the ship's purser, but she's a lot more than that. In addition to handling every penny we take in and send out, she sends out a few special delivery items of her own. She's the baddest door-gunner you'll ever meet. When you see her on the Minigun in the Little Bird, you'll grow a whole new respect for accountants."

Gator stuck out his hand, and Ronda shook it.

"It's nice to meet you, Ronda. I'm Clint Barrow, but apparently, I'm Gator now."

She giggled. "It's nice to meet you, Clint, and I can't wait to hear the story that stuck with that name. Whatever it was, get used to it. They dubbed me Ronda No-H, and it stuck just because my mother spelled my name the correct way instead of sticking an H in it."

"I'm already getting used to it," he said.

I took a seat. "If you have time, will you take Gator through the pay chart?"

Ronda grinned. "You betcha. Come around here, Gator."

He stepped behind her desk, and she pointed toward a screen. "This is your account, and"—she opened her desk drawer and slid a card toward our newest operator—"this is your card. Don't lose it. But if you do, tell Skipper immediately. We'll shut it down and get you a new one right away. Did Skipper give you a phone and tablet?"

He pulled the phone from his pocket. "The tablet is in my gear, but here's the phone."

Ronda opened an app that looked like a restaurant menu. "You can check your account from here. See? This is your balance, and as you use the card, a list of the one hundred most recent expenditures will appear. If you need to track farther than one hundred, it requires a security code. Skipper will give that to you if you need it."

He said, "Wait a minute. Go back to the balance page."

I laughed quietly to myself, and Ronda tried to hide her smile. She pointed toward the icon. "Just tap that."

He thumbed the phone, and disbelief consumed his face again. "That can't be right. That says two hundred thousand dollars."

Ronda said, "You've worked your butt off for the past eighteen months, haven't you?"

"Well, yes, ma'am. But . . ."

"No but," she said. "When you work, you get paid."

He glanced up at me. "Is this right? Will I really make two hundred grand every eighteen months?"

"Oh, no," I said. "Not even close. You'll do much better than that."

He furrowed his brow. "Are you serious?"

"Welcome to your new world. Do your job, stay alive, keep the man beside you alive, and you'll be well compensated."

"I don't know what to say. They didn't tell me anything about this at The Ranch, and I was too scared to ask."

"How many times have we told you to ask when you don't know?"

"Yeah, but nobody told me that at The Ranch."

"We're not in Kansas anymore, Toto."

Ronda cleared her throat. "Sorry to interrupt, but we've got a few more things to discuss. If you've got time, we need to fill out a W-Four. You don't have any dependents, do you?"

"No, ma'am. It's just me. My family . . ."

I laid a hand on his shoulder. "Can we do this later, Ronda?"

She stroked a few keys and clicked her mouse. "Of course. I know you boys have to go save the world or whatever you're doing this time. Let me know if you need me and my Minigun to come pull your butts out of the fire again."

I said, "Hopefully, you can stay nice and clean on this one."

She recoiled. "Oh, God forbid. Nice and clean is boring. I'll take hanging out of a chopper any day."

"In that case, I'll see what I can do to get my butt into a fire, just for you."

She bowed ever so slightly. "Thank you, kind sir, and I'll do my best to pull it out."

We stepped from the office and back into the corridor, where Gator promptly took me by the arm. "I'm not taking money from the rest of the team, am I?"

"What do you mean?"

"Like, the rest of the guys aren't giving up part of their pay for my salary, are they?"

My respect for the new kid just vaulted a few steps. "No, that's not how this works, but I like that you asked. That says a lot about your character."

He shrugged. "I haven't done anything yet except learn and get a new nickname."

"The nickname will likely stick, but the learning will never stop. Let's go check on the RHIB."

We made our way to the stern deck, where we found Hunter and Mongo prepping the boat. "How's she look, guys?"

Mongo said, "Shipshape, boss. What's the plan?"

I gave the starboard tube a press with my knee, and it pressed back. "Give it a push, Gator." He did, and I said, "That's how it should feel. If it's softer than that, fill it up. If it's firmer than that, let it be. The overpressure valve will take care of it. Did you do any RHIB ops at The Ranch?"

"No, sir, not really. We had one day of water recovery, and they used a RHIB to pick us up, but that was it."

I paused. "You said *we*."

Gator nodded. "Yeah, there were four of us in the water that day. We did the water survival course together, and we were ordered to never disclose our name or anything about ourselves."

"Did you do other training events with other students?"

"A few," he said, "but not many. The same rules applied every time we were with anyone else. A couple of times, I was pretty sure the other students were really instructors sent to see if they could get anything personal out of me."

"You were probably right, and if you'd given up any information, you wouldn't be here today."

I motioned for Hunter. "Give Gator a down-and-dirty RHIB briefing. He only did high-speed recovery at The Ranch. He's never worked from inside."

Hunter stuck out his hand, and Gator reached for him. Before the new guy could grip my partner's hand, Hunter grabbed Gator's wrist, spun him around, and yanked him into the boat backward. He landed on the deck with his legs and arms spread.

"That's lesson number one," Hunter said. "If you're getting into the boat under fire or being pursued, that's how you do it. Don't step in, don't jump in, don't dive in. Land on your back so you can continue to return fire and watch for anyone following you into the boat."

I left Gator in Hunter's capable hands and headed for the combat information center, where, just as I expected, I found Skipper.

"Hey, Chase. I'm glad you're here. I've got some satellite footage you'll want to see."

She pulled up the video playback, and I watched closely as she pointed to the screen, where two small specks bounced across a black background.

"What am I looking at?"

"Those are the two boats that left Gi-Gi's docks the night the cigarette boat came in. I'm not saying he told us the whole truth, but take a look at this." She zoomed into the northernmost speck, and it blossomed into at least a fifty-foot boat. "That one matches the description you got out of Gi-Gi. If you look closely, you'll see the dark stripe on the hull. It was almost dark, so it's impossible to know if the stripe is blue, but I'm willing to bet it is."

"How far did the satellite track it?"

"Only eleven minutes, but because I'm a super analyst, I found another satellite—well, several more actually—that caught the boat's turn."

"Turn?" I asked.

"Exactly. Even though they headed toward the coastline, they didn't land in Nicaragua." Almost before she finished, she pulled away. "Don't even think about kissing me on the forehead again. That was nasty."

"Not even a little peck?"

"Only if you want me to slug you."

"Okay, okay. Deny my love if you must."

She rolled her eyes. "Yeah, that's it . . . love. Anyway, here's what they're doing."

She pulled up a nautical chart of the Western Caribbean with a yellow dashed line running northward and parallel to the coastline of Central America.

"They're running the coast? Why?"

She let out a long sigh. "I only have a guess, and it's not a good one."

"Let's hear it."

"I think it's a contingency plan. These guys are smart. There's no way they would let a terror plot be foiled by having one element of it screwed up. I think they had fail-safes built into the plan at every turn."

"Keep talking," I said.

"I think when they got rolled up by Kennedy's team, they had another team waiting to intercept them, eliminate the good guys, and continue the mission. I believe that's what happened in San Andrés."

I closed my eyes and played out the scenario in my head. "Okay, I'll buy it, but where are they headed?"

"Toward their goal. They've got a reliable boat that's capable of taking them as far as they want to go as long as they can find fuel."

I didn't like anything about Skipper's theory, mostly because I believed she was right. "How far will you be able to track them with satellites?"

"I plotted their likely course if they continue hugging the coastline, and I'll have relatively good satellite coverage until they get about halfway up the eastern seaboard of the States. Of course, all of that is weather-dependent. If they get beneath a cloud layer, all I can do is predict where they'll pop out and wait for them to show up again."

"Stay on that," I said. "But when you can, find some footage of the crossing to San Andrés. Maybe that'll show us what happened to Kennedy's team."

"I'm not sure I want to see what happened to the other team."

"Me neither," I said. "But we need to know."

"I'll keep digging, but we really need to get on that cigarette boat at the docks if it's still there."

"That's the plan," I said. "Do we have a forensic guy on board?"

"I don't know, but I'll bet the captain does."

He answered my call quickly.

"Captain."

I said, "Barry, we need a forensic tech. Do you happen to have one of those hanging around?"

"Not really, but Dr. Shadrack has a couple of lab guys who are pretty sharp. Check with him."

I made my way to sick bay, where Dr. Shadrack was working furiously on his computer. "Hey, Doc. Can I interrupt you for a minute?"

He pushed his glasses on top of his head. "You already did, so go ahead."

"Sorry."

He waved a hand. "I'm just messing with you. What can I do for you?"

"I need the closest thing you've got to a forensic tech."

"Do you mean like matching bullets to a gun barrel or lifting fingerprints?"

"Hopefully no bullets," I said. "We're planning to spend a little quiet time this evening aboard a go-fast boat that may have been used to transport some bad guys. I need to know if anything sinister happened aboard that boat."

"Oh, *that* kind of tech. I've got just the guy for you. Hang on."

He hopped up and slipped from his office, but he was back in minutes with a man in scrubs. "Chase, meet Trip Collins. He was an NCIS tech in the Navy before he became a nurse practitioner."

I shook his hand. "Nice to meet you, Trip. I'm Chase Fulton, and I run the tactical team."

"I know who you are. Everybody knows who you are. You should know, though, I'm not a very good field medic, so if that's what you need, I'm probably not your guy."

I said, "I've got two former Eighteen-Deltas, so we've got all the Special Forces medics we can use. What I need is a crime scene tech."

"In that case, I'm your boy. Tell me about the scene."

"It's a boat. Something in the sixty-foot range. There may have been a pretty good skirmish on board. I need a set of eyes that can tell the difference between normal operations on the boat and a nasty little fight that may have ended with at least six dead bodies."

"Dead bodies are easy to spot," he said. "How long ago was the event?"

"Seventy-two hours or maybe a little more. Is that doable?"

"Sure, unless somebody who really knows how to clean it up took care of it."

"Can you spot a fight even if it's been cleaned up?"

"Probably, depending on how thoroughly they cleaned. Where's the boat?"

"It's on San Andrés, about twelve miles south of here."

He checked his watch. "Let's go have a look."

"We will," I said, "but I want to do it in the dark. Are you good with that?"

"Sure. It's all the same to me. The luminol is easier to see in the dark anyway. Are we choppering over?"

"No, we'll take a RHIB. Put your kit together, and plan to hit the water about twenty-three hundred tonight."

"Done. I'll see you then."

All that remained was waiting for our side of the Earth to spin from beneath the sun, and it would be time for Team 21 to play ball.

Chapter 17

In for a Penny

We grabbed dinner as a team in the ship's mess, and Skipper sat staring at her empty fork as if mesmerized by the stainless-steel utensil.

I leaned toward her. "Are you all right?"

She pulled herself from her stupor. "I've got a crazy idea."

"That's my favorite kind of idea. Give it up."

"I know it's going to sound insane, but hear me out. The *Lori Danielle* can catch that cruiser, no problem. We could run an interdiction and roll up everybody on board."

"That's not a crazy idea. It makes perfect sense. The problem is, we don't want to gun them down, and if they're willing to kill an entire ops team, they're not going to roll over if we show up and say, 'Show me your hands.'"

Skipper said, "I told you to hear me out. I wasn't finished. We could easily catch them, but if we tried an interdiction, just like you said, it would get bloody, and we'd never gather the intel we need and want. Here's my idea. I say we chase them until we catch up and then shadow them until they make a fuel stop. Taking on as much fuel as that thing can carry can't be a quick operation. That would give us time to put a couple of divers in the water and plant a GPS tracking device on the hull. With a tracker in place, who cares about the cloud cover and visibility? We'd still be able to track them precisely without worrying about being able to physically see them from twenty miles in the sky."

I leaned back in my chair and stared at my own fork. "That's gutsy for sure, and it just might be crazy enough to work. I've got an idea to take it one step further and make it even crazier. If we can plant a tracker, we can also plant a charge to disable the boat anytime we want or need."

"Why not? In for a penny, in for a pound . . . of C-Four."

I turned to Clark. "See? That's how you *properly* screw up a saying. Learn from her."

"It's not going to work," he said. "You can lead a horse to water, College Boy, but you can't make him drown."

I so badly wanted to come up with a witty retort, but he wasn't wrong.

Hunter stuck a finger in the air. "Me and the new kid will do it."

Gator whipped around. "We're going to drown a horse?"

That got a good chuckle from everyone except Hunter.

He said, "Nope, just a few jackasses."

I knocked on the table in a pitiful attempt to call the room to order. "Okay, okay. That's enough. How fast are they moving, and what's their range?"

Skipper said, "They're averaging twenty knots, and at last check, they were about three hundred fifty miles out."

I closed one eye and let the numbers run in my head. "Here's the plan. We'll scrub the cigarette boat tonight with the tech and then chase the bad guys. Any guesses where they're headed?"

Gator had a new look on his face, and that intrigued me.

"What's on your mind?" I asked.

He shrank in his seat. "Nothing. I was just . . ."

I said, "No, it's not nothing. Something hit you. What is it? Do you think you're not ready for a real dive mission with Hunter? If that's what it is, get that out of your head. We wouldn't put you in the water if you weren't ready."

"No, sir. That's not it. I was just thinking, what if that boat is already loaded with more C-Four than we can stick to the hull?"

Silence overtook the mess, and all eyes were on the new guy.

He stared back at us wide-eyed. "What? It was just a thought."

"It was more than just a thought," I said. "It's the thought every one of us should've had the instant we knew they were on board a big cruiser."

Clark leaned in. "We need some guesses on where they're headed."

Skipper spoke up first. "New Orleans, maybe?"

Tony said, "The Northrup Grumman shipyard in Mississippi?"

"There are a thousand beach towns full of tourists up and down both coasts of Florida," I said. "There's no way to know with the information we have now. We're so far behind the power curve, we may be chasing our tails before this is over."

Singer checked his watch. "It's dark, and we're falling further behind by the minute. I say we get to the cigarette boat now and head toward the bad guys ASAP."

I said, "I agree. Let's move."

Hunter, Kodiak, Gator, Trip, and I climbed aboard the RHIB, and the deckhand lowered us over the side. We left the davit lines in place until both engines were running smoothly and every piece of electronics was alive and well. With everything in shipshape, we cast off the lines and motored away from the security of the *Lori Danielle* with Gator at the helm.

As the lights of San Andrés came into clear view, I said, "Don't stare at the lights. It'll screw up your night vision. Keep your eyes moving, and keep our speed up. I'll tell you when to slow down."

He nodded his understanding and managed the RHIB like an old pro.

Half a mile from the docks, I tapped Gator on the shoulder. "Bring her back to about fifteen knots, but use whatever speed you need to keep us up on plane."

He pulled the throttles back, and our speed bled off until we settled on eighteen knots with the keel still cutting across the surface of the Caribbean.

At a quarter mile from the docks, I said, "The yard is blind to the west, so maneuver that direction and set up for an approach from the southwest. We want to remain as invisible as possible."

He brought the boat around to the southwest of the docks and waited for my signal to turn inbound.

I watched the angle form. "Okay, make your turn and bring the engines to idle." He followed the order, and I said, "Look for a pair of white lights stacked on top of each other. Do you see them right there on the point?"

He studied the scene in front of us. "Yes, sir. I've got 'em."

"Bear on those lights, but don't stare at them. Keep your eyes moving, and watch for motion. Report any movement." I motioned toward a covered panel on the console of the RHIB's helm. "Open that panel, and flip both switches upward."

He did as I instructed.

I said, "Kill both engines."

He looked at me as if I'd lost my mind, and I took a step closer.

"Don't question orders in action. Follow the order, and ask questions later."

He pulled the kill switches, and both engines fell silent. All that remained was the hum of the twin electric motors pushing us through the water at eight knots.

I said, "Nothing changes except our noise signature and our speed. The throttles still work the same, and the steering remains true."

"Oh, that's cool," Gator said. "I had no idea we had electric propulsion."

"If you were designing a stealthy craft, wouldn't you want some nearly silent motors pushing it around?"

He grinned. "Yes, sir."

I pointed over the windscreen. "There's our objective. Put us alongside that cigarette boat at idle speed. I'll take Trip aboard, and Hunter and Kodiak will pull guard."

"What about me?" Gator asked. "Am I staying with the boat?"

"Not only are you staying with it, but you're going to move it back out the reciprocal course we came in on and wait for our signal to pick us up."

We conducted a comms check, and everyone's earpiece worked flawlessly. Hunter, Kodiak, and I enjoyed the high-quality sound from our bone conduction devices.

Gator brought us alongside the cigarette boat at less than one knot and held the starboard tube less than an inch away from our target.

"Nice work," I said. "Don't forget to come back and get us. If you hear gunfire, bring both main engines back online, and get us out of there as fast as possible. Got it?"

"Yes, sir."

Trip grabbed his gear bag and stepped from the tube onto the gunwale of the cigarette. I followed one step behind. Hunter bounded from the bow of our boat onto the foredeck, and Kodiak took the stern. Both men hunkered into kneeling positions with their rifles at the ready. We didn't want a gunfight, but if somebody onshore wanted one, we'd be happy to oblige.

Trip wasted no time. Before we'd been on the boat thirty seconds, he had a spray bottle of luminol in one hand and a black light in the other. He sprayed every surface he encountered, and the interior of the boat lit up like a Christmas tree under the black light.

He glanced over his shoulder at me and raised an eyebrow. "See that? That's blood."

"Human blood or fish blood?" I asked.

"Do you see any fishing gear?"

"I sure don't."

He continued spraying and waving the black light until we were confident a bloodbath had occurred on the boat.

"Can you get any prints?"

He twisted the nozzle of the luminol bottle and shoved it back into his bag. "We'll know soon."

He began with surfaces around the helm. "Somebody had to drive, so we'll probably find some prints here." A minute later, he sighed. "Nothing. It's been wiped clean of prints."

"How about the fuel caps?" I asked.

"Good thinking."

He dusted the two fuel caps and lifted three well-defined prints. "That's a start."

I agreed and motioned toward the stern. "As much as I hate to ask, can you find where the bodies were thrown overboard?"

His luminol bottle emerged back from the bag, and the fingerprint kit vanished. In less than a minute, he had bloody slide marks glowing in the dark.

The thought of what happened aboard that boat sickened me as my mind pictured the massacre. "Is there enough blood left for DNA testing?"

"Maybe. I'll take some samples, and we'll find out."

Even though the boat had been thoroughly cleaned, the trace evidence was all but impossible to erase without burning the boat to the waterline.

Trip took several swabs and deposited them into clear plastic bags. He leaned against a seat. "Do you know what I *don't* see?"

I studied the scene. "What?"

"Bullet holes. I don't know how they killed these guys, but it wasn't with guns. There's no way you make this much blood with bullets without hitting something inside the boat. If I were a betting man, I'd put my salary on this being a knife fight. A nasty one."

"There's no such thing as a good knife fight," I said. "What else do you need to do?"

"That's up to you. I can roll for hair and fibers if you want."

"Do it. Everything we can use to identify the victims is important."

He worked feverishly for several minutes until Kodiak said, "We've got company. Two men with flashlights."

"Are they guards?" I asked.

"Don't know, but I'm going in the water." Kodiak slipped from the stern and into the water beside the hull. From his position, he could keep an eye on the pair of men while remaining practically invisible.

I felt the boat move slightly, and Hunter said, "I'm in the water at the bow."

Trip and I pressed ourselves beneath the console of the vessel and froze as flashlight beams danced across the boat.

The two men spoke in calm patois as they continued walking. When they were almost to the bow of the cigarette boat, one of them said, "Did you hear something?" They stopped, and the two beams of light returned.

Trip and I regulated our breathing to remain as silent as possible, and one of the men said, "What dat be der by da wheel o' dat boat?"

The other man said, "Don' know. Go down der and check it out."

"I not gone in dat boat. No way."

If they stepped aboard the boat, we were busted, and there was nothing we could do about it.

At the perfect moment, Kodiak made a splashing sound from the stern of the boat, and one of the men on the dock said, "What was dat?"

The other man laughed. "'Twas jus' a fish jumpin'. Why you so nervous?"

The moment was apparently enough to make both men forget about what they'd seen by the helm, and they continued their rounds.

Peeking over the console, I watched them make the turn to the east, behind the same shipping container Clark used for cover only a few hours earlier. I said, "Get us out of here, Gator."

Chapter 18
That's My World

I scanned the surface of the Caribbean and listened carefully for the sound of the approaching RHIB slicing almost silently through the water with Gator at the helm. A flash of motion caught my attention, and I moved my eyes in a figure-eight pattern to make optimum use of my natural night vision. Turning to Trip, I said, "There he is. Get ready to jump. He won't stop when he comes alongside."

As Gator and the RHIB drew closer, the outline of the boat became clear, and I asked, "Are you ready?"

Instead of answering, Trip did the last thing I could've expected. He leapt forward, plunging into the water feetfirst, leaving me in absolute disbelief.

Why would he do that?

No answer came to mind, but a reaction from the docks showed up in spades. The two men who'd shone their lights into the cigarette boat a moment before, spun and sprinted back toward the boat. As they ran, I assessed my situation and didn't like anything about it. I had three men in the water, and one of them made no sense at all. I was all but burnt, with the beams of the two men's lights swinging wildly and certain to find me in no time. Finally, I had a rookie operator behind the wheel of our only way out of the situation.

"Dat don' be no fish."

I checked over my shoulder one final time to gauge how much time I had to come up with a plan, and the second hand wound down. I was out of time, out of ideas, and down to only one option.

I joined Trip in the water, but before I stepped from the boat, I said, "Gator, all four of us are in the water, and the guards are approaching."

I made far less noise than Trip as I slipped into the water, but it didn't matter. The damage was done, and we were in a run for our lives.

"Who dat be?"

The excited patois from the guards only added to the exhilaration of the moment until the crack of a rifle split the warm Caribbean night. The first round was followed by a dozen more in rapid succession, and tiny fountains of water sprang up all around us as the rounds struck the surface of the water. Instinctually, the four of us swam for the cover of the cigarette boat. The guards wouldn't be able to shoot through the hull, but by taking cover there, we'd eliminated any chance of a safe and silent retreat.

Continued yelling came from the dock as the two men searched frantically for the four of us.

Hunter slithered beside me. "Do you want us to take 'em out?"

I whispered, "Only if there's no other option. I don't want to start leaving bodies in our wake just yet."

At that moment, rifle fire erupted from the dock to our left. At least one of the men had repositioned himself into the perfect killing angle. We were seconds away from being cut down, and I took a long packing breath in preparation for the coming minutes of my life that would be, out of necessity, spent underwater, but before I made my descent, the sweetest sound I'd ever heard echoed through my head.

Automatic rifle fire ripped through the darkness, and arcing sparks of 5.56mm rounds colliding with the concrete and steel of the docks sparkled like little stars hung by our guardian angel. Gator abandoned any attempt at stealth and fired up the twin engines of the RHIB. His suppressive fire continued raking the docks and sending the two guards scampering for their lives.

He roared toward our position and threw the engines out of gear to stop the props as he allowed his stored momentum to carry the boat past us fast enough to avoid coming to a complete stop. The light of the docks gave us an excellent view of everything Gator did, and I couldn't have been more pleased. He tossed a line across each side of the RHIB and leaned himself over the starboard tube with a hooked arm extended toward Trip, our forensic tech. Unfamiliar with the extraction technique, Trip grabbed at Gator's arms like a drowning man surging for any rescue.

Gator's plan had obviously been to hook Trip's arm and swing him aboard as he passed, but instead, the tech clumsily clawed at him and the side of the RHIB until he pulled Gator out of the boat.

At the same instant Gator hit the water, one of the guards from onshore engaged again, sending round after round toward our RHIB. Hunter and Kodiak returned fire, pinning the man down and sending him retreating for cover.

Gator grabbed Trip's shirt with one hand and the line he'd thrown into the water with the other. As the line came tight, he shoved a section of the floating line toward the tech. "Grab this, and don't let go!"

Trip followed the order and wrapped the line around both hands as the RHIB pulled him through the water. Gator pulled, hand over hand, until he reached the stern of the RHIB and climbed aboard. The rest of us grabbed the line that didn't hold our CSI Aquaman.

Gator grabbed the line and pulled furiously, dragging Trip toward the boat. "A little help would be nice, there, big-time crime buster!"

Trip got the message and joined Gator in hauling himself toward the boat. It was awkward, but our new guy finally got the tech back aboard. He shoved him to the deck and commanded, "Stay down."

Kodiak covered Hunter and me as we pulled ourselves toward the RHIB. When I reached the portside tube, I looked up to see Gator shaking the salt water from his rifle that had been draped across his shoulder by its sling for the whole adventure. He raised the weapon to his shoulder and yelled, "Come on, Kodiak! I've got you."

Kodiak, our former new guy, powered toward the boat on the drag line while Gator bounced a few more rounds off a shipping container to keep the guards' heads down. We dragged ourselves aboard, and I scampered my way to the helm.

In Gator's haste to get us out of the water, he failed to shut down the electric motors, so I powered those down before pressing the throttles forward. With a quick glance across my shoulder, everything I expected was confirmed. Gator was hauling in the remaining drag line, and Hunter and Kodiak were kneeling in the stern with rifles at the ready to suppress any aggression from ashore. Trip remained on the deck, exactly where Gator put him.

The bow rose as I pressed the throttles forward, and the RHIB felt sluggish and awkward in my hands. Something clearly wasn't right, but the priority in that moment was to put as much distance and darkness between us and the aggressors onshore as possible. I watched the bow climb and slowly fall as we limped to the surface and the boat finally planed out. A scan of the instrument panel told the story I didn't want to hear. The portside engine was producing no power, but the ignition switch was in the running position. I cycled the switch, and the ammeter showed a drain as the starter engaged, but the engine never came to life.

Rather than troubleshooting the engine in the heat of our escape, I thumbed the tilt control and raised the foot of the portside engine out of the water. Without the drag of the dead engine, we gained five knots of speed, and the ride smoothed considerably.

With things calming down, I grabbed Gator's shirt. "Take the helm!"

He slid into position, and I moved to my team. "Is anybody hurt?"

Hunter shook his head. "I'm good."

Kodiak gave the okay sign, and I knelt beside Trip. "Are you hurt?"

He stared up at me with wild eyes. "I don't think so, but I'm cold."

"You'll be all right. Why did you jump in the water?"

He looked baffled. "You told me to jump."

"I told you to get ready to jump into the RHIB, not the ocean. We were ten seconds away from being gone in silence, and you nearly got us killed."

He scowled. "I'm a lab tech and a nurse practitioner, not a commando like you guys."

I laid a hand against his chest. "You're right. I should've been clearer with the instructions. You did a good job tonight, right up to the point you did a gainer. Where are the blood samples?"

"They're in my bag."

"Where's your bag?"

Trip sat up and peered over the stern. "Back there."

My frustration rose, but I did my best to keep my cool. "Is your bag waterproof?"

He shrugged.

"Will it float?"

"I don't know."

"All right. Stay down out of the wind, and you won't get any colder. We'll have you back on the ship in a couple of minutes."

I stepped behind the console with Gator, and he slid to his right.

"Stay where you are," I said. "I'm not taking the helm. You're the driver. I'm just trying to get out of the wind."

Gator brought the boat alongside the *Lori Danielle* like an old pro, and the crane operator lowered the davit lines. Hunter and I rigged the lines, and I gave the signal to hoist away.

A few seconds later, we settled into the RHIB's cradle, and a deckhand walked around the boat, running his hands along the tubes. "You must've had a little excitement."

I climbed down from the damaged RHIB. "You could say that. We took a little fire, but nobody got hit."

"The RHIB should be so lucky," he said. "It looks like that port engine took at least two to the head."

"That would explain why I couldn't get it to make any power."

He chuckled. "Yeah, that'll do it. Looks like you took a few to the bow as well. We'll get her inside and patched up. We've got a spare engine, so we'll throw it on. It looks like this one has seen its last fight. Are you sure everybody's okay?"

"We're all right," I said. "Who's on the bridge?"

"The captain. He's always on the bridge when we're running an op from the deck. He lives for this stuff."

Gator and Kodiak helped Trip from the RHIB, and I stepped in front of him. "You did well tonight. I'm sorry for putting you in harm's way when you weren't expecting it. It was my fault for not realizing you weren't an operator."

Trip said, "I'm sorry I dropped my kit. Are you going back for it?"

"No, we got the verification we needed. Whatever happened on that boat was a bloodbath, so we have to assume the worst and treat it like another breadcrumb in the terrorists' wake."

"Look, I'm really sorry for getting us shot at out there. I was out of my element, and I screwed up. I'm sorry."

"Stop apologizing. Imagine the damage one of us knuckle-draggers could do in your lab. We live in two different worlds. Now, get down to sick bay and have them check you out. Sometimes we're hurt and don't realize it when our adrenaline is pumping."

He smiled. "Yeah, I know. *That's* my world."

Chapter 19
The Chase Is On

With salt water still dripping from every inch of me, I jogged my way to the navigation bridge. "Permission to come aboard the bridge?"

Captain Sprayberry looked up. "Come aboard. This is your ship, Chase. You don't have to ask."

I said, "Oh, no. You're not hanging this monster around my neck. This is *your* ship. I'm just a soggy passenger."

"You are a little damp. How'd it go out there?"

I looked down and couldn't disagree with his assessment. "Not bad. We took a little damage to the RHIB, but we got what we needed. I think we scared Trip out of his skin, but I suspect he'll never forget the experience."

"I look forward to hearing that story," he said. "Are you ready to start the high-speed chase scene?"

"That's why I'm here. Did Skipper give you everything you need?"

"She did, and then some. We've already plotted an intercept course, and we're ready to move on your command."

I waggled a finger. "We already covered that command thing. It's still your ship, and I'm still a passenger, but I would like to put in the formal request to chase that sucker down."

Barry turned and gave the order. "Helm, all engines to ninety percent. Lay in the course to intercept target. Weigh anchor, and make ready for high-speed operations."

The young officer at the helm said, "All engines to ninety, lay in intercept course, weigh anchor and make ready. Aye, sir."

I watched the exchange and said, "It's just like in the movies."

Barry laughed. "We only do that when you're around since this is your ship. Most of the time, we just wing it."

"Okay, then. If you insist on it being mine, I say we head back to the Straits of Florida and do some more scientific sampling since you love that work so much."

The captain glared at me across his glasses. "Get off of *my* bridge before I throw you off *my* ship. And for God's sake, get some dry clothes. You're a mess."

I gave the thumbs-up and backed through the hatch. I was still several minutes from clean, dry clothes when I stepped into the CIC.

Clark and Skipper looked over their shoulders, and Clark said, "I hate I missed the excitement. What did you find?"

"We found a couple of trigger-happy roving guards, but they were no problem. The boat looked like a slaughterhouse. Somebody tried to clean it up, but the luminol glowed like fire. A lot of people lost their lives on that boat."

"That's what I was afraid of," he said. "How did Gator do?"

"He got yanked out of the RHIB by a terrified lab tech with the electric motors running."

"I really hate that I missed that. I'm glad you went back to get him."

"That's the best part," I said. "He was the only one in the boat, but he had the presence of mind to toss over a pair of drag lines before abandoning ship."

Clark gave me a nod. "He's going to be all right, isn't he?"

"I think so. He got to send a few rounds downrange, too. We looked like the A-Team. We fired ten thousand rounds and didn't hit anybody."

Clark said, "Nicely done. We don't need a trail of dead bodies behind us yet."

Before I could say anything, the ship accelerated and turned to the northwest.

Skipper said, "That must mean the chase is on."

"It is," I said. "Now, if you don't need me, I'm going to rinse off and throw on some dry clothes."

She said, "I was just about to throw you out for dripping on my floor."

I took a step back. "It's called a deck."

She hurled a paperweight toward me, and I caught it with one hand. "Until you can throw a ninety-five-mile-per-hour slider, you're wasting your time throwing things at me. I'll see you in a few minutes."

By the time I made it back to the CIC, the rest of the team had assembled in clean, dry clothes. We ran through the after-action review and took turns bragging on Gator.

"You did a nice job out there," Hunter said.

I gasped. "What? Was that a compliment from Stone Hunter?"

Hunter rolled his eyes. "I hand them out when they're earned. They're just rarely earned. I will say this, though. The next time you let anybody yank you out of a boat, you better hope they drown you before I get to you. That was sloppy, dangerous, and stupid."

"There it is," I said. "I knew you couldn't stop after doling out a compliment."

Gator said, "Yes, sir. You're right. I expected that guy to know how to get in a boat."

Hunter jumped in before I could. "And we expected you to know how to keep a forensic geek from jerking your football-playing butt out of a boat."

"Walked right into that one, didn't I?"

"Welcome to the team," I said. "I assure you the plunge won't be the last thing you do wrong, but I need you to understand how serious it could've been. If you hadn't deployed the drag lines, we would've been in a gunfight without a boat with a panicked tech to deal with. We all make mistakes. I made a big one assuming Trip understood what was going to happen. I started the chain of insanity, and I learned from it. We all need you to do the same."

"Yes, sir."

I continued. "Nice job not killing anybody tonight, guys, but the rules of engagement have changed. As you can feel, we're running as fast as this old girl can run to catch the boat with the terrorists. The next encounter we have won't be against Caribbean island guards. It'll be with enemies of America who are determined to complete a mission we can't allow."

Mongo raised a finger. "Do we have any new ideas about what that mission might be?"

I turned to Skipper, and she said, "We're still working on it, but the Board is still convinced it'll be a symbolic attack and not a serious threat to American lives."

I cut in. "That's just a theory, and we don't restrain ourselves on theories. These people have a plan to harm the United States and its citizens, and we have one task—to stop them at all costs. We want to capture at least two of these guys alive."

"Why two?" Gator asked.

"Because if we interrogate one person, we have no way to validate his intel. If we have at least two of them, we can compare stories and piece together the plan. In a perfect world, we'd capture all of them, but based on what we saw on that boat tonight, they're obviously not going down easy."

Hunter asked, "What's our ETA to intercept?"

Skipper brought up a chart. "If everything stays the same, we'll intercept them just south of Cozumel in a little over twelve hours. If that boat is typical of vessels that size, she'll be low on fuel by then, and Cozumel makes a nice gas station."

"Are we going to cut them down?" Kodiak asked.

I tapped my fingertips against the table. "No, not at first. If they stop for fuel, we're going to tag them with a tracker and a nice little remotely detonated boom-boom in case they get away from us. I want to know what their target is, and the best way to find out is to let them think they're getting to it. We can lie back, watch, and listen, and when they move in, we'll be right behind them to roll them up."

Hunter said, "It's still me and the kid, right?"

"If you want," I said. "You're the best underwater tag-you're-it player we've got."

He turned to Gator. "You up for it?"

"Yes, sir."

Hunter said, "Quit calling me sir. You can call Disco and Clark sir because they're old, but I'm just a knuckle-dragger like you."

Kodiak said, "When we were Gator's age, everybody was old. But I've got a question. What's our plan if they don't stop for fuel?"

I said, "They have to stop sometime, but if they don't stop in Cozumel, we'll follow them until they do."

Kodiak cocked his head as if playing out the scenario in his mind. "What if their fuel stop is their target?"

That stopped me in my tracks. Each of us sat in silence considering Kodiak's question.

Mongo finally said, "What if we sink them slowly?"

"Keep talking," I said.

He leaned toward the table and rested on his elbows. "There are a thousand things that can force a boat into port, or at least shallow water. A small hole is high on that list. If we can cripple their boat but not destroy it, they'll have only three options: let it sink and abandon ship, run for a port, or stick her on a sandbar. No matter which one they choose, we'll have them at our mercy."

"I like it," I said. "Unless they run into a port and disappear into mainland Mexico."

The big man shrugged. "What if they do? That just makes this a footrace instead of a boat race, and we're good at both."

"Point taken. How do we punch a hole in them without ripping their keel in half?"

"That's Singer's department," he said.

I gave our sniper an eye. "Can you do it?"

"I can. But I may not be the best man for the job."

I said, "Nobody on this boat can outshoot you, so if anyone can do it, you're the guy."

"With a rifle, you're right, but what if our magic carpet is a better shot than me?"

"What are you suggesting?" I asked.

"I'm suggesting we get the weapons officer down here and see what tricks he has up his sleeve."

Skipper was on the phone almost before Singer stopped talking, and as if he'd been waiting in the passageway, the man we needed stepped through the hatch and into the CIC.

He scanned the room and motioned toward the new guy. "I know everybody except him."

I made the introduction. "Gator, meet retired Commander Ted LeGrange, our weapons officer."

Gator stuck out his hand, and Ted shook it.

"Nice to meet you, Commander."

"Nice to meet you, too, Gator, but call me Weps."

"Yes, sir."

Weps said, "Skipper told me you needed a weapons capabilities briefing. Is that right?"

"Sort of," I said. "We're pursuing a fifty-foot motor yacht with suspected terrorists aboard. They're running north about twenty miles offshore of the Central American coastline. We want to force them into port or shallow water. We need to know what the *Lori Danielle* can do to make that happen."

He took his seat at the weapons systems panel and spun to face us. "We've got a few options. First, may I assume we're faster than the target vessel?"

I said, "Yes, by at least twice."

"Thought so. We could just muscle them ashore. The smaller boat can probably outmaneuver us, but she can't outrun us. With some patience, we could push her anywhere we want her to go."

"We're looking for something a little less overt."

He said, "We've got four anti-ship missiles on board."

"Still too overt."

He pressed his lips into a thin line. "Torpedoes?"

I said, "I may not have explained the situation very well. We want to poke a hole in that boat that won't destroy the vessel but will force her to stop."

"Oh," he said. "Sure, that's easy. We'll hit her with an unarmed torpedo if she's fiberglass or wood, and if she's a steel-huller, we can arm a penetrating torpedo without a high-explosive warhead. That'll poke a six-inch entry wound and exit wound in the hull. She'll sink, but not fast."

Singer snapped his fingers. "See? I told you I wasn't the best shot on the boat."

Weps said, "What are you going to do when she stops?"

I said, "We're going to invite everyone on board to come over and have a little chat."

Weps said, "Oh, it's that kind of party."

"It is, but there's one more caveat. Part of me wants to lag behind and see where they're going before we bust them. It's possible that we could roll these guys up and turn Clark loose on them, and they never say a word."

Gator scoffed. "Not likely. I've been interrogated by Clark, and I was ready to tell him everything I knew in the first hour."

"I'm glad you brought that up," I said. "What you endured was a training scenario. Yes, it sucked, but you knew we weren't going to cut your fingers off or put bullets through your kneecaps. Even though you were scared and injured, you weren't going to die. That's an entirely different mindset than the guys on that boat have. They want to die for their cause. Crazy stuff starts happening in the gray matter when a person is looking forward to dying."

Gator said, "I got it. I'm sorry for interrupting."

"Never be sorry," I said. "Your input is just as valuable as mine when we're planning and scheming. That changes a little when people start shooting at us, but don't be afraid to join the discussion in here. On the battlefield, do what you're told for now, and we'll explain it when we all come home in one piece."

"Yes, sir."

"Now, back to my idea. If we take these guys and they don't talk, we've stopped the threat, but we've not learned anything. It's important to do both. We want to know what they were thinking, planning, and anticipating. We don't get any of that if we shoot them in the face or stop them before they're ready to strike. I want to find a way to walk that fine line between approaching the target and striking the target."

Weps crossed his legs. "That's not my area. I'll kill whatever you tell me to kill when you tell me to kill it."

Mongo jumped back into the fray. "What if we make this a variable plan? If they stop, we stick a bomb and a tracker on the hull. If they don't, we chase them with our torpedoes and anti-ship missiles locked and loaded and cut them down when we believe they're on the verge of striking. Can we maintain that level of readiness, Weps?"

The weapons officer said, "I can do anything from nothing to blowing that bath toy out of the water at the drop of a hat. All you have to do is say the word."

I panned the room. "Does anyone have a better idea?"

Heads shook, and no one spoke.

"Okay, then. That's the game plan. We'll catch her, tag her if she stops, trail her if she doesn't, and keep our finger on the trigger."

Chapter 20
I Didn't See That Coming

Mike Tyson said it best: "Everyone has a plan until they get punched in the mouth."

I stopped counting missions a long time ago, but I never remember contact with an enemy that followed my plan. The coming days of our lives would be no different. Something—possibly everything—would change. Somebody would do something we didn't expect, or we'd make an error that demanded an immediate change of plans.

We slept, ate, and conducted weapons drills while the *Lori Danielle* carried us across the Caribbean at almost a mile a minute.

During a break for Gatorade and calories, Gator said, "I really appreciate you guys taking the time to work weapons drills with me. I'll get up to speed, and we won't have to do this stuff all the time."

Singer gave his protégé a knowing grin. "That's the most rookie thing you've said since you've been here."

"What do you mean?"

Singer said, "We're not running drills for you. We're running drills for the team. This is exactly what we'd be doing even if you were still playing ball in Kansas. This is what we do. We train, train, and train some more. Then, when the fight comes, the training takes over and we come out with fewer bullet holes in us than the bad guys have in them. If you don't like weapons drills, you're in for a long, hard road with this team."

"Seriously?" Gator asked. "This is routine?"

Singer said, "Yes, sir. Everybody on this team hopes he never has to pull another trigger in anger, but we all know that hope ain't a plan. Because of that, we're going to be better trained, better equipped, and harder hitting than anybody we face. That's how we stay alive."

The drills continued until our bellies demanded groceries.

As we finished lunch—or "noon chow" as they call it on the ship—Skipper plucked her phone from her pocket, listened, and said, "Thanks." She dropped her fork and looked up. "We're within radar range of the target vessel."

We abandoned our plates and piled into the CIC. "There she is," Skipper said, pointing toward monitor number two.

"How do you know that's her?" Hunter asked.

"Because the radar target correlates with the satellite data. When we get within visual range, we'll launch a drone and get some hi-def video of her."

As if on cue, the ship slowed and settled into the water as the hydrofoils retracted into their wells inside the hull. Every eye was glued to the radar screen as we pulled ahead of the yacht by at least a mile.

Gator asked, "Why are we moving ahead of them if our plan is to follow?"

Skipper spun around. "You're asking good questions, new guy. The position out front gives us two advantages. First, nobody thinks they're being chased by somebody in front of them, so we appear to be a coincidental parallel track, but not a chaser. We'll vary our position over the next few hours to appear even less threatening."

"That makes sense," he said. "What's the second advantage?"

She drew a triangle in the air with her fingertip. "It's geometry. If we're going to fly a drone over there to get a closer look, it would chew up the batteries if the poor little thing had to catch up to the yacht from behind, but with us in front, it'll be a leisurely flight. When we recover the drone, we'll reduce speed, fall behind, and make the return trip nice and easy, as well."

"You guys think of everything," Gator said.

Skipper spun back to her workstation. "Not everything, but we're learning. I suspect you'll have that feeling a lot in the next few days and weeks. You're well trained, but there's always so much more to learn . . . even for us."

Just as Skipper predicted, whoever was in command on the bridge brought us into perfect position to launch the drone, and Dr. Mankiller released her creation into the afternoon sky. Skipper initiated the program to direct the flying photography platform into position over the yacht.

A perfect high-definition shot of our ship appeared on the screen in front of our analyst for a few seconds and then went disturbingly black.

Kodiak gasped. "What was that? Did it crash?"

"Calm down, gunslinger. I shut down the camera to conserve the batteries. We want as much time on station as we can get. The longer I can loiter over that boat, the more details we should be able to glean from the video."

The flight took just over three minutes and felt like an eternity, but when the camera began broadcasting again, the reward was well worth the wait.

Every pair of eyes in the room leaned toward the monitor, and I said, "Zoom in on that guy!"

Skipper shot a glare across her shoulder. "Take it easy. I'm on it."

As the image grew on the screen, I couldn't believe my eyes. "Who is that?"

"I'm working on it," Skipper said.

Mongo was the first to make the connection. "Forget trying to figure it out. Bring up the headshots from the dossiers the Board sent us."

Skipper froze and let out a heartbroken sigh. "No. It can't be."

"Don't vapor-lock," I said. "Stay in the game, and bring up those dossier photos."

The second monitor populated with the six pictures, and my heart sank. "That's him. Get me everything you can find on that traitor. I want to know who his first babysitter was and what he had for breakfast."

Skipper said, "I can't fly the drone, operate the camera, and dig into that guy's world at the same time. You've got to pick one."

Instead of making that decision, I yanked my phone from my pocket and thumbed the speed dial.

Dr. Mankiller answered immediately. "Hey, Chase. What's up?"

"I need you in the CIC now!"

I didn't wait for an answer and shoved the phone back in my pocket. "Fly the drone, and get me the name of that boat."

Celeste came through the hatch as if she were being chased. "What's going on?"

I shoved Gator and Disco out of the way. "Get in here and fly the drone."

She didn't argue, and in seconds, Skipper was free to dive into the American on that yacht.

She said, "His name is Evan Brewer. He did six and a half years in the Army. The final three was with the Ranger regiment as a sniper. Three deployments, Bronze Star, Purple Heart, medical discharge PTSD and chronic back pain."

I glared at Singer. "Get on the phone."

He gave me a sharp nod and headed for the door.

I laid a hand on Skipper's shoulder. "Keep digging."

She didn't react, but her fingers moved like lightning across the keyboard. Her screen filled with lines of text, and she said, "Ex-wife, child support . . . Wait a minute. This could be duplicate data, but it looks like he's paying child support to two different women."

"Debt?" I asked.

"Yeah, a bunch."

My gut felt like someone stuck a knife in it. "Is there any chance he's a hostage?"

"Nobody's guarding him, and he's not restrained."

"I don't want to believe this guy is a traitor."

Skipper groaned. "Neither do I, but everything is pointing in that direction."

"Keep digging. I need everything."

Singer came back through the hatch and stepped beside me. "He was a good soldier. He had twenty confirmed kills, and everybody liked him. Apparently, it got to him, and he started drinking. He hurt his back on a night jump gone bad."

"Combat jump?" I asked.

"Yeah. I guess he rubbed some dirt on it and embraced the suck instead of getting it checked out."

I stepped into the corridor and tried knobs until I found an empty open compartment where I could hide and think. I played everything I knew through my head and tried to understand what we faced. I was dealing with three terrorists in custody, who turned into six or seven bad guys, with a dead team of American operators who were probably passing through the digestive systems of a few sharks in the Western Caribbean. The haunting element was the American in dire money trouble with a headful of trauma and a screwed-up back. I wasn't over my head, but I was neck-deep in a pool in which I didn't want to swim.

My phone chirped, and I ignored it. I needed two more minutes or perhaps two more centuries to process what I was facing.

Can I shoot this guy if he shoots at me? Did he play a role in the deaths of his teammates? How deep is this thing going to get before it makes sense?

The phone alarmed again, and I slapped my pocket. Nothing could be so important that I had to hear it immediately. Everything inside me wanted to sink that yacht, drag the survivors out of the water, and carve the truth out of them, but the mission would never give me such luxuries. I was in for the long haul, and the task ahead of me would leave its indelible mark on all of us.

"Chase! Are you in there?"

Clark pushed open the hatch and leaned in. "They just made a turn."

I stood and stepped toward him. "Well, that's the only thing that makes sense so far. I guess Skipper was right. They must be out of gas."

Clark said, "They didn't turn for Cozumel. They turned northeast."

"Northeast? Toward the Keys?"

"Exactly."

"What is it, four hundred miles to Key West?"

"Yeah," he said. "Something like that."

I drew the map in my head. "That leaves out the Gulf Coast as a target."

"You're right, but just because we eliminated a few targets doesn't mean we're any closer to knowing where they're headed."

I stared into Clark's face. "Is Evan Brewer in on this thing?"

He looked away. "Up to his ears, my friend. Up to his ears."

I followed him back to the CIC, and Skipper started talking almost before we were inside. "They're headed for the Keys, Chase."

"I heard. What have we learned about the boat?"

Celeste said, "It's a custom sixty-five-footer christened the *Scimitar*. She's owned by a cousin of the Saudi royal family."

"Well, that's not good," I said. "Do we know who built her?"

She said, "A French shipyard who isn't likely to answer the phone when we call."

"Are we ever going to catch a break on this mission?"

I took in the faces of the men and women around me and the thousand bits of data on the screens in front of me. The video of the yacht was still rolling on Celeste's monitor, and two more men appeared on deck. They were not Americans.

I leaned down and asked Celeste, "How much battery life is left on that drone if it's not broadcasting video or flying?"

"I think I know what you're really asking, but it won't work with that drone. It doesn't have the endurance, but I've got three more."

I squeezed her shoulder. "Park one on top of that yacht, and turn off the camera."

She said, "I need to recover this one. It's going to die in seven minutes."

"Let it die and crash into the ocean," I said. "We've got the video. We can sacrifice the drone. Get another one in the air."

She typed in a few commands and abandoned her station.

I called the bridge. "Put us in position to launch another drone."

The maneuver was flawless, and the second drone climbed into the sky as if it were built exclusively for this mission.

Celeste returned to the CIC and flew the device toward the fleeing yacht. With the dexterity of a surgeon, she planted the drone on the highest point of the boat and shut down everything except the GPS tracker built into the craft.

I leaned against the bulkhead and dialed the bridge again. "Put us twenty miles ahead of the *Scimitar* and lay in a course for Key West."

We accelerated and soon had the twenty miles I ordered. Steaming northeast, matching the speed of the yacht, we settled in for the seventeen-hour, four-hundred-mile trek.

I dismissed the team and said, "Get some rest if you can. If they plan to hit the Keys, I'll need you well rested and ready to run and gun."

I didn't expect sleep to welcome me, but she did, and I drifted off after half an hour in the sack.

Long before my body and mind wanted to be awake, a knock at my door drew me from my sleep. "Yeah, come in."

Skipper stuck her head into my cabin. "They're not headed for the Keys. They just took a turn into Havana."

Chapter 21
I Remember This Place

I swung my single foot over the edge of the bed and reached for my prosthetic. "Havana? Cuba?"

Although I couldn't see her, I could almost feel her rolling her eyes. "How many other Havanas can you think of in the Straits of Florida?"

I positioned my prosthetic in place and pulled on a pair of pants. "Who else is awake?"

"Just you and me. I figured there was no need to wake up the others until you make the call."

I followed her through my hatch, and she pointed at my bare foot. "Are you going with that look?"

It was my turn to roll my eyes. I stepped back into my cabin, planted myself on a chair, and pulled my left boot onto the one human foot I had left. Once in the CIC, I checked the screens for our position and the position of the *Scimitar*.

Skipper said, "I flew the drone off when they made the turn into the harbor. There's only one way out of there, and we can cover that with radar. I didn't want to risk anyone finding our drone if they went crawling around on top of the yacht for some reason."

"Good thinking. Is it safely back aboard?"

"It made an automatic landing on our helipad without incident. I'll change its batteries before sending it back out."

I rubbed the sleep from my eyes and poured a cup of coffee. "Please tell me you have a satellite in position to see what's going on."

She turned to a monitor and checked her watch. "I'll have one in place for twelve minutes starting in fifteen minutes, but we're blind right now."

"Is there enough light in that harbor for us to see anything?"

She sent her fingers flying across the keyboard, and soon the main monitor filled with the unmistakable image of Havana Harbor. "The next satellite in position has the identical camera to this one that came over forty-five minutes ago. It'll look just like that with the addition of one *Scimitar*."

I scanned everything on the wall of monitors and built a mental image of the situation. "Wake 'em up and tell the deck crew to ready the SDV. I'm going to see the captain."

She said, "He's not on watch. The first officer is . . ."

It didn't matter. Anyone on the bridge would do, and I covered the distance in record time. I made no request to board the navigation bridge. Instead, I sprinted into the space, catching the crew off guard.

The first officer leapt from his seat and reached for his sidearm, immediately sending both of my hands above my head.

"It's Chase."

Niles Milton, the *Lori Danielle*'s second-in-command, resecured his pistol into its holster. "It's never a great idea to come running onto the bridge."

"I know. I'm sorry. It won't happen again. I need to know how close you can get me to the mouth of the harbor without having the Cubans send out a welcoming party of gunboats."

Niles stepped to the radar and motioned toward every return on the screen. "I don't see any gunboats on patrol. That's not unusual. Diesel is expensive, and parts are scarce, so the Cubans tend to leave their engines quiet and their gunboats in port most of the time. I can put us within a mile of the mouth of the port as long as it's dark, but I can't loiter there for long. What do you have in mind?"

I said, "I plan to put our SEAL Delivery Vehicle under that yacht with four personnel. It'll be a drop-and-go."

A grin claimed half of his face. "I'll wake up the skipper."

I checked my watch. It was 3:44 a.m. "What time is sunrise?"

Niles said, "Six thirty-five, but the sky will be light enough to silhouette us at six."

I played out the mission timing. "How close can you get us without waking up the captain?"

"I won't break territorial waters without the captain's okay."

I said, "Twelve miles is too far for the mini-sub. It's just too slow."

Niles turned to a young man with binoculars pressed to his face. "Perry, you have the bridge."

"Aye, sir. I have the bridge."

Niles stepped through a sliding hatch and knocked on the captain's cabin door. "Captain, sir. It's the first officer. You're needed on the bridge."

A muffled reply came from the other side, and Niles reclaimed his position. "First officer has the bridge."

The young man at the window said, "Aye, sir. No changes."

"No changes," Niles echoed.

A few seconds later, Barry stepped onto the nerve center of the ship, and Niles said, "Captain's on the bridge."

Captain Sprayberry wiped his eyes. "As you were, Mr. Milton. The bridge remains yours. What do you need?"

Niles glanced at me, and the captain said, "I should've known. What have you done now, Chase?"

"I didn't do it, Captain, but I'm going to. I need Mr. Milton to stick us in the mouth of Havana Harbor so I can launch the SDV."

"Oh, is that all? You want to violate the sovereign waters of a communist country at four in the morning and launch a mini-sub into the harbor of the capital city so you and your band of merry-men can, no doubt, unleash some manner of havoc on the unsuspecting inhabitants of that city."

"When you put it that way . . ."

The captain said, "Somebody pour me some coffee. The captain has the bridge."

A cup of steaming coffee materialized in Barry's hand, and Niles gave the pass-down briefing.

When he was finished, Barry said, "Thank you, Mr. Milton. The ship is mine. Helm, lay in a course for the mouth of the harbor, and proceed at twenty-five knots."

The helmsman answered, "Dead on to the harbor at twenty-five knots. Aye, sir."

Barry turned back to me. "That'll put us one mile outside the harbor in twenty-eight minutes. Is that fast enough?"

"That depends on the crew readying the SDV."

Barry turned and picked up a handset from the console. "Moonpool, Bridge."

I could only hear his end of the conversation.

"How much time do you need to ready the SDV?" He waited a few seconds and said, "Thank you. Bridge out. It'll be ready to splash in ten minutes."

I asked, "How fast can we go without being on the foils?"

"Thirty knots."

"Then make it thirty knots," I said. "My team will be ready to hit the water on your hack."

He waved the back of his hand in a shooing motion. "Get off my bridge, and get ready to get wet."

I left the navigation bridge almost as quickly as I'd arrived. When I reached the moonpool on the lower deck of the ship, the SEAL Delivery Vehicle rested on its cradle with davit lines leading to the overhead crane. Hunter, Gator, and Clark waited in wetsuits and full scuba gear. A fourth set of gear lay on the deck beside them, and it just happened to have my name stenciled onto the tag. Clark handed me the diving prosthetic Mongo built for me. It didn't have any electronics, but it had a built-in Scubapro fin that made me feel almost like a frogman.

I was in my gear and aboard the mini-sub in ten minutes. Clark slid behind the control panel of the sub and oriented the GPS, then he spun the propeller and cycled through the controls. The rudder and dive planes functioned flawlessly, and he gave the signal to take up the slack in the davit lines.

Hunter patiently took Gator through the operation of the SDV's compressed air system and proper ingress and egress techniques. The new guy had to learn, but I wanted to be the one to plant the explosive charge on the *Scimitar*. Perhaps my days of doing such things were fading and I was being slowly replaced by my betters.

The ship slowed and stopped, and I eyed the chief deckhand.

He cupped a hand over his ear and looked up at me. "Captain says we're three quarters of a mile outside the harbor and centered on the mouth. We're go for splash on your order."

Clark gave the okay sign, and I turned to Hunter. He gave the same signal, and my eyes fell on Gator. He sat motionless, and Hunter gave him a shove.

"Tell Chase you're good to go."

He flinched and yelled, "Good to go!"

Hunter slugged him again. "Not with your mouth, dummy. Give him the okay sign."

The verbal call was good enough for me, and I signaled for the crane operator to hoist away.

We pulled on our full face masks and connected the lines from the sub's air system. The electronic comms clicked, and we conducted a communications check. Everything was working perfectly, and I gave the signal to splash the sub.

The crane operator skillfully lifted us over the opening of the moonpool and lowered us into the sea.

Hunter said, "Don't forget to breathe, kid."

The Caribbean rushed into the confines of the SDV, and we slid the hatches closed. There was no way to keep the water out since the sub was designed to be wet inside and out. Clark performed one more overall systems check before I gave the command to cut us loose, and we were away.

The water penetrated our wetsuits, and our bodies adjusted to the temperature change. At eighty degrees, it was well below our body temperature, but it was warm enough for us to survive and thrive for several hours without shivering.

Clear of the ship, Clark turned us on course and floated the GPS navigation buoy. The buoy would float on the surface above the SDV connected by a tether. The antenna buoy was about the size of a child's shoe and would be impossible to detect on the surface. Alongside the navigation buoy was a commo buoy giving us radio communication with the bridge and CIC.

Clark made course adjustments for the current and started a timer while I made our first radio call. "CIC, Alpha One. We're wet and away. ETA twenty-one minutes."

Skipper's voice sounded distorted and hard to understand. I glanced over at Clark. "Does Skipper sound bad in your comms?"

"No, she sounds normal to me."

I wiggled the connection to my mask and tried again, but she still sounded terrible.

Hunter said, "We've got her loud and clear back here."

"It must be my mask. Something's definitely wrong."

Skipper spoke slowly. "Did you take your hearing aids out?"

I pressed the push-to-talk button. "Order me a new pair, and ask if they have a waterproof set."

I fished the waterlogged hearing aids from my ears and stuffed them into a pocket of my wetsuit. Suddenly, Skipper sounded like Skipper again.

Halfway to our target, I double-checked Clark's navigation and said, "Hey, Gator. How are you doing back there? You sure are quiet."

"I'm good. This is just a little freaky."

"Welcome to your new normal," I said. "You'll get used to it. This thing freaked me out the first time I was in it, too."

Clark brought the SDV to periscope depth, and I deployed the simplistic tube that would allow us to see above the waterline. It took a minute for my eyes to adjust, but I soon found the *Scimitar* and fed Clark course corrections to maneuver directly toward the target.

I reported. "Alpha Element is on target and securing comms."

I reeled in the nav/com buoy and secured the periscope while Clark descended beneath the *Scimitar* and allowed the SDV to settle onto the muddy bottom against the seawall.

We slid open the hatches, and I gave the order to disconnect from the SDV's air system. Hunter was first out of the sub, and he spun to watch Gator and me work ourselves clear of the vehicle. Clark stayed with the SDV to ensure that our ride home would be where we expected when we completed the mission.

I pointed toward Hunter and gave him the signal to lead. Gator fell in on his left and followed Hunter toward the hull of the yacht, only a few feet over our heads. In order to remain neutrally buoyant and avoid rising to the surface, we allowed air to escape our buoyancy compensation devices as the reduced pressure of the shallower water caused the air trapped inside our BCDs to expand.

Operating in the relative darkness of the port presented a set of challenges unique to our environment. The small amount of light filtering through the dirty water around the hull of the *Scimitar* painted an eerie silhouette of the yacht looming above us. Depth perception was accomplished only by use of our hands.

The three of us reached upward until we felt the hull touch our fingertips. Hunter brought his mask-mounted light online at its lowest setting, and the white beam cut a narrow, short swath through the water and reflected dimly from the hull of the boat. With his eyes adjusted to the dim lighting, Hunter reached toward Gator and held up one finger. The new guy pulled a small package from a pouch and placed it in Hunter's palm.

Hunter held the device close to his face and examined the explosive charge before feeling his way to the stern of the vessel. Careful to remain well clear of the pair of propellers that could turn him into fish food in an instant, he pressed the adhesive magnetic charge near the rudder and laid the small uplink cable along the keel until the bottom of the hull became the transom. Nothing about the mission was easy or inherently safe, but running the antenna cable just above the waterline so the satellites could see the receiver was, by far, the most dangerous part of the task. He doused his mask light and let himself rise slowly toward the surface. Silently, Hunter lifted his head and eyes out of the water only far enough to scan for prying eyes from the seawall. No one was there, so he continued running the cable and securing it in place.

After double- and triple-checking his work for secure adhesion to the hull, he descended back beneath the vessel, where he set three more small explosive charges and a pair of GPS trackers before motioning for Gator to come close. He took our newest brother by the hand and traced the wiring and devices. Under normal conditions, we would've set the circuit and run for the hills, but Hunter couldn't let a teaching moment of such real-world quality pass without taking advantage of it.

After two passes through the circuitry, Hunter and Gator descended away from the hull and back toward the darkened seabed where our limo waited.

Back inside the SDV, I checked my watch, and we settled in for the long ride home. With the sun due on the eastern horizon in less than an hour, we didn't have the luxury of running the *Lori Danielle* back into the twelve miles of Cuban territorial waters for our recovery. We had no choice but to ride our undersea missile back to the ship some thirteen miles offshore. At eight knots, the ride would last ninety agonizingly boring minutes.

Clear of the harbor, we floated the buoy again, and I called home. "CIC, Alpha One."

"Go for CIC," came Skipper's quick response.

"Mission complete, clear of the harbor, and coming home."

"Roger, Alpha One. We'll be waiting with coffee and towels. How did Gator do?"

I couldn't resist having a little fun. "We didn't bring him. It's just Hunter, Clark, and me."

Silence filled my mask for several seconds, and I poked the bear a little more. "Apparently, he didn't get up when you roused everyone. As far as I know, he's still asleep in his bunk."

That took it one step further than Skipper could swallow, and she said, "You were right. He was still in his bunk, so I shot him twice and ordered the crew to dump his body overboard."

"Outstanding," I said. "That's one less mouth to feed. We'll be home inside ninety minutes . . . all four of us. Alpha One, out."

Chapter 22
Outside the Wire

Clark surfaced the SDV precisely in the center of the moonpool, and in seconds, the deck crew attached the lines leading to the crane. The crew of the *Lori Danielle* could teach a master class on efficiency. Two minutes after the lines were made fast, we landed in the cradle designed to hold the mini-sub in even the roughest of sea conditions.

The four of us climbed down and shucked off our dive gear and wetsuits. The deck crew collected our wet gear and inspected everything for damage before taking it away for cleaning, drying, and staging for the next mission. Having a support crew of such competence gave my team and me the ability to operate and deal with the critical tactical elements of the mission without spending time washing and repairing gear. Every time we operated from the *Lori Danielle*, I fell more deeply in love with the process.

After showers and calories, we assembled in the CIC, where Skipper wasted no time. She stuck a shiny new pair of hearing aids in my hand. "There's something you have to see."

"This doesn't sound good."

She said, "You're the boss, so you can make the call. I'm just the girl who digs up things to make your day worse than it already is."

I took a seat. "It's been a good day so far. The mission went off without a hitch. In fact, it went so well, I've got that nagging feeling that we missed something. Did your satellite get anything interesting while it was in the neighborhood?"

She pointed to a monitor. "Have a look for yourself. It's only six minutes long, but that's better than five minutes."

The dark video played on the screen, and I found myself expecting sound, but of course, the satellite was just as deaf as me from twenty miles high.

Skipper shined her laser pointer at the screen. "That's the port of Havana, and that's the *Scimitar*."

"Can you zoom in?"

She made several keystrokes, and the image grew in size but not clarity. Although the yacht was tied alongside the seawall, no one seemed to be interested in refueling it. For the most part, it appeared the boat was being ignored.

"Does anything happen in these six minutes?" I asked.

Back to the keyboard Skipper went, and the clock in the lower corner of the video picked up speed. When the video returned to normal speed, she said, "Just this."

Two people stepped from the yacht and jogged along the seawall. The satellite must've been directly overhead because the angle gave me no indication of either person's height. I assumed both were adult males, but I had no way to be certain.

"Here it comes," Skipper said.

A van pulled up beside the two men, and they climbed inside. The van disappeared to the southeast, and Skipper said, "That's it."

"Any ideas?" I asked.

She sighed. "I've got some thoughts and questions, but nothing concrete."

"Let's hear it."

She leaned back in her chair. "The first thing that caught my attention was that nothing about the arrival of the *Scimitar* seemed to catch anyone by surprise. They were expecting her."

"I saw the same. What about the two guys and the van?"

She raised her eyebrows. "That one has me stumped. Obviously, someone was expecting them, and whoever that somebody is dispatched a van for them. To me, everything about it looks like a planned, coordinated stop."

"I agree. Are they still in port?"

She held up a finger. "Not only are they still in port, but I think they've shut down the engines."

"What makes you think that?"

"Try to stay with me," she said. "This is all an educated guess, but when you were carrying the GPS tracker, it was perfectly stable and providing a one-hundred-percent solid position return. When you or whoever placed it on the hull, that stability fluctuated. It wasn't by much, but the returns weren't as clear as they were before the device was planted on the yacht."

"I'm still tracking."

She continued. "Within seconds of the tracker being affixed to the yacht, the oscillations started. I believe that was a side effect of the vibrations of the engines. Were the engines running when you were underneath the vessel?"

I replayed the dive in my head. "Yes, at least one of the engines was running. I remember the vibration."

"That's what I thought. About thirty minutes after you placed the tracker, the oscillation stopped and the signal was dead on again. I think they shut down the engines."

I considered her theory. "Could the tracker have fallen off? Wouldn't that explain the absence of vibrations?"

"Sure it would, but it wouldn't explain how I can still see the tracker. If it fell off and sank to the bottom, I wouldn't receive any signal from it at all."

"Have you talked to Dr. Mankiller about it?"

"Not yet. She's still sleeping, but it's on my list."

I changed gears. "Okay, enough about the engines. What were you going to show me when I walked in?"

The monitor turned dark and was soon filled with a frozen image of a well-dressed man standing behind a podium.

I said, "That's Congressman Claven, chair of the House Select Committee on Intelligence, right?"

"Yep, and dear old daddy to Richard Andrew Claven III, our blue badger from the CIA." She started the video and sped through the opening remarks. "The first two minutes are meaningless. Here's the part I want you to see."

The video paused and then resumed as Congressman Richard Andrew Claven II poured out a crock of crap.

". . . . that's why, ladies and gentlemen, I am proud to sponsor the bill that will provide hundreds of millions of dollars in desperately needed funding to large cities across this great country of ours to create, train, and operate teams of patriotic Americans to detect, deter, and defeat significant terrorist threats aimed against our most important cities—cities like Miami, San Francisco, Chicago, and of course, New York City, my hometown."

The gathered crowd cheered, and the congressman took a drink of water while basking in the adoration of his constituents. When the applause wound down, he held up his hand and continued. "Don't get too excited yet, for there is a roadblock—a major roadblock standing against this bill and standing against the safety and security of the American people. My colleagues in the House of Representatives who sit across the aisle are vowing to block this legislation by every means available to them. Can you imagine such a potentially treasonous stance?"

He shook his head and paused. "Now, I know some of you shuddered when I used the word *treason*, but think about what that word means, and think about what those elected officials are saying when they pledge to stop this legislation that will, no doubt, save millions of American lives in some of our greatest cities across the country. They're ideologues who'd rather watch Americans suffer and die than work in a bipartisan way with me and my colleagues to protect you and millions of Americans just like you. Americans who trust the federal government—and rightly so—to protect them from all enemies, both foreign and domestic."

More water. More clapping.

"Furthermore, neighbors, hear me when I say this. I will never stop fighting for you and your security, no matter how tall my esteemed colleagues on the other side of the aisle build their beloved wall of opposition against this bill and against the idea of securing and protecting massive populations of Americans just like you."

Skipper struck a key and froze the video. "What do you think?"

I furrowed my brow. "I'm confused."

She laughed. "Me, too. Claven has never supported a spending bill for national security. In fact, he's rallied against every spending bill specifically for the purposes he now seems to champion. Something doesn't pass the smell test to me, but I don't know what it is yet."

"Has Mongo seen this yet?"

She said, "No, but I like where your head's at. I'll play it for him and get his reaction."

I turned to Clark, Hunter, and Gator. "Let's do the after-action review and get some sleep. From my point of view, everything went off without a hitch. No injuries, no loss or damage to equipment, and the mission was accomplished exactly as planned. Other than congratulating you on a job well done, I have nothing else to report. Do you guys have anything?"

Clark bit his lip and said, "I don't like it."

"What's not to like?" I asked.

He scratched his face through his beard. "I don't like the fact that the Cubans were obviously expecting the *Scimitar*. I don't like that they didn't immediately start bunkering fuel. I don't like that they've shut down the engines and not moved. It almost looks to me like they're retreating and regrouping."

"I agree," I said. "The only thing we can do now is watch and wait. Until they make a move, we can't jump in the game. It's not like we can blast into Havana with guns blazing and roll up half a dozen bad guys."

"Why can't we?" Clark asked.

"Are you serious?"

"Why not? We've done crazier stuff. We could put together enough satellite imagery to find them, roll in there high-speed and hard, grab them up, and run to Gitmo."

I said, "Our orders are to detain and question at sea, not drop them off at Guantanamo."

"Then we can do that," he said.

I crossed my ankles and stared at the ceiling for a long moment. "No, I don't like it. Too much can go wrong. If we get busted running an op on Cuban soil, we'll never see home again."

He said, "I get it, and I agree. It's risky, but it's an option."

"Not yet. For now, we'll sit tight, watch them leave the port, and keep following them. Once we know their target, we'll have a much better position, and the Board will have some solid intel to feed up the chain—wherever the chain goes above them."

Clark said, "You're the team lead, so it's your call. I'm just here to . . . I don't know. Maybe I'm just here to look good."

I leaned in to examine his face. "There's a lot more gray in that beard than there used to be. You may be reaching the end of your looking-good phase, and I can't imagine anybody calling you 'distinguished looking.' You'll just be old."

He grabbed his chest. "Words hurt, and that's mean-spirited. I'm finding some ice cream so I can eat away my pain."

"I'm finding a bed so I can sleep away mine. Oh, and just so you'll know, ice cream at six in the morning won't take away your pain. It'll just make you fat in addition to being old."

He stuck out his bottom lip. "See? Just hurtful."

"Get out of here," I said. "I need to talk with a guy at the other end of his career."

Clark made his exit, and Hunter stood to leave, but I said, "Hang on. I need to talk with both of you."

Skipper looked up. "If you need to have a private conversation, this is my office, and I'm not leaving."

I said, "I'll never have a conversation with anyone that you can't hear."

She turned back to her computer and continued doing whatever she does while I debriefed Gator.

"You did a good job tonight. Your buoyancy control wasn't stellar, but at least you didn't breach out of the water like a whale. We'll work on that when this is over."

Gator nodded, and I continued. "Did you understand what Hunter showed you about installing the explosives and tracker?"

"Yes, sir. That's pretty straightforward."

"Do you have any questions for us?"

He shot a look between Hunter and me. "Just one. What would've happened if we got caught out there tonight?"

I took a long breath. "The United States would've disavowed any knowledge of us or our operation. We would've been arrested, interrogated, possibly tried, and imprisoned. That's why your buoyancy control is so critical. If you shoot to the surface, where everybody can see you, you're busted."

He frowned. "*I'm* busted? Or *we're* busted?"

"Excellent question. You're learning. We're never going to surrender as a squad. If they bust you, we'll do everything in our power to get you back because you're one of us. It's likely no one else will come pluck us out of there, so we have to rely on our team to do what it takes to get you back. Does that answer your question?"

He nodded. "It does."

"Hunter, do you have anything?"

He said, "Like Chase said, you did a good job tonight, but don't start thinking every operation will be like that. Things usually go wrong. In fact, I can't remember the last time everything went as smoothly as tonight. What I'm saying is, don't get complacent. Keep your head in the game and stay vigilant. The next time we go outside the wire, it's likely somebody's going to start a fight."

Chapter 23
Muzzle Thump

When I landed on my bunk, my body realized how tired it was, and still dressed, I collapsed onto my pillow. Congressman Richard Claven's speech played on a continuous loop in my dreams, or perhaps my subconscious mind, until I awoke, unable to think about anything else.

Back in the CIC, I found Mongo, Clark, and Weps. "Have you guys seen the congressman's video yet?"

Mongo looked up. "Yeah, we saw it. That's what we were just talking about."

I slid onto a chair. "Is it just political lip service?"

Mongo spun a legal pad and slid it toward me. "Normally, I'd call it lip service, but we've been doing a little digging. It appears the good congressman's brother-in-law just opened a business called Analytical Systems, Incorporated, with offices in DC, Seattle, and New York."

I glanced at Mongo's legal pad. "Okay, so what does that have to do with this?"

Clark said, "Maybe nothing, but when you hear zebras running, don't expect to win the Triple Crown."

I squeezed my eyes closed and tried to turn that into something meaningful, but it wouldn't come. "Would somebody else please answer the question?"

Mongo chuckled. "What Clark's trying to say is that it's a mighty big coincidence that the congressman would sponsor a billion-dollar funding bill to hire security consultants for major cities at the same time his brother-in-law opened that exact type of business."

Suddenly, the hoofbeats did sound like zebras. "Oh. This thing is getting messy."

"Indeed, it is," Mongo said. "But we're still in limbo here. The *Scimitar* hasn't moved since it showed up last night."

The room was silent for what felt like an eternity before I said, "We're not seriously thinking that a sitting senior congressman, the chairman of the Select Committee on Intelligence, is coordinating a terrorist attack to bolster support for his family-owned business, are we?"

Weps was first to answer. "I'm not thinking anything. I'm here to keep you guys up to date on how hard we can punch."

My eyes fell on Clark, and he said, "We're just floating facts, College Boy. What do you think?"

I said, "Two things. First, I say we sit on the *Scimitar* for another twelve hours. If she still hasn't moved, we have to board her and take a look. I've got a nasty feeling about that boat."

"What's the second thing?" Clark asked.

I lowered my chin. "We need a face-to-face with Congressman Claven."

Clark perked up. "Oh, how I love a good face-to-face. Remember Moscow?"

I knocked on the table. "How could I forget? That was the night you got shot by a Russian general."

He scowled. "That's the night *you let* me get shot."

"Yeah, well, I had my hands full. And besides, you lived."

Mongo said, "Let's stroll down memory lane some other time, all right, guys? Let's talk about the boarding party."

I said, "Me, Hunter, Kodiak, and Gator."

"Gator?" Clark said. "Are you sure about that?"

"I'm sure. We can't protect him forever. He has to get his feet wet at some point, and he's a strong swimmer. If we have to bail out, I won't worry about him keeping up."

Clark said, "Okay. What about overwatch?"

"I'm working on that," I said. "Have you seen Celeste this morning?"

Mongo said, "She and Skipper are grabbing lunch. They should be back any minute."

I pulled my phone from my pocket and sent out a team-wide text calling everyone to the CIC.

Three minutes later, the room was full, and I started talking. "Listen up, everybody. We've got some new intel that isn't exactly actionable, but we're going to act on it anyway because that's what we do. For now, we're waiting and watching, and all of you know how terrible I am at that."

A few chuckles rose from the team, and I continued. "If the *Scimitar* doesn't leave the harbor before midnight, I'm leading a boarding party made up of Hunter, Kodiak, and Gator. We'll take the sub, just like last night, but this time we'll board and search the yacht."

Hunter asked, "How do we get the prisoners back to the ship when we find them?"

"I'm still working out the details, but it doesn't make sense for that boat to sit still for twenty-four hours. Something's going on, and I don't like it."

That seemed to satisfy Hunter, so I turned to Celeste. "Dr. Mankiller, I need overwatch while we're on board the *Scimitar*.

Do you have a waterproof drone we can carry in with us and launch from the surface?"

She cocked her head. "They're all waterproof when sealed inside a plastic bag. I'm sure the galley has a vacuum sealer."

I gave her a broad grin. "I expected a high-tech answer, but sometimes simplicity saves the day."

She said, "Overcomplication is never necessary, but so many people fall into the trap of believing complexity equals quality."

"Did Skipper talk with you about the engine vibrations affecting the GPS tracker on the yacht?"

Celeste said, "Yes, and I agree with her assessment. I can build in a dampener to the next one if you want. That'll eliminate the phenomenon."

"No, leave it the way it is. I think it's a handy coincidence."

"As you wish. You're the boss."

The afternoon was spent digging into Analytical Systems, Inc. and the congressman's brother-in-law. The paper trail wound its way through a complex web of LLCs and holding companies, and I found myself wishing for Dr. Mankiller's simplicity principle.

As I sat alone at the stern of our ship, staring into the endless blue of the Caribbean Sea, I slowed my breathing and closed my eyes. The enlightened would've called it meditation, but knuckle-draggers like me simply thought of it as calming the madness inside of our heads. Men like me tend to collect voices. Many of those voices seem to be the relentless cries of the men we've put in the ground, but some of the echoes are more distant and even more haunting. Those are the voices yet to come, and perhaps even of my own dying wails. Would those voices relent when I became the vanquished, or would I carry them with me throughout all eternity as penance for my brutality? In those moments, I envied those fortunate men who never have to press a trigger in anger or draw a razorlike blade through the flesh of an enemy. I wondered if the minds of such men are purer, quieter, and saner than my own.

Sometimes, in those moments of external quiet and internal chaos, I could make sense of the world in which I lived. Sometimes, I could see evil simply as evil without justification and without reason. That afternoon, such a moment of clarity came as if on the wings of an angel and consumed me as few comforts can. I would do what must be done, and I would lead my team into temporary hells, where our souls would once again be tempered in the fires of battle, and our will would be honed against the steel of our enemy's blade. Freedom demanded such sacrifice of men and women who walked beneath the banner of warriors—men and women like me and the team I called my family.

* * *

We like to believe our world is the center of the universe and that everything happens around us, but nothing could be further from the truth. The rock on which we live is little more than one of billions of rocks spinning around stars throughout all of creation, but watching our particular star disappear across the western horizon only served to reinforce that flawed view of the vast, endless sea of all that exists.

Our star disappeared, and darkness consumed my side of the planet. A dim glow rose from the south and hung over the floating communist island harboring our foe. I didn't want to pluck that foe from Castro's grasp, but if that was the opportunity I would be given, I wouldn't squander the opening. Part of me hoped the yacht would be vacant when we climbed aboard, but somewhere deep inside the recesses of my mind, I knew nothing good waited for us on that vessel.

* * *

Evening chow was pork chops, mashed potatoes, and peas. I pushed the peas around my plate with my fork, expecting to hear my mother scold me for not eating them first. The table was quiet as the team pondered and tried to predict what the night would hold. Regardless of what any of us expected, we were in for a night we'd never forget, on the edge of the Caribbean, in a pit of economic and political despair, aboard a yacht that belonged anywhere other than Havana Harbor.

I finally dropped my fork, determined to keep the peas out of my mouth. "Listen up, guys. I'm moving up H-hour. We're going to prep the SDV for a twenty-three-hundred departure. That'll put us on the *Scimitar* by midnight, if everything goes well. High tide is twenty-three thirty and starts receding an hour later. With any luck, we'll ride the tide in and back out. I'm taking Hunter, Kodiak, and Gator. We'll conduct the mission brief prior to departure. Any questions?"

Gator looked around the room, his nerves blatantly on his sleeve. "Uh . . . What are we going to do with anyone we find on the *Scimitar*?"

Singer grinned, and I said, "Good question. I'm still working on that one. Hopefully, we won't—"

Clark broke in. "*Hope* ain't a plan, man."

I gave him a nod in silent acknowledgment. "Let me rephrase. I don't want to have to put anybody down on that boat. I would prefer to get in, collect intel, and get out without anyone knowing we're there. The rules of engagement on this one are simple. Shoot only to save your life or the life of one of your teammates."

"What if they run?" Gator asked.

I let out a long sigh. "Okay, it looks like we're doing the mission briefing now."

Gator said, "Sorry, I didn't mean to—"

I waved him off. "No, it's not you. We need a solid plan and a definitive contingency plan. We're the only ones in the mess deck other than the cooks, and they're too busy back there to listen, so let's work through this together."

Clark checked over his shoulder. "We're alone for now, but the crew will be filtering in for chow. Why don't we take this to the CIC?"

We reassembled in the combat information center, and Skipper checked the status of the *Scimitar*. "She still hasn't moved."

I mumbled, "What's going on with that boat?"

Clark slid beside me. "I've got a hunch."

"Let's hear it," I said. "I can't come up with anything."

He said, "My money is on an empty boat."

"What?"

He nodded. "Yep. I think they're bugging out, and the easiest way to get back to the Land of Sand is a flight out of Cuba."

"You think they're giving up?"

"No, not giving up. Just delaying. They got busted on this attempt, so they probably think we know the plan. I think they're running home to Daddy to rethink the plan and try again later."

"If you're right, we've wasted a lot of time, money, and assets chasing them around the Caribbean."

He said, "Was it really wasted if we sent them packing?"

"I would've rather rolled them up and invited them over for a nice little chat."

He grinned. "We all would've preferred that, but we have to consider it a win if we stopped an attack."

"We may have delayed it, but we didn't stop it."

Everyone settled into the seats of their choice, and I kicked off the briefing. "As I mentioned earlier, we'll depart at twenty-three hundred, in drysuits this time. The plan will be to board the *Scim-*

itar from the port stern quarter, away from the seawall. From that point, we'll launch the drone for overwatch and split into two teams. Gator, you're with me on the port side, and Kodiak and Hunter will clear from starboard."

I glanced at each of them, and three nods returned.

I continued. "We're working a theory that the yacht may be abandoned, but I don't want us to walk in there expecting to see nothing. We have to expect resistance. In their minds, these guys are fighting a holy war, so they won't cling to life or behave rationally when confronted. The true believers will welcome a bullet in the brain, but with any luck, we'll have at least one with some doubts about his seventy-two virgins. That's the guy we want. If we can get him back to the ship, he's the one who'll eventually tell us everything he knows."

Hunter raised a finger. "So, we're going in with the intention of taking prisoners, right?"

"That's right."

He pursed his lips. "How do you intend to get them back to the ship?"

"I'm glad you asked," I said. "That's my favorite part. Just like the first insertion, we'll run in with the *Lori Danielle* as close as possible and deploy the SDV and the RHIB. I want Singer and Disco on the RHIB and to lay off half a mile from the mouth of the harbor. If or when we encounter humans, we'll make the call to run in. We'll roll them up, package them for shipping, and drop them over the port side, where the RHIB will be waiting."

Something seemed to strike Hunter, and he said, "Wait a minute. We got the RHIB shot up pretty good. Is it operational yet?"

"It is," I said. "The engineers replaced both engines and the damaged tube. They patched the bullet holes in the fiberglass, and she's ready for action."

Kodiak said, "I want to make sure I fully understand the ROE. We're in and out with intel, only if possible, right?" I nodded, and he said, "Secondarily, we're taking prisoners, if possible."

"Yes."

He continued. "And if they put up a fight, we can shoot back, right?"

I said, "I'd prefer muzzle thumps, but if you have to pull a trigger, make it count."

Gator screwed up his face. "Muzzle thump?"

Clark spun around. "They didn't teach you the muzzle-thump maneuver at The Ranch?"

He shook his head. "I've never heard of it."

Clark scanned the room. "I need a rifle."

Skipper unlocked a compartment and handed an M4 across the table.

Clark cleared the weapon and showed Gator that it was clear and safe. "Now, imagine you're sound asleep and dreaming about whatever Islamic terrorists dream about, and you wake to see me standing over you like this." Clark stepped in front of Gator and shouldered the rifle.

When the new guy looked up, he instinctually grabbed the barrel of Clark's M4.

Clark said, "Perfect. That's exactly what scared, startled bad guys do. From here, the easy way out is to pull the trigger, but even with a suppressor, that makes some noise and leaves a dead body that could've been full of valuable intel. The better option is the beloved muzzle thump."

He leaned forward and drove the muzzle of the rifle into the center of Gator's chest, sending him backward, gasping for breath, and grabbing his chest.

When the kid stopped making dinosaur noises, Clark said, "That's a muzzle thump at twenty-five percent. When you do it, make it one hundred percent. It's impossible to ignore, and it leaves a lasting impression of love."

Gator rubbed the center of his chest aggressively. "If that was twenty-five percent, full speed would kill a guy."

Clark handed the rifle back to Skipper. "Okay, maybe it was twenty-six percent."

I said, "I guess that does it for muzzle-thump training. Let's get back to business. If it all goes wrong and bullets start flying, I want the RHIB coming hard and fast. If we get shot up, that will be our primary exfiltration method."

Hunter looked up. "Are we abandoning the SDV if everybody gets hit?"

I thought about the possibility. "Everyone except Gator can fly the sub, so even if it's a single-man operation, I want the SDV back aboard the ship. It's too valuable to leave on the bottom of Havana Harbor."

Singer said, "Maybe we should include Clark on the RHIB crew in case we need him to recover the SDV."

I gave Clark an eye, and he nodded.

"Good plan. Clark is on the RHIB crew."

I turned to Skipper. "Get Ronda and Gun Bunny down here, please."

They showed up in minutes, and I recapped the mission. "Here's what I need from you two. I want you and the chopper ready to fly with the Minigun locked and loaded. If this thing goes south, we may need you to cover our retreat."

Ronda stood wide-eyed. "You know I love to shoot, but is this authorized by anyone with any authority?"

I gave her a wink. "Me."

She smiled. "That's good enough for me. Gun Bunny and I pulled you off a beach on the south side of that island one morning with bullets filling the air. Why should the north side be any different?"

"Yes, you did," I said. "And we appreciate the work. I don't think this'll turn into that, but just in case, I want to be ready."

Weps said, "Don't forget about the mother ship. If things get seriously bad, we can sink the whole island if necessary."

"If it gets to that point," I said, "too much has gone wrong."

"I just want you to understand the toolbox you have at your disposal."

"Thank you, Weps. With any luck, the op will go off without having to unleash the arsenal."

Chapter 24
¿Plata o Plomo?

With the briefing complete and everyone in go mode, I grabbed Gator. "Come with me. It's time for a little upgrade for the newest arrow in our quiver."

He cocked his head. "What does that mean?"

"That means you're the arrow, and you're about to become part cyborg."

He followed me to Dr. Shadrack's sick bay, where Celeste waited with gloved hands and a tray of tools in front of her. Gator looked like a scared child at his first vaccination appointment.

"Have a seat," Celeste said. "This won't hurt a bit."

"What are you going to do to me?"

She gave me a covert wink. "I'm going to remove your gallbladder and appendix. You don't really need either of them, so we remove them from all of our operators to eliminate one more internal organ that might catch a bullet."

"What? Wait. I'm not sure that's such a good—"

Celeste put a hand on his chest and encouraged him to take his place on the surgical table. "It's no big deal. Everyone else on the team survived it, and we've got the added benefit of having a real surgeon on board in case I screw it up."

Gator made his stand. "I'll take my chances with the bullet. I don't want to do this, especially with the mission tonight. It just doesn't seem like a good time."

Celeste threw up her hands. "Oh, okay. Have it your way. I'll just insert your bone conduction communication device on your jawbone tonight, and we'll deal with the guts later."

I couldn't hold back the laughter any longer, and Gator's face morphed from temporary terror to embarrassed anger.

He reached for a scalpel from Celeste's tray. "You'd win, but I'd get a few slices in before you beat me down."

I raised both hands in surrender. "Nobody wins in a knife fight, so I'll surrender now."

He dropped the scalpel. "Excellent decision."

"You can relax," I said. "This is extremely minor and only takes a couple of minutes. You'll be amazed how this thing works."

Less than five minutes later, Gator's implant was affixed to his jawbone, and his tiny incision was glued closed.

A few minutes later, Celeste had his cell phone and sat-com programmed to communicate with his bug.

After a radio check, Gator said, "This is the most amazing thing I've ever seen. I had no idea anything like this existed."

I said, "And you get to keep your appendix."

"You guys really had me going."

"Oh, we know. Dr. Mankiller is a PhD, not an MD, but I still think she could take out your gallbladder without killing you."

His eyes widened. "Are you serious? I assumed she was a real doctor."

"Don't ever let her hear you say that. She *is* a real doctor, just not a medical doctor."

He glanced over his shoulder to make sure she wasn't within earshot and pointed toward the tiny wound on his jaw. "Does this mean you're keeping me?"

"We're keeping you until you give us a reason not to."

He put on a somber expression. "I'm not very good at saying things like this, but I want you to know I really appreciate you and Clark picking me up for the team. I wouldn't have done well on my own. I've got a few demons I'm still fighting, and being part of this is making it a lot easier for me."

"We're all glad you're here. And everyone has their battles to fight. If you ever want to talk about it, I'm always available, and Singer is a great listener."

He dug at the deck with the toe of his boot. "Yeah, I've talked a little with Singer. He's got it together. Thanks for everything."

I turned for the door. "Come on. We've got a lot of work to do before the mission tonight. After whatever happens at midnight, you may want to turn in your new body part and go back to playing football."

He said, "I doubt it."

* * *

The world kept turning, and eleven o'clock approached to find Hunter, Kodiak, Gator, and me in drysuits and rebreathers in the moonpool with our SEAL Delivery Vehicle poised and ready. On the stern of the ship, Disco, Clark, and Singer stood ready beside the RHIB. Barbie and Ronda No-H were conducting the preflight inspection of the MH-6 Little Bird and her accompanying General Electric M134 Minigun. All of the pieces were falling together, and I prayed we wouldn't need those extra pieces.

In the moonpool, we each carried a Glock, an M4 rifle, and plenty of ammo for both. Each of us wore a body camera designed and built by Dr. Mankiller to capture everything we saw, said, and did. A pair of drones were vacuum-sealed inside plastic bags and ready to be released into the wild to provide video to the CIC and boat crew when we surfaced in Havana. The occupants of the RHIB were similarly armed, and everything was coming together for the launch.

With our comms connected to our bone conduction devices, we climbed aboard the SDV and conducted communications checks with the CIC, Bridge, the RHIB, and Gun Bunny in the Little Bird.

I said, "CIC, Alpha One."

Our analyst said, "Go for CIC."

"Skipper, it's your operation. Call the go times."

"Roger. Oh, and Chase, don't forget to take out your hearing aids before you go swimming this time."

"I'm never going to live that down, am I?"

The next words out of her mouth were the command for the *Lori Danielle* to activate radar-absorbing capability and run for the entrance to Havana Harbor.

The SDV swung like a pendulum beneath the crane as the ship accelerated, and we waited for the one-mile mark. The two-minute warning came over the radio, and we donned our facemasks. The ship slowed, and the water beneath us in the moonpool splashed onto the deck, but due to the flawless design of the ship, it drained away just as quickly as it arrived.

One limit of the SDV deployment was that the ship had to be fully stopped before the crane operator could lower us into the water. The moonpool opening was only slightly larger than the body of the SDV, so we had to descend without any forward motion to avoid striking the hull with the skin of the SDV.

We came to rest, and I gave the signal to lower away. The darkness beneath the waves accepted us again, and we were clear of the ship. Skipper gave the command to launch the RHIB, and although we couldn't see or hear the boat hit the water, just knowing she was there was a confidence we didn't have on our first run into the harbor.

Minutes passed like molasses, but we finally hit the mouth of the harbor, and I brought the SDV to periscope depth. Nothing had changed in the past twenty-four hours inside the port, and only one boat appeared to be moving. I maneuvered the sub beside the *Scimitar* and brought it to a hover. Hunter untied the boarding ladder from the SDV and extended it over the portside rail of the yacht. He emptied the salt water from his rifle, press-checked for a round in the chamber, and started up the ladder.

I watched him go and positioned Gator at the foot of the ladder. Just as Hunter had done, Gator cleared the water from his rifle and gave me a nod. The instant Hunter stepped over the rail and swept the deck for targets, I tapped the new guy on the leg, and he climbed the ladder in silence. Kodiak didn't need any direction. He was up the ladder and on the deck in no time. I tossed a line from the SDV to Hunter, and he secured it around a deck-mounted cleat.

I reached up for the ladder at the same instant I programmed the sub to sink, and the vessel submerged itself to the bottom of Havana Harbor for the second time in as many nights. I climbed the ladder, crossed the rail, and released the drone.

When the tiny flying machine was out of sight, I cut open the second bag and launched the number-two drone. "CIC, Alpha One. Drones released, and we're aboard the target vessel."

Skipper said, "Roger, Alpha One. RHIB is in position. I have good comms with both drones. And the Little Bird is at flight idle."

"Roger, CIC. Alpha team is commencing clearing the vessel."

We shucked off our rebreathers and staged them on the deck. I laid a hand against Gator's side and positioned him behind me to my right and whispered, "Don't shoot me."

Hunter and Kodiak rounded the stern and took a position on the starboard rail. Hunter reported. "Seawall is clear. There's nobody anywhere."

I said, "Roger. Activate body cam and move ahead."

We moved in unison, and I stepped through the first opening and into a companionway with dim lights glowing just above the deck. At every opening, I moved with practiced precision to cut the pie and take in the next space in small slices as I searched for targets. Everything about the yacht felt empty, and everything I saw reinforced that belief.

Gator and I cleared three spaces on the main deck and ended up in a common area near the bow with Hunter and Kodiak. I expected them to come through the opening on the starboard side, but Gator apparently did not. When he picked up their motion on the opposite side of the space, he raised his rifle and seated the butt against his shoulder. It happened too quickly for me to stop him, so I sent up a wordless instant prayer that he wouldn't press the trigger. Thankfully, he did not.

Hunter motioned toward a pair of companionways at the rear of the space, and we moved toward them. A stairwell is the ultimate fatal funnel when conducting room-clearing operations, and the companionway was no exception. It was only wide enough for one of us, leaving no space for Gator to shoot around me if we befell fire while descending. I moved as quickly as possible while remaining silent, and my partner moved in locked step with me all the way to the lower deck.

We continued moving just as we'd practiced time after time in the shoot house back at Bonaventure, and Gator never faltered. When we'd cleared every space on that deck, I motioned for Gator to move to the lead position. I had every reason to believe the boat was completely abandoned, so I thought it would be the perfect opportunity to get the new guy some actual experience with being the first man through the door. Being a few inches taller than him, I could see and maneuver around him without difficulty, so I was confident we could handle any encounter we faced.

On the third deck, a soft hum filled the air, and I assumed it was a small generator powering the dim lights throughout the yacht. Gator moved slower than I would have, but his caution spoke volumes about his thinking process. I remembered the mantra Clark had beaten into my head about room-clearing. *Never put your body anyplace your brain hasn't already been.*

If Gator was thinking through the coming space before stepping through doorways, that was precisely what he should've been doing. We cleared two spaces and came to a narrow doorway marked "Sala de Máquinas." A narrow corridor led in each direction, left and right, and we cleared both directions before Gator pressed his hand against the engine room door. He gave a tiny twist of his head, and I tapped his shoulder, indicating that I was ready to press through the door. He took a half step backward and cupped the doorknob in his palm. I held my rifle at the high-ready position, just above his left shoulder. The instant before he twisted the knob, everything in our world changed in the blink of an eye.

"*Alto!*"

Gator and I spun to our right and leveled our rifles directly into the face of a uniformed Cuban soldier with an AK-47 bearing down on us. He spoke in rapid-fire Spanish, and I studied every inch of him in an instant. It took only a glance for me to feel a sense of ease when I saw the safety lever on his AK in the position that rendered the rifle harmless.

Gator hadn't fired yet, but every muscle in his body was flexed, and he powered forward with his M4 leading the way. He slapped the soldier's AK away with the forearm of his rifle and drove the muzzle directly into the center of the man's chest. The thump wasn't forceful enough to send the man to the ground, but he backpedaled, unbalanced, until his body was pressed against the portside gunwale.

Gator leaned into the man, pressing the muzzle harder into his sternum, and growled, "*¿Plata o plomo, amigo?*"

The wide-eyed soldier dropped his rifle. "*Plata, señor. Plata, por favor.*"

Gator gave the command "Down" in Spanish, and the soldier obeyed. We soon had him flex-cuffed and his ankles tied.

I spoke quietly. "Contact. One Cuban soldier disarmed and secured on deck two near the engine room."

Hunter said, "Secured, as in dead or captured?"

"No shots fired," I said.

Hunter answered, "Roger. Bridge and upper deck are clear. We're moving to you."

Kodiak took over guarding the Cuban while Gator and I cleared the engine room. Confident we'd found the only soul aboard the boat, we returned to the corridor.

I took a knee in front of our prisoner, drew my pistol, and pressed the muzzle against his forehead. In soft Spanish, I asked, "Whose boat is this?"

The man swallowed hard. "*El barco del General Castro ahora.*"

Three of us laughed, and Hunter said, "What's so funny?"

Gator said, "He says it's General Castro's boat now."

I asked, "Who brought it here?"

The soldier had no idea. He was nothing more than a junior enlisted soldier who'd been tasked with guarding the yacht and failed.

I continued questioning in Spanish. "Where are the men who arrived on this boat?"

His eyes crossed as he stared at my pistol still pressed into his forehead. "They are gone."

"Gone where?"

Sweat poured from the man's face. "I don't know. I don't know. Just gone."

"When did they leave?" I demanded.

"Many hours ago."

"How did they leave?"

"On the other boat."

I pressed harder. "What other boat?"

"*El barco negro.*"

"What black boat?" I growled.

The soldier, who couldn't have been older than seventeen, squeezed his eyes closed and trembled.

I withdrew my pistol a few inches from his head. "Relax, and tell me what you know. You'll be fine if you tell me. I need to know about the black boat."

He said, "Fast boat, smaller than this one. Very fast. They left while it was still dark. Maybe eighteen or maybe twenty hours ago."

"How many men were on the boat?"

"*Seis o siete.*"

I looked over my shoulder and met Hunter's gaze. "Get Skipper working on finding that black boat."

I rolled the soldier onto his side and slipped his wallet from his pocket. I made a show of going through every item inside the worn leather wallet, then held up his national identification card, memorized his address, and smiled. I pulled five hundred dollars from my pocket and slowly slid the American bills into his wallet. "Five hundred American dollars, and you never saw us, right?"

He nodded in exaggerated motions and grinned.

Gator lifted the AK-47, emptied the thirty-round magazine of the five rounds it contained, and tossed them overboard. I cut the flex-cuffs almost all the way through, making them easy to break, and stood.

A minute later, we were descending through the murky water with our rebreathers providing all the air we needed and our slow ride home waiting just a few feet beneath us.

When we reached the SDV, I put Gator in the driver's seat and took my position beside him. Baptism by fire isn't always the best teaching method, but he had to learn sometime. I talked him through the controls, and he soon had the hang of the vessel.

When he appeared to be comfortable behind the controls, I said, "Nice Pablo Escobar back there. Where did that come from?"

He shrugged. "I heard that *plata o plomo*, silver or lead, was one of Escobar's favorite things to say when he had a gun in somebody's face. Clark told me the only thing more important than accomplishing the mission was accomplishing the mission while looking and sounding cool, so I thought I'd give it a try."

I shook my head. "Maybe you shouldn't listen to Clark so much."

Chapter 25
Tag, You're It

As we plowed through the water at eight knots, everything inside me wanted to be back aboard the *Lori Danielle* and chasing the mysterious black boat with a twenty-hour head start to somewhere.

As my patience grew thinner and finally nonexistent, I called the mother ship. "Bridge, Alpha One."

Captain Sprayberry said, "Go for Bridge."

"Come get us."

A momentary pause came, and Barry's tone changed. "Alpha One, do you require emergency assistance?"

I rolled his question around in my head, trying to make sense of it, and then it finally hit me. I said, "Affirmative, Bridge. Alpha Element request emergency assistance. We are in peril and unable to exceed eight knots."

"Roger, Alpha One. Research Vessel *Lori Danielle* is responding to your call for aid and en route to your location."

"What was that all about?" Gator asked.

I said, "We record every word that's spoken through our comms aboard the ship. If Captain Sprayberry gets busted in Cuban territorial waters, he's subject to arrest, and his vessel is subject to seizure by the Cuban government, unless . . ."

Although I couldn't see it, I could hear Gator's grin through the comms. "Unless he's responding to a vessel in peril, which he's required to do under international maritime law."

"You've been studying," I said.

"Just because I've been landlocked all my life doesn't mean I've never read a Cap Daniels book."

The ship arrived and hovered in position with her bow in the wind as Gator tried to replicate the masterful job Clark had done in surfacing the sub precisely in the center of the moonpool. Although he didn't succeed, nothing was broken, and that was a victory. The deck crew plucked us from the water and secured the moonpool doors in short order.

We climbed from the sub, dropped our gear to the deck, and I grabbed Gator. "Go with the deck crew, and learn how to clean and service the rebreathers. Then get with Singer to learn how to save your rifle and sidearm before all that salt water turns them to stone."

"Yes, sir."

My first stop was the CIC. "Have you found it yet?"

Skipper didn't turn around. She said, "Maybe, but I can't believe we let that thing slip out of the harbor."

"It was a rotten mistake that's one hundred percent my fault," I said. "I never dreamed they'd change boats."

"We're in this together," she said, "and I should've been monitoring traffic in and out of the harbor more closely."

"None of that matters now. The damage is done, and all we can do is find that boat. You said you may have found it, so let's hear what you've got."

She cleared her throat. "First, you should know that finding a small, fast black boat on a trillion square miles of open ocean is practically impossible."

I rolled my chair close to hers so I could see her screen. "Yeah, I know, but you do the difficult immediately, and the impossible takes just a little longer."

"Yeah, that," she said. "I found six possible targets, and I think two of them may be duplicates. I'm waiting for daylight to confirm. Satellite coverage is pretty good through the Straits of Florida, but it gets a little shaky up the eastern seaboard in places. We really need to make some guesses where they're headed and how fast they're going."

I shuddered. "That's a lot. Let's break it down. With the wind out of the northeast and the Gulf Stream running from the southwest, that makes for a bumpy ride. That's good news for us. It means the go-fast boat can't go so fast without beating its passengers to death. If they're making more than fifty knots, it would be exhausting and torturous."

"That helps, and it eliminates two of the possibilities," she said. "Now, how about some target guesses?"

I planted my elbows on my knees and my temples in my palms. "I'm thinking." I ran everything I knew, believed, or considered through my noggin. "Miami, the nuclear submarine base in St. Marys, DC, Navy facilities in Jacksonville or Norfolk, New York City, and the sub base at Groton, Connecticut. Is that enough?"

Skipper slumped in her chair. "One would be enough if it were the right one."

I said, "Set up a video call with the Board for eight a.m. Eastern time."

"Consider it done."

"Now, back to the tracks," I said. "You told me you have six possible targets, and the speed eliminated two. That leaves four, right?"

"Yeah, and of those four, I think two might be duplicates, or they're running side by side."

"Either way, we can treat those two as one possible target. Will our course change significantly between those three?"

She studied the chart and the satellite overlay. "No, just a few degrees."

"That solves it, then. We run as hard and as fast as we can toward all three targets until we pick one."

She said, "We can't close the distance on these guys as quickly as we did with the *Scimitar*, but we've got a few knots on even the fastest of the three."

"When did you sleep last?"

She checked her watch. "I don't remember."

I said, "Get Tony down here, and you get some rest, even if it's just a couple of hours. I'll need you at your best when this thing comes to a head."

"Chase, I can't sleep right now. There's too much to do."

"I'm not asking," I said. "I'm making a command decision. I'll have someone from sick bay bring you something to help you fall asleep."

She huffed. "I've got Ginger working this issue from Silver Spring, and she's liable to call at any time."

"Does Tony know how to answer the phone?"

She let out an exasperated sigh. "You're impossible sometimes. Do you know that?"

"I know, but I also know this thing is going to turn into an international incident in a few hours, and every one of us has to be at our best. Sleep."

She gave me a mock salute. "Aye, aye, Captain." Skipper thumbed her phone and stuck it to her ear. "Tag, you're it. Chase ordered me to get some sleep and put you on watch in the CIC." She listened for a moment and hung up. "He'll be here in five minutes."

Before she could put away her phone, it chirped. "What have you got?" She listened and then said, "Hang on. I'm putting you on speaker." She pressed the button and laid the phone on the console.

"Who's there?" Ginger asked.

"It's just me and Chase. Go ahead with your intel."

The brilliant analyst who taught Skipper the trade said, "Hey, Chase. You're going to love this."

"Let's hear it."

"In addition to tracking every fast mover northeast of Cuba, I've been tapping a few phone lines—legally, of course—and I came across an interesting conversation between Jack Flannery and his personal assistant."

I said, "Wait a minute. Who's Jack Flannery?"

"Congressman Claven's brother-in-law," Ginger said. "I thought Skipper explained the connection."

"She did," I said. "I've got a billion things going on in my head, so give me a little latitude."

"Anyway," she continued, "I just happened to be included on a call between Flannery and his personal assistant. I'm sure it was just some electronic glitch that patched me into their call. I'm sure you understand."

Skipper said, "Oh, yeah. It happens all the time. Go on."

Ginger cleared her throat. "It turns out that the congressman and Flannery are having a meeting at four this afternoon."

"Where, and with whom?" I asked.

"Apparently, it's just the two of them, and they're meeting at Flannery's house on Hilton Head."

I couldn't stop the grin. "You just made my day, Ginger. The only thing that could make this news better is if you had a nice little bow to put on top of it."

"Oh, I've got one of those, too," she said.

"I can't wait to hear it."

"About twenty minutes ago, the Coast Guard and DEA intercepted one of the targets we've been tracking. Four arrests were made, and the vessel was seized for drug trafficking. All four of the arrestees were Nicaraguan, not Middle Eastern. That whittles down our possibles to three or maybe two. We're tightening the noose."

I glanced at Skipper, and she said, "What? I would've found out about the arrest, too. I've been busy."

"I wasn't blaming you for anything. I was waiting for you to celebrate. We're making progress."

Tony came through the door, and Skipper pressed a finger to her lips. He took a seat but didn't say a word.

Skipper worked frantically on her keyboard as Ginger continued the briefing.

When she'd given me everything she had, I said, "Thank you, Ginger. Let us know if anything changes. In the meantime, shoot me Flannery's address. I feel the need to crash a party."

Skipper snatched the phone. "Thanks, Ginger. Talk soon."

She briefed Tony on what to expect in the next couple of hours and looked up at me. "I've arranged a Citation jet out of the Ocean Reef Club for Hilton Head. They'll be on the ground and waiting in an hour."

"You're the greatest," I said. "I'll see if I can catch a ride ashore."

She stood. "You do that. I'll see you when you get back."

She pecked Tony on the cheek. "Try to stay awake. There's some important stuff going down."

He watched her go. "Love you, too."

She waved over her shoulder. "Yeah, yeah. You, too."

I called Clark. "Hey, where are you?"

"In my rack, why?"

"Crawl back out, and put your boots on. We're going on a field trip."

"A field trip to where?"

"Hilton Head," I said. "It looks like Congressman Claven and his brother-in-law, Jack Flannery, are having a powwow this afternoon, and we're invited."

"You don't say."

I shrugged. "Well, maybe we're not *officially* invited, but I feel like they'd want us there, don't you?"

"Oh, absolutely," he said. "But how are we getting there?"

"Get a shower, and meet me in the hangar bay in half an hour."

"See ya there."

Tony slipped onto Skipper's chair and read through the log of the previous twelve hours. "Things are getting hot."

"It's about time," I said. "I'm tired of chasing. I'm ready to catch."

He asked, "So, what's going on with this thing in Hilton Head?"

"It's apparently an off-the-books meeting between Claven and Flannery. It sounds like the perfect time to put the screws to them and see what comes squirting out."

"You're taking Clark, right?"

"Of course. He tightens the screws better than anybody I know."

"How about Gator?" Tony asked.

"I hadn't thought about that. What do you think?"

"He's got to learn sometime."

"I'm not sure he's ready for a gig like that. I think it'll just be Clark and me on this one."

"You're the boss."

"It's not all it's cracked up to be, but regardless of that, I want you to keep chasing the possible targets as fast as the captain is willing to push the ship in this rough water. We'll plan to hook up with you when you're off the coast of South Carolina."

Tony nodded. "What if they hit a target somewhere in Florida before we catch them?"

"That's the gamble we have to take. We'll play the hand we're dealt, but if they make a hit before Clark and I are back aboard, Mongo is in command."

"Where do you really think they're headed?"

I took a seat. "Don't let me screw up your objective look on this thing, but my money is on New York City."

Chapter 26
Naming Demons

Gun Bunny had the MH-6 Little Bird out of the hangar, un-chained, and situated on the helipad when Clark and I climbed the ladder.

I said, "Good morning. Thanks for the quick start."

She wiped her hands after finishing the preflight inspection. "You don't have to thank me for doing my job. I get a paycheck every week, and that's just a bonus. My real pay is getting to fly this thing as much as I want."

"She's a fun little thing, isn't she?"

She ran a hand across the fuselage. "I've never flown anything I enjoy more. I hear we're headed for Key Largo."

"That's right. We're meeting a Citation at the Ocean Reef Club."

"I'll have you there in no time. Are you ready now?"

We all climbed aboard and took off aggressively against the speed of the ship, and the chopper shuddered as we transitioned from the lee of the ship's superstructure and into the wind. Barbie made the takeoff look like child's play, and we were soon making a hundred knots toward Key Largo. She even let me do some of the flying to knock the rust off of my helicopter skills. I'd flown so few hours in a chopper in the previous months, it was almost like learning to walk again. She complimented my work, even though it was sloppy, and my ego appreciated the gesture.

I flew the approach and landing at the Ocean Reef Club, and most of the big pieces stayed on the helicopter during my rather aggressive contact with the ground.

Hank, the airport manager, watched us shut down and climb from the Little Bird. In keeping with his lifelong love of the ladies, he approached Barbie first. "Hello, ma'am. Have these two scoundrels hijacked you and forced you to bring them here?"

She grinned and stuck out her hand. "I agree with your assessment of these two, but they're paying customers this morning. I'm Barbie, but you can call me Gun Bunny. Everybody does."

"And I'm Hank, the chief cook and bottle washer on this ship."

"It's nice to meet you, Hank. You don't happen to have a truck full of jet fuel, do you?"

"Of course I do. I'll top you off as soon as I harass your passengers a little."

I gave the old man a hug, and he dusted himself off. "Easy there, young fellow. Don't get any of that spy dust on me."

"How are you doing, my friend?"

"Oh, I'm getting better every day. It's good to see you, Chase. How come every time you show up, you've got a better-looking woman with you?"

"It's how I roll, but I figured this one would be safe from your advances since she's not Eastern European."

He sighed. "They sure can make 'em over there, can't they?"

"I'm going to go without comment on the grounds I might incriminate myself."

He laughed and turned to Clark. "I thought you were too smart to run around with a spook. You need better friends."

Clark shook his hand. "If I run around with people like Chase, it makes me look like a good guy. Have you seen a Citation this morning? We're supposed to meet our ride."

He pointed to the northern sky. "She's inbound. I heard her on the radio a few minutes ago. Go on inside and have a cup of coffee, and get rid of your last cup. I'll squirt a little fuel in your chopper, then I'll come in and join you."

We did exactly as he suggested, and the Citation landed minutes later. Two ununiformed pilots trotted down the stairs and into the terminal.

One of them spotted me. "Are you Mr. Fulton?"

I stuck out a hand. "Call me Chase. You must be my ride to South Carolina."

"Indeed, I am. We'll be ready to go in two minutes."

"We'll meet you on the plane," I said, and turned to Barbie. "Thank you again for bringing us ashore. I hope your flight back to the ship is nice and boring. We'll see you a few hundred miles up the coast."

We settled into a pair of seats in the Citation, and Clark said, "I remember these seats."

I slid my hands across the leather. "They do feel a lot like our old Citation. You know, we would've never met Disco if we hadn't bought that plane."

"It's funny how those things work out sometimes. He's turned into a pretty good operator, especially being an old guy like me."

"When we brought him on, I thought he'd just be a pilot for us. I never imagined he'd turn into a knuckle-dragger, but I'd be proud to dig in with him beside me in a gunfight anywhere in the world."

"We've got a pretty good team," he said. "What do you think about Gator so far?"

I grabbed a bottle of water from the cooler and tossed one to Clark. "I think he's going to be all right and that we made a good choice."

He caught the bottle and spun the lid. "I agree. He's not showing any signs that give me any reason to doubt him."

I swallowed half the bottle. "He's mentioned fighting demons a couple of times. I want to sit down with him and poke around in his head when this is over."

Clark said, "We all fight those battles."

"I think his are a little different, though."

Clark chewed on his toothpick. "All demons fight the same. They just use different names."

The two pilots bounded up the stairs and sealed the door. "Sorry for the delay. We'll have you on the ground in Hilton Head in less than an hour."

I thumbed the button and reclined, hoping to catch a few minutes of sleep on the way, but Clark had other ideas.

He jabbed me in my side. "What are you doing? You know your tray table and seat back must be in their full upright and locked position for takeoff."

"I'll take my chances."

He said, "We need to talk about the plan."

I pressed the button and sat up. "Fine. How do you think we should play it?"

"You know what I think. I say we string him up by his heels until he tells us everything we want to know."

"That may not be the best plan for this one," I said. "I brought a goodie bag full of toys from Dr. Mankiller."

"Did she send any rope?"

"I doubt it," I said. "This isn't the time for a freight train on Main Street. I think the best option is for them to never know we were there."

"How do you plan to pull that off? You know the place will be crawling with security."

"I'm not so sure. Something tells me this meeting is so far off the record that even Claven won't have his entourage with him."

Clark cocked his head. "Do you really think an ego like that would travel without the goons?"

"We'll see. With any luck . . ."

He rolled his eyes. "There you go with that luck garbage again. You've got to get that trash out of your head, College Boy. We're way beyond luck."

"All right, then. Luck or not, here's the plan. We'll recon, assess, and adapt based on security, location, and access. Plan A will be to listen without detection. If we can glean the intel we need, we'll slip away and go to work. If we can't, we'll move to Plan C."

"Wait a minute," he said. "Two things. First, stop using words like *glean*. Nobody knows what that means. And B, what happened to plan B?"

"There is no plan B. It's just Plan A and Plan C for Clark."

He grinned. "You know how much I love plan C."

"Yes, I know. Now, leave me alone so I can get a few minutes of sleep before whatever this turns into."

I woke up as the wheels of the Citation touched the runway on Hilton Head Island, and I stretched myself back to life. "That was quick."

Clark was already on his feet and leaning into the cockpit. "Nice job, guys."

The first officer glanced over his shoulder. "Thank you, sir. Shall we wait for you?"

Clark said, "No, we've got it from here. Have a good flight home, wherever home happens to be."

The young man patted the panel of the Citation. "This is home for me."

"I remember those days," Clark said. "No matter where I was, that was where I lived. Enjoy the ride, but don't forget that there's life beyond that windshield and that our ride on this rock floating around the sun is short."

The wisdom of Clark Johnson.

"Do you have a card?" Clark asked, and the pilot produced one from his shirt pocket. Without examining it, my partner stuck it in his wallet and asked, "Do you have any Gulfstream time?"

"Not yet, but I'm always willing to go back to school."

Clark shook his hand. "Maybe we'll see you around."

The pilot nodded. "I'd like to be seen around."

I opened the hatch, and we stepped from the plane and into the muggy island air. Hilton Head is a bit unique among the islands of the South Carolina Lowcountry. It's a hodgepodge of tax brackets from the calloused hands of the men and women who ended every day covered in dirt and sweat, to the manicured nails of the elite who barely noticed the former.

My partner and I could buy and sell most of the privileged few on the island who believed themselves superior to everyone around them, but we'd always prefer having a beer and a cheeseburger across the table from the men and women who toiled and labored their way through life instead of a glass of champagne with the better-than-you crowd.

Something told me we were about to spend the afternoon sticking our noses into the world of two men who believed themselves not only superior to the working class, but also untouchable and above the law. My job was to help them understand just how wrong they were.

We picked up keys for the prearranged rental car at the FBO and chuckled when we saw Ginger's choice for us. Black Suburbans were our vehicle of choice on more operations than I could count, but on that day, I became the common driver of a common Toyota Camry on an uncommon mission on an uncommon island.

"Well, isn't this invisible?"

Clark slid a hand across the dash. "It's you, College Boy. Embrace it."

"I think you're right. I just might keep this one."

He said, "Leave it to Ginger to pick the perfect ride for the job. Nobody will give us a second look in this thing."

We drove through a posh neighborhood of homes belonging to those who needed to impress their neighbors and to the address Ginger gave us for Jack Flannery's property.

Clark groaned. "Wouldn't you know it? There's always a security fence."

I rolled past the estate, studying it well as we went. "I wonder if it extends all the way around the property."

"There's only one way to find out," Clark said. "Make the block, and maybe we can see it from behind." I did, and Clark kept his eyes on the property. "It looks like a perimeter fence. The sun is on the wrong side of the planet for this op."

I said, "We don't get to pick the time, but we're hard-core operators, old man. If anybody can pull this off in the daytime, it's the two of us."

"I like the confidence," he said, "but I'm not looking forward to the dogs on the other side of that wall."

"How do you know they have dogs?"

He said, "Have you ever climbed a wall like that and not found dogs on the other side?"

"I'm not worried about the dogs as much as the security cameras."

He tugged his phone from a pocket. "Ginger or Skipper?"

"Ginger. Skipper's got her hands full on the ship."

He dialed the number and pressed the speaker button.

Ginger's voice filled the car. "Hey, boys. I thought you'd be calling about now. How was your ride?"

Clark asked, "The Citation or the Camry?"

"Both."

"Perfect," he said, "but we've run into a little issue at Flannery's house. He's got a twelve-foot security fence running the entire perimeter, and we need to know what's inside the walls."

"That's why you have me, boys. Have no fear. I'm already recording the security camera footage so I can play it on a constant loop while you're inside the walls. They'll never know you were there."

"How about dogs?" Clark asked.

Ginger said, "Oh, yeah. There are dogs, all right. Two of them, in fact. They're ferocious killers. According to Flannery's veterinarian bills, one is a cocker spaniel, and the other is a shih tzu, but their privileged little paws never touch the ground outside the house. Do you think you can survive those beasts?"

"We'll do our best," Clark said. "How about personal security?"

"That's the best part. Claven left his gun-toters behind. I guess he doesn't want any prying ears on this one."

"That's too bad for him," I said. "Our ears are poised to pry."

She giggled. "I know they are. If you need me to, I can open the gate for you."

Clark glanced at me, and I shook my head. "No, we'd rather go over the wall in the back, but it would be nice to know where they're planning to meet inside the house."

Ginger said, "Even I have my limits. I got you the address and a nice cushy ride. The rest is up to you."

I asked, "Is Claven here already?"

"Yep. He got there about thirty minutes before you."

"I guess that means it's time for us to go to work."

The sound of Ginger clicking keys almost as quickly as Skipper rattled through the phone. "Have fun, boys. I'm looping the security video now, so do your thing and let me know when you're clear."

Chapter 27
Stay the Course

We stashed the car in the driveway of a house that appeared to be well sealed for the season, and I grabbed Dr. Mankiller's bag of tricks from the back seat. With no traffic or pedestrians in sight, we crossed the street and wound our way through a stand of trees to the rear of Flannery's property. The corner of the stone security wall made a perfect ladder, and Clark and I were across the fence and on the ground inside in seconds.

"I'm getting too old for this fence-climbing business," Clark said.

"With any luck . . ."

Clark gave me a shove. "If I hear you say those words one more time, I'm going to finish the job Anya started and cut out your tongue."

"Sorry. What I meant was, here's hoping the rest of the op goes as smoothly as the entry."

We crossed the well-manicured lawn diagonally to avoid exposing ourselves too long to any one of the multitude of windows lining the back of the house. Against the wall of the structure, I unzipped the bag and pulled out a handful of small suction cups attached to blocks about the size of dice. "It's time to turn those windows into microphones."

I lifted the receiver control from the bag and programmed it to communicate with our bone conduction devices, then I dropped six of the suction cup cubes in Clark's hands.

He said, "Let's do it."

I lowered myself to the ground and crawled beneath the windowsills across the back of the house. With a brief peek inside every third window, I pressed one of the suction cups to the glass panes.

Sound is nothing more than vibrations traveling through the air. Flat glass windows are rigid enough to capture those vibrations and flexible enough to transmit them to our devices that would convert the vibrations back into the original sound and broadcast it to our receivers secured to our jawbones.

With the back and one side of the house wired for sound, we moved slowly to the other side to finish the job. Ten minutes after climbing the wall, we nestled ourselves behind a row of hedges and brought the window devices online. We could hear every noise generated inside the house, and the cacophony of sound was maddening. At least three televisions played inside our heads, coupled with a roar of other sounds we couldn't identify, but somewhere amidst the chaos, two voices appeared in the background.

Each window device had its own volume setting on the master control panel, and I changed levels until the televisions faded away and the voices became the predominant element of the broadcast. The small talk was meaningless until the sound of ice falling into glasses caught our attention.

"Things are getting serious," Clark said. "They're pouring drinks."

"If we listen closely, we might be able to tell what they're drinking."

Clark rolled his eyes. "I'm sure you're right."

The voices grew softer until they were inaudible, and I began the task of adjusting levels on the control module to find them again. It took several attempts, but soon, both men could be heard clearly, and the rest of the echoes from inside faded into the background.

A voice I assumed belonged to Jack, the congressman's brother-in-law, started the show. "Listen, Rich. You worry too much. It's going to work. We've got every detail planned, down to the smallest possibility."

Claven said, "I don't think you understand what we've got to lose. The Arabs are fanatics and impossible to control."

"Exactly my point," Flannery said. "They're on autopilot and will complete the mission no matter who or what gets in their way."

Claven groaned. "You said nobody was going to get hurt when all of this began. You said it's just a matter of material things. That statue is more than just a material thing, Jack. It's a symbol, and it's been standing in New York Harbor since eighteen eighty-six."

Suddenly, my heart pounded as if it were on the verge of an explosion, and I almost couldn't get the words out of my mouth. "They're going to take out the Statue of Liberty."

Clark flushed pale and let his face sink into his hands. Everything inside of me wanted to catch the Citation before it took off and head straight for New York City, but we were committed to gathering as much intel as possible before rejoining our shipmates.

Flannery said, "This is not the time to get sentimental, Rich. The ball's in motion. You committed to this plan eighteen months ago. It's too late to get cold feet now. They'll take out the statue while nobody is on the island. That'll give you a talking point when you get all weepy-eyed on national television. I can hear it now . . . 'Thank God no innocent lives were lost *this time*, but can we honestly believe these savages won't strike again?' You'll have them eating out of the palms of your hands, so relax and stick with the plan."

"What about the commandos?" Claven said.

"What about them? They got in the way, and they had to be eliminated. Brewer upheld his end of the plan, and he had to murder five people he was supposed to be protecting. Think about that. All you have to do is make a speech, cry in your handkerchief, and pretend to be outraged. The country will be outraged, the appropriations bill will pass by a landslide, and we'll be wealthy beyond anything we could've ever imagined. Trust me, Rich. The money is as good as in the bank."

"That money in the bank won't be any good to anybody if we're locked up. This thing's getting out of hand, and I'm not—"

Flannery cut in with a tone that left little doubt who was calling the shots. "You're not *what*, Rich? You're not on board any longer? You're not man enough to follow through with your commitment? Let me tell you what you're not, Congressman. You're not backing out. You're not walking away. It's too late, and you're in too deep for that. We're seeing this thing through to the end, or you're going down in flames. I've got enough on you to bury you under a federal prison, maybe even Guantanamo. You've seen what I'm capable of doing. Trust me, Congressman. I'm not the kind of man you walk away from. I leave smoking corpses and scorched earth in my wake, and I don't care who those bodies belong to. I'm going to be wealthy when this is over, and you've got two choices. You can either ride the high with me, or you can burn down without me. It's up to you."

Silence overtook the scene, and ice filled my veins. The thousand-yard stare in Clark's eyes told me exactly where he'd gone. It's a rage that can't be captured by words. It's a wild animal behind the immovable bars of the cage. It's a yearning unlike any other, an unyielding need to step into the fire and feed your hungry soul the only morsel it cries out to devour: the heart of evil. We'd stepped into that fire, side by side, and come out the other side changed, and perhaps having become more like the demons we'd devoured than the people we were protecting. Perhaps that was our lot, our calling, our purpose for walking the Earth.

Claven said, "You listen to me."

Flannery stopped him with a calm, determined tone. "I'm finished listening to you, Richard. This is the last time we will ever speak of this. You will stay the course. It's too late for anything less."

Movement inside the house filled my head, but the discussion was over. Everything about our mission had changed in an instant. We were destined for far more than learning what happened to a team of operators, and the thought of the terrorists running home to regroup was forever abandoned. We were now the only thing standing in front of the ultimate enemy: greed. Stopping the terrorists was only the first step in what would become our solitary purpose in the coming days. Flannery, Claven, and every living soul who played any role in the conspiracy and ultimate betrayal of the American people would crumble beneath our boots, and we would stop at nothing to fulfill that noble purpose.

It took only ninety seconds to reclaim our receivers from the corners of every window and make it back across the wall. We were driven by a new mandate, a revived necessity, and that drive fueled us as if we were unstoppable. I prayed we were.

Back in the car, Clark took the wheel while I called the CIC. "Skipper, I'm uploading the audio now. I need you and the team to pore over it, dissect every word, and make certain you hear the same thing I hear."

"The file is coming in now," she said. "Are you and Clark clear?"

"We are, and we're exfilling now. Where are you?"

She clicked a few keys. "We're north of Lauderdale off West Palm."

"Have you narrowed your target?"

"Oh, yeah," she said. "We've got 'em right in our sights, and high-res satellite imagery confirms it's them."

"Well done," I said. "Listen to the audio, and we'll be at the airport. Dispatch the chopper when you're in range, and we'll be standing by, I don't want to discuss the audio until we're back aboard."

She said, "If my math is correct—and it always is—we'll be off Hilton Head in seven hours. We'll launch the Little Bird to pick you up and rendezvous in the most efficient timing. What else do you need from me?"

I said, "Don't lose the target. Keep Congressman Claven's movement on the radar, and don't waste a second picking us up."

"Consider it done."

I shoved the phone back into my pocket, and Clark said, "I think we should kill them now."

"Who?"

"Claven and Flannery."

I huffed. "I'd love to, but that wouldn't stop the attack. You heard what he said back there. The ball is already in motion, and killing the masterminds won't stop gravity."

"I still want to kill them."

"Yeah, I know. Me, too. But we've got the audio, and the things we can do with that little morsel are so much more painful than a bullet to the brain."

He drummed his thumbs on the steering wheel. "They still need killing."

"Yes, they do, and I hope you and I get to be there when it happens."

With more than six hours to kill before Barbie and her chopper would appear on the eastern horizon, my mind spun out of control, imagining what was to come. The Board would dictate the general plan under which we would operate, but when our boots hit the ground, the men around me would make a thousand decisions every minute and find a way to prevent the coming attack.

In the pilots' lounge at the airport, Clark pushed the heavy oak door closed with the toe of his boot and slid onto the oversized lounge chair designed to give weary pilots a place to catch a nap before the next leg of their charter. "Why don't we just sink 'em, pick 'em up, and have a little heart-to-heart on our way to Gitmo?"

"That would stop the attack," I said, "but what we're doing here is a lot deeper than that. The foot soldiers are dangerous, but the real terrorists were inside that house today. New Yorkers keep electing Claven, and he's the real enemy in all of this."

Clark thumbed the button to recline his seat. "Don't forget about his brother-in-law, Flannery."

"I've been thinking about him. I don't know if he's the mastermind behind this thing, but he's definitely a ground-floor guy. He's obviously been in on it from its inception, and I don't see a political motivation."

"What do you mean?" Clark asked.

"I don't think Flannery—or even Claven for that matter—hates America. They don't want to bring down our country. They just want to get stinking rich, and they lack the moral fiber to do it legally. That changes the way I look at this thing."

"What are you talking about, College Boy? These guys are worse than the ideologues who want to bring us down."

"I don't see it that way."

He retracted the footrest and sat up. "Are you going soft on me?"

"No, nothing like that. I just want to make sure we're looking at this thing through the right lens. We're not saving American lives. We'll stop the attack on the Statue of Liberty. I have no doubt about that. But that's not the job. The real mission is stopping Claven, Flannery, and whoever else they've got in bed with them. That's police work, and we're not cops."

He rubbed his eyes. "Listen to me. I'm going to get your head right about this thing. Regardless of their motivations, those guys are the bad guys in all of this. It doesn't matter if they're doing it for love, hate, or indifference. They're still doing it, and they have to pay. I know there's a thousand more just like them lined up to take their place when they go down, but we'll fight them another day. We've got a task. It's our job to stop the shooters and yank the leadership out by its roots. It's that simple. If you keep trying to turn this thing into philosophy or whatever, you're going to hesitate when it's time to press the trigger, and the fighters around you, including me, deserve better than that from their leader."

"I won't hesitate," I said. "There's too much at stake."

Clark returned to his feet-up position and pulled his University of Alabama Crimson Tide cap over his eyes. "I know."

Chapter 28
Build Another Fire

No matter how hard I tried, I couldn't join Clark in the spirit world. Whether it was his snoring or my mind's inability to relax keeping me awake didn't particularly matter. I was left dangling somewhere between consciousness and utter absence.

A distant, strangely familiar sound tugged at me, and I slipped my phone from my pocket. "Yeah?"

"Why weren't you answering the sat-com?"

Skipper's tone left me feeling like an errant child.

"Sorry. I didn't hear it."

"Is it on?"

I thumbed the slim transceiver in my pocket. "It is now."

She huffed. "Why was it turned off? Oh, never mind. Is everything all right?"

"Clark's sleeping. Imagine that. And I'm thinking."

"Neither surprises me," she said. "Wake him up. Barbie's on her way."

I checked my watch. "ETA?"

"Twenty minutes."

"We'll be waiting on the ramp."

"Chase, there's something else you should know."

"That sounds ominous. What is it?"

"The *Scimitar* is on the move. She pulled out of Havana Harbor an hour ago and turned north."

"Well, that's not good," I said. "Keep an eye on her, and figure out where she's going."

"I'm on it, but there's no way to know if it's still part of the mission or if she's just going home."

"For now, we have to assume every move is sinister. Consider her hostile until we know otherwise. Does Ginger have an opinion?"

"She's taking the same posture as you. All we can do is watch and guess."

"Is there anything else?" I asked.

"Hang on. They're changing course."

My curiosity exploded. "Which direction? Where are they heading? Which boat?"

"Jeez. Calm down. I'm talking about the lead vessel. It looks like they're pulling into St. Simons. Maybe it's a fuel stop."

I recalled the nautical chart around St. Simons. "What's your range?"

"We're twelve miles in trail."

"Get Mongo," I said.

"He's right here beside me."

Our giant said, "What do you want me to do?"

"You're in command while I'm ashore. What do *you* want to do?"

He didn't hesitate. "I want to close the distance, launch the RHIB, and get eyes on that boat. If the timing and position is right, I want to mark it and plant enough C-Four to blow it to the moon."

"It's your show," I said. "But I'd do exactly the same."

I neither expected nor received a response. Instead, I heard the big man push himself from his chair and cross the floor.

I kicked Clark's boot. "Get up, Ranger. Things are happening."

He lifted his hat and stretched. "What? I wasn't asleep."

I ignored him, and Skipper said, "We're spreading ourselves pretty thin with two away teams."

"I agree, but we can't let the chance to mark that boat slip out of our hands."

She said, "I know. It just feels like we've got too many irons in the fire."

"Then build another fire."

"I think they're building themselves," she said. "I'll see you when get back on board."

Clark retied his boots and stood. "Weren't there some cookies around here somewhere?"

I motioned toward the countertop by the back wall of the pilot's lounge. "Hurry up, Cookie Monster. We've got a chopper to catch."

I chuckled as Clark shoved a collection of cookies into his pocket.

"What? You never know when you're going to need a cookie. We could crash on the way back to the ship, and you'd wish you had a pocketful of cookies."

"Always the Boy Scout, huh?"

He gave me the three-finger salute. "Semper Fi Cookies."

"Yeah, I don't think that's the Boy Scouts, but let's go."

We parked ourselves on an aluminum bench outside the terminal and panned the southeastern sky for our approaching chariot. We didn't have to wait long to watch Barbie touch down as gently as a hummingbird a few feet away.

We were aboard and airborne in seconds, with Hilton Head Island shrinking behind us.

Barbie pushed the Little Bird as hard as she'd go, and we landed on the *Lori Danielle*'s helipad just offshore of St. Simons Island.

We stepped from the flying machine, and Clark held out a handful of crumbs toward Barbie. "Want a cookie?"

She stared down at his palm. "I'll pass, but thanks."

Clark shrugged and crammed the whole mess into his mouth.

In the CIC, a monitor displayed a high-definition video of the vessel we'd been chasing.

"Who's out there?" I asked.

Mongo said, "Hunter and Kodiak are in the water. Gator's running the RHIB under Disco's watchful eye."

"Great call," I said. "How long have they been in the water?"

He pointed toward a counter in the corner of the monitor. "Nine minutes."

"Are they on diver propulsion vehicles?"

"No, we're doing a line recovery."

"I like it," I said. "But does Gator know how to rig it?"

Mongo said, "Hunter briefed and demonstrated it on deck, but Disco won't let him screw it up."

"What do you think about him so far?" I asked.

Mongo gave a sharp nod. "He's good, Chase. You made an excellent decision on that one."

"I think so, too, but we have to make sure we don't get overconfident in him too early."

Minutes passed like hours as the counter ticked upward until Hunter's distorted voice rang through the overhead speaker. "Their port prop shaft is warped, and the bearing is coming apart."

I leaned toward the microphone. "How much longer will it survive?"

"It's hard to say, but if they get another day out of it, it'll surprise me."

I said, "Roger. Say expected time on station."

"We'll swim away in two minutes, but I wish I had brought a prop shaft bearing with us. We could've replaced this one and given them another hundred hours."

"You're quite the good Samaritan," I said. "Just set the explosives and get out of there."

The view on the monitor changed from the image of the vessel to a shot inside and over the stern of our RHIB. A pair of lines led from pad eyes through fairleads on spreaders and into the water behind the boat. The spreaders would keep the lines away from the RHIB's propellers, even in a turn. At the running end of each line was a small disk just large enough for each diver to either sit or stand on while tightly gripping the line. In that position, Gator could motor away with no one noticing the lines descending into the water behind the RHIB until they were far enough away to recover the divers out of sight of prying eyes.

The procedure worked exactly as planned, and Hunter and Kodiak emerged from the water and slithered over the tubes and onto the deck of the RHIB.

Gator said, "Divers recovered, mission complete, exfil underway."

Skipper gave me a wink. "He's even starting to sound like an operator."

The crane operator hoisted the RHIB over the rail and deposited her into her cradle.

Gator was last out of the boat, and Mongo caught his arm when he hit the deck. He said, "Listen. I wasn't doubting your ability in the water by sending Kodiak with Hunter. I was concerned about our window of time, and I didn't want Hunter to get caught up in teaching you something new under there."

The new kid looked up at Mongo. "You don't have to explain your decisions to me. You were in command, and I followed your orders. That's what I'm here to do."

Mongo said, "I just didn't want you to think . . ."

Gator smirked. "I'm not smart enough to think, so I'll just keep doing what I'm told."

Mongo gave him a slap on the back with his massive palm, and Gator collected the used dive gear.

Hunter caught him. "You don't have to clean the gear."

Gator said, "I know, but I'd like to go through it one more time with the techs to make sure I understand the rebreathers a little better."

Mongo chuckled. "You're making the rest of us look bad. You need to stop being all conscientious and stuff."

"Maybe one day."

The team assembled back in the CIC for the situation report to the Board.

The faces appeared on the monitors, and Clark took the floor. "Good evening, gentlemen and lady. Did you receive the most recent brief timestamped twenty-three forty-five Zulu?"

"We did. Are you requesting additional assets?"

"That depends on what assets are available," Clark said. "Do you have a waterborne team who can pursue the *Scimitar* and free us up to stay with the lead vessel?"

"Unfortunately, no, we do not. Are you prepared for us to brief Homeland and the Pentagon?"

Clark turned to me as if that call lay solidly in my lap.

I said, "I need some parameters before I make that call. Is it your intention to make this event public?"

The Board members exchanged glances, and one said, "Give us a moment."

They silenced their conversation, but a skill they taught me made their effort pointless. As I watched their lips, my eyes replaced my deafened ears. I caught Skipper's eye and pressed a finger to my lips. She silenced our mics, and I covered my mouth. "They're saying that keeping it out of the news is impossible. Does anybody agree with them?"

My eyes slowly met every other pair in the room, and each echoed a resounding no.

I nodded to Skipper. "Make us hot again." She hit the keys, and I said, "You may think it's impossible to do this covertly, but I—we—believe it can be done. We can stop the attack, capture the terrorists, and apprehend Congressman Claven without a single camera seeing us do it."

That stopped the Board in their tracks, and every head turned back to the cameras.

The man said, "What about Evan Brewer, the American? Can you snatch him now?"

Almost without conscious thought, I turned immediately to Hunter, and the corners of his mouth turned slightly upward. That's all I needed from my partner, and I said, "Yes, sir. We can."

Before he could respond, Hunter and I were on our feet.

I said, "Kodiak, find Gator. You two are on rebreathers and with us. Disco, you're on the helm. Let's move."

Clark ordered, "Launch a pair of drones. Get me overhead video, and find Brewer."

Skipper stepped way outside her typical spicey attitude and said, "Aye, sir. Drones in the air in sixty seconds."

I said, "Get Weps down here, and get a starburst ready to fly."

Skipper paged the weapons officer, and Clark looked up at the camera. "We'll have Brewer inside thirty minutes unless you give the stand-down order now."

The Board member said, "Happy hunting, gentlemen. Keep us off CNN."

We sprinted to the RHIB, and Kodiak showed up with Gator and every piece of dive gear we could need for the mission.

"Get us in the water," I ordered.

The crane operator leapt into position and yelled down at us. "Is the pre-deployment checklist complete?"

I locked eyes with him. "Put us in the water now."

Without another word, the crane whirred to life, and we rose from the cradle and across the rail faster than we'd ever done before. The instant the feet of the engines hit the water, Disco had the props spinning, and Kodiak cast off the lines.

The boat was on plane and racing across the waves in no time while Kodiak and Gator climbed into their dive gear. I briefed the plan over the howl of the engines and waves, and everyone gave the thumbs-up.

I powered up the sat-com. "CIC, Alpha One."

Skipper answered. "Go for CIC."

"Where's our target?"

"He walked into the structure fifty yards from fuel point two minutes ago. It'll be dark in minutes, and the drone video will be weak."

I said, "Roger. Send the video. And we're counting on the sun going down." The panel-mounted monitor bloomed with the overhead view from one of our two drones, and I drove a finger into the screen. "Put the divers in the water here, and put me and Hunter on the dock there."

Disco nodded, and I curled a finger, calling Kodiak and Gator close. With a finger still on the monitor, I said, "If the timing works, we'll put him in the water right here. You two do your thing and deliver him to the RHIB at the end of the pier."

Gator asked, "What if he fights?"

Kodiak and I laughed.

"Oh, he'll fight, but you two have a constant supply of breathable air. He has only what you give him."

Disco glanced over his shoulder from the helm and yelled, "Divers ready!"

Kodiak took his position face-down on the portside tube, and Gator matched his posture on the starboard tube. Just as the world's closest star took her bow for the day, I slapped Gator's shoulder, and Hunter slapped Kodiak's. The two rolled away, striking the water with their backs first, and vanished beneath the darkening surface.

Disco brought the RHIB about and headed for the second drop point. Our dismount was far less dramatic and much drier than Gator's and Kodiak's. Disco slowed to idle, and Hunter and I stepped from the port tube and onto the dock.

A few boaters and tourists were scattered about the marina, and their presence made me glad I ordered the weapons officer into position. Through my sat-com, I said, "Weps, Alpha One."

"Go for Weps."

"Stand by with starburst, and configure to deploy five hundred yards northeast of my position."

Weps said, "Starburst ready and standing by."

Skipper said, "We're dark, Alpha One. The drone video is fading."

"Roger. It's an eyes-on operation now. Get medical standing by on the aft deck."

"Roger, Alpha One."

Hunter gave me a smirk. "You think Brewer's going to hurt somebody?"

I returned the expression. "No. I'm afraid Gator might try to drown him."

"That's valid, but I'd like to rip his legs off before Gator gets him."

I said, "I'll see what I can do. Are you ready to go?"

Hunter nodded. "Always."

We moved into position, fifteen yards from the door of the marina office, and began our wait. To our surprise, we didn't have to wait long. Evan Brewer emerged from the door with a two-liter bottle in one hand and a plastic bag in the other.

I called the CIC. "Weps, Alpha One. Launch the starburst."

"Alpha One, Weps. Starburst away."

The flight time of the harmless exploding round was thirty-five seconds, and I watched every one of them tick off in slow motion.

At twenty-nine seconds, I gave the order. "Go!"

Hunter and I burst from our position and into a sprint down the dock. We wouldn't see the explosion, but I expected everyone else on the dock would. A dozen strides into our attack, the air-splitting crash thundered through the darkening sky. Before another second passed, Hunter's shoulder hit Brewer just below his belt, and mine collided with his chin.

I'll never know what became of the shopping bag and two-liter, but I know exactly where Brewer's most recent breath went. It had huffed into the night in a massive evacuation from his lungs.

Hunter and I performed the opposite maneuver with our diaphragms. Our lungs were full to overflowing when the three of us hit the water. Clark may have been the master of getting prisoners to talk with a little water up their nose on dry land, but he was no match for Hunter's ferocity in the water. Brewer fought, just as I knew he would, but I hadn't expected him to stay calm. Most people panic when they find themselves suddenly and unexpectedly forced underwater, but Brewer kept his wits about him and lashed out in perfect blows.

I caught an elbow to my jaw that sent watery stars circling my head. Disoriented but still holding on, I followed Brewer back to the surface, and my mind raced.

Would he yell for help when his head broke the surface, or would he take a breath and continue the fight? Maybe both.

When our heads found the air, he didn't call out for assistance from his Arab friends. Instead, he packed his lungs with air and continued fighting.

Underestimating an opponent is a deadly sin, and I was guilty. Knowing Brewer to be a treasonous traitor to his country, I let myself believe his hand-to-hand skills were as weak as his allegiance to Old Glory.

Hunter landed a blow to Brewer's gut hard enough to empty his lungs again, and we dragged him under for a second time. Returning to our plan, I gained control of his left arm while Hunter wrestled with his right. At the height of the skirmish, a lightning bolt struck my left hip, and electricity coursed through my spine, leaving me sickened and momentarily dazed. I couldn't understand why or how, but I was temporarily out of the fight as my body dealt with the shock. I retched and then pawed at my hip like a wounded animal. There was no apparent reason for the pain that had surged through my body, so I refocused and dug deep for the continued will to fight.

By the time I reclaimed my hold on Brewer's arm, his wrists were tied together, and Hunter had the man well controlled. Although I was mentally and physically prepared to keep the punishment flowing, it was far from necessary. Four unseen hands from the depths grasped Brewer and dragged him from our grip. Blind in the dark water, I reached for Hunter and met his outstretched hand. We swam to the surface and caught our breath.

"What happened to you? Where'd you go?"

I spat a mouthful of water. "He landed a sharp one on my hip, and it felt like a rifle shot."

He held up a small, curved blade. "It was a karambit. Roll up, and let me see how bad you're cut."

Instinctually, I reached for the wound, but underwater, it was impossible to assess the damage. I followed my partner's instructions and rolled onto my side, trying to thrust my hip out of the water.

When I could no longer hold the posture, I raised my head from the water. "What do you think?"

"I can't tell, but we need to get you out of the water."

"No," I demanded. "We can't blow our cover. We're sticking with the plan and waiting for the pickup."

Hunter groaned. "Okay, but I'm not letting you bleed out."

He moved to my left side and wrapped his arms around my waist, clamping pressure against the wound on my right hip.

I said, "You could've at least bought me dinner before taking our relationship to this level."

"Shut up, and stop getting hurt. I don't like this any more than you do."

"Do you think I get hurt on purpose?"

He laughed. "Which one of us has a fake foot, a fake wrist, and hearing aids?"

"Touché."

Anyone who's ever suffered a serious injury knows that the more the brain tries to minimize the pain, the more agonizing it becomes. I may have been stabbed through the joint, or it may have been nothing more than a scratch, but the part of my brain devoted to keeping me alive kept screaming for a medic, and all I had was Hunter, the hip-hugger.

In what might have been two minutes or two decades, Disco and the RHIB finally showed up, and Hunter reached over the starboard tube for Gator's offered hand.

"Chase was stabbed. Get him on board first. It's his right hip."

With a mighty pull, Gator hoisted me from the water and deposited me on the deck of the RHIB beside the hogtied Brewer. Kodiak rolled me onto my side and cut away my pants at the same instant Hunter planted a knee in the center of Brewer's chest.

"You stabbed my friend, you traitorous piece of crap. Now I'm going to cut out your spleen with your own knife."

Gator threw an arm around Hunter's neck and pulled him from Brewer's chest. "Easy, big fellow. His day will come."

Kodiak laid a hand on my shoulder. "It's not good, Chase, but there's not a lot of blood. We'll have you back to the ship in no time. Do you need a morphine hit?"

"No, I'm okay. But I think I might be pregnant after Hunter's hands-on first-aid technique."

Chapter 29
Let's Have a Chat

I wasn't in pain, but I was mad. I wanted to bury Evan Brewer's karambit in his neck, but most of my anger was directed at myself for not controlling his arm during our skirmish in the water. I was complacent when I should've been vigilant, and that's the deadliest sin in the world in which I lived. I'd like to say it would never happen again, but making such a statement was just as foolish as the sin itself.

Everybody on the boat had flex-cuffs tucked away somewhere on his body, but watching Hunter's 550 cord cut into Brewer's flesh at his wrists was far more satisfying than seeing him endure the relative comfort of the plastic bindings. Everything about the man lying beside me on the deck of the RHIB repulsed me, yet somewhere deep inside, I felt a measure of pity for him. The coming hours and days of his life would be more uncomfortable in every way possible than he was capable of imagining, and I would never want to experience what lay in his future.

We were hoisted aboard, and Hunter threw me over his shoulder.

"Put me down," I demanded. "I can walk. It's just a flesh wound."

He groaned under my weight. "I'll put you down when the doc says I can. Until then, enjoy the ride."

Fortunately, for Hunter, a medic met us at the base of the superstructure with a wheelchair, and my bearer hesitantly released me into his care. I refused the chair and followed the scrubs-clad corpsman to sick bay.

"What have you done to yourself now?" Dr. Shadrack asked as he pulled my sliced pants away from my wound.

"I got lazy and let a traitor stab me."

"Not a great plan. Let's have a look." He examined the wound and let out a sound I didn't like.

"What does that noise mean?"

"It means you're getting an MRI and some X-rays. You're lucky he missed your kidney, but I suspect he got into the hip joint, and that could be bad enough to send you to a real surgeon."

"You *are* a real surgeon," I said.

"Not that kind of surgeon. I can put you back together when pieces start falling out, but big joints like the hip are a specialty all their own."

I reached up and took him by the sleeve. "I'm not leaving the ship, no matter what the X-rays show, so I suggest brushing up on your ortho skills."

He patted my chest. "Oh, Chase. It must be nice to believe you're always in charge."

In the next instant, a tech wheeled me toward the tiny radiology department aboard our ship. She said, "I'm sorry, sir, but we need to get you out of these wet clothes. Can you stand?"

"Yeah, I can stand, but don't freak out when you see me pull off my pants." She frowned, and I chuckled as I realized what she must've thought I meant. "No, it's not that. I have a prosthetic leg."

She nodded. "I know. It just sounded funny. You're not the first man I've ever seen without his pants."

"You know about my leg?"

"Yes, sir. We all know every detail of every member of your team. If you'll excuse me for saying so, you seem to get hurt more than everyone else combined."

"I'd like to say that's because I do more work than everyone else combined, but that's not the case. I tend to be a little clumsy."

"Based on your wound, I doubt this one was clumsiness. It looks a lot like a stab wound to me."

"It is," I said, "but I got it because I was being clumsy."

"No matter. We'll fix you up. Here's a towel and a gown."

I dried off and pulled the cotton gown around my shoulders. "Sorry. I probably don't smell very good."

"Just lie down on the table," she said. "We'll stick you in the shower after we figure out how badly you're hurt."

"It's not bad. It's just a flesh wound."

She ignored me and situated me on the MRI table. "Are you claustrophobic?"

"Everyone is claustrophobic if the space is small enough, but I think I'll survive the MRI machine."

"Here's the bulb, just in case. Give it a squeeze if you get uncomfortable."

I squeezed the bulb several times in rapid succession, and she rolled her eyes and plucked the device from my hand. "On second thought, just suffer through it."

The machine buzzed, and the table moved me inside the tunnel. The clicking, clanging, and thumping were disheartening, but I never felt like I needed the bulb.

When it ended, I spent a few minutes on the X-ray table, and I was finally returned to Dr. Shadrack's capable hands.

"Good news," he said. "The hip joint looks okay. The blade must've been relatively short."

"It was. It's in the pocket of my pants, wherever they are."

He glared down at me. "So, you got stabbed, then you took the knife away from the guy?"

"Not exactly," I admitted. "Hunter took the karambit from the guy."

"Is he still alive?"

"Hunter?" I asked.

"No, the stabber."

"I hope so. I've got a long list of questions I intend to ask him."

"That'll have to wait," Dr. Shadrack said. "I've got a little work to do to get you closed back up."

He spent the next half hour cleaning and closing the wound. When he was finished, he leaned away and stretched his back. "That should do it. I'm supposed to tell you to stay off your feet for forty-eight hours and limit your walking to only necessary movement for a week, but something tells me I'd be wasting my breath."

"I'll do what I can, Doc, but we've got a lot of work to do. What'll happen if I don't exactly follow your orders?"

He pulled off his gloves. "I had absolutely no faith that you'd follow medical advice, so I double-sutured everything. Knowing you, it probably won't hold, but I can always do it again."

I sat up and spun, letting my legs hang down from the gurney. "Thanks, Doctor. I'll try to be careful."

"No, you won't, but I appreciate the sentiment. Now, go get a shower. You smell like a rotten goat."

"I'll get to that," I said. "I've got a few errands to run first."

The tech who'd x-rayed my hip held out her hand with Brewer's karambit resting in her palm. "I thought you might want this."

I lifted the curved blade from her hand, slipped my index finger through the ring, and spun it through the air. "Thanks. I think I'll use this to make a point or two."

She grinned. "I thought you might. When you're through with him, we'll put him back together if we can."

"Thanks for understanding."

There were a lot of things I loved about the *Lori Danielle*, but the fact that an interrogation cell was necessary aboard such a vessel somehow felt like a blemish on her otherwise beautiful existence. Inside that cell is where I found Evan Michael Brewer trussed up like a piñata. Clark sat silently in the corner of the cell, arranging the tools of his horrific trade.

Stepping into the space, I ignored Brewer and dragged the toe of my boot across the drain situated conspicuously in the deck. Clark didn't look up, and I didn't look at him. Instead, I stood in front of Brewer and stared through him as if he weren't there.

I pulled a Velcro patch of the American flag from my pocket and held it in front of his face, then slapped it against his nose several times. "Does the sight of this flag disgust you as badly as you sicken me?"

He stared back into my eyes and worked his lips, trying to convince his mouth to produce the saliva he wanted to spit in my face.

I sidestepped the assault and drew his karambit, then pressed the point of the blade against his Adam's apple. "Does that feel familiar?"

He raised his chin as if offering himself to the blade, and I laughed. "Oh, you'd love that, wouldn't you? You'd love feeling your blade pierce your flesh and the life drain from your body. That would be merciful, and we're not big on mercy for people like you."

He pressed himself forward against the curved blade, but I pulled away with his every advance.

"You have some decisions to make, Brewer. There's nothing you can say that will make the coming hours pleasant, but you can avoid a great deal of pain by cooperating."

His expression didn't change, so I continued. "I'm your only hope on this ship. Everyone else, and especially him"—I motioned toward Clark with his towels, buckets of water, and collection of terrifying probes—"wants to disembowel you. I want to learn from you."

The slightest break in his frozen expression came, and I noticed.

"You know how these things work, Brewer. We're supposed to give you an opportunity to talk before we start inflicting pain, but we're not exactly the traditional kind of operation. You see, Evan, we enjoy our work." I glanced at Clark. "Some of us more than others. There are all sorts of reasons a person would turn his back on his country and his countrymen. I'm sure you found a way to justify your treason, and I look forward to hearing your reasons, but, unfortunately for you, I don't get to go first."

I searched for any degree of submission in his eyes, but no matter how deeply I looked, it wasn't there. "I'm a scientist and a philosopher, but the rest of my team isn't quite so sophisticated. They speak a different language—a language I think you probably understand."

I held his knife between our faces and watched a tiny droplet of blood trace the spine of the curved blade. "On second thought, maybe I will give you a chance to avoid the ugliness that neither of us wants. So, this is your singular chance. Tell me the plan."

I thought I caught a glimpse of fear behind his defiant eyes. "Don't fight it, Evan. Tell me everything, and I'll see that you're treated with some dignity."

His eyes fell, and my heart sank.

"Bad decision, Evan. Bad decision."

My hip throbbed as if a thousand clawing animals were digging their way from within my body, but I turned and walked away, forcing myself to avoid the limp my body so desperately wanted to employ.

As I strode past Clark, I said, "Try to keep him alive. I'll be back."

As if I'd never entered the cell, Clark showed no reaction to my leaving or my instruction.

Although a two-way mirror stood between the interrogation cell and the observation room, I didn't watch and went in search of Gator instead. I found him in the CIC, and he stood when I walked in.

"Are you okay?" he asked.

I patted my hip. "Just a flesh wound. Come with me."

Gator followed without a word, and I parked him inside the observation room.

"Watch, and don't look away."

He groaned. "Yes, sir."

"Everything we do has a purpose, and this is no exception, but it is the most difficult to watch."

He reached up and grabbed my arm. "You're a psychologist, right?"

I nodded, and he asked, "Does it make sense that I'd feel a little sorry for that guy?"

I pulled his hand from my arm. "If you didn't, I wouldn't want you on my team."

I left Gator alone in the room and found Hunter.

He asked, "Are you okay?"

"I will be. It's just a stab wound, straight in and straight out. Doc sewed it up, and I'll be as good as new in a few days."

"When do I get my turn with Brewer?"

"Clark goes first, and if he doesn't open up, you're next."

Hunter said, "It's gonna be hard for me not to kill him."

"I know, but we need him alive. He's got intel we need."

Hunter looked away, and I said, "The mission comes first. We're not in the revenge business."

Singer stepped beside me and asked, "Are you making Gator watch?"

"Yes."

"Do you mind if I go in with him?"

I nodded toward the interrogation observation room, and our Southern Baptist sniper walked away.

Chapter 30
You Have the Right

I made my way back to the CIC, where Skipper sat, frantically scanning half a dozen monitors.

"What are you doing?" I asked.

Without looking up, she said, "Everything."

I sat beside her. "Stop whatever you're doing, and get Ginger on the phone."

"Chase, I don't have time for that."

"Do it."

She huffed and made the call. When Ginger answered, I didn't give Skipper a chance to speak. "Ginger, are you working on anything that can't wait?"

"Well, I'm doing—"

I cut in. "Will people die if you pull off?"

"No, but—"

"Good. Set it aside, and cut Skipper's workload in half."

"Okay. I can do that."

I laid a hand on Skipper's shoulder. "Brief her on the *Scimitar* and anything else that isn't directly tied to the lead vessel. I want you on that boat and nothing else."

"It's not that simple."

"Yes, it is," I said. "I need you at full strength on this thing. We've got a traitorous combatant in custody and a direct threat against the United States. It's exactly that simple. Now, brief Ginger, and focus on our direct mission."

She nodded reluctantly, and I sat back to listen to the briefing.

When she was finished, Ginger said, "Sure. No problem. I've got it. I'll update you with any significant changes. What else can I do?"

Skipper turned to me as if asking what I needed, and I said, "Get us everything you can find on the status of the Statue of Liberty in the next five days."

"The Statue of Liberty? What's that got to do . . . ? Wait! Are you serious?"

"I couldn't be more serious. Just get me the information."

"I'm on it," she said.

I stood and squeezed Skipper's shoulders. "Don't do this to yourself. I need you sharp and clear."

"I've got this."

"Yeah, I know."

When I stepped into the observation room, Singer sat with his eyes cast to the deck, and Gator watched the gruesome scene in front of him as if he couldn't look away.

I stepped beside our new guy. "It's your turn."

"My turn? What am I supposed to do?"

"You're supposed to go in there and pull Clark off the guy. He'll make a show of resisting, but he knows the game. Be forceful if you have to. Shove him around and act like you're in charge."

He looked up and furrowed his brow. "Shove Brewer around?"

"No," I said. "Shove Clark around. Like I said, he knows the game. When you get him off of Brewer, spend a little time examining his wounds and pretending to care. Ask him if he's ready to talk. He'll spit at you and curse, if he does anything. It's possible he'll show no reaction at all. Either way, feign indifference. Make him believe his life has no value."

Gator said, "Are you sure I'm the right guy for this?"

"This isn't about Brewer. It's about you."

Singer pressed his palm against Gator's back. "Go do as Chase says. You have to do it. It'll get easier in time, but the first one is always the hardest."

As if driven by Singer's encouragement, Gator rose and pressed through the door. Clark delivered three blows with his baton to the muscular section of Brewer's thigh, where the strikes could do no damage other than superficial bruising. A few inches lower at the kneecap, the blows would've been devastating and permanently crippling, but we were several hours away from that approach.

Gator stepped between Clark and Brewer. "That's enough! Step back."

Clark shoved him out of the way and delivered a crushing blow to Brewer's ribs. The man gasped and lurched.

Gator shoved Clark backward. "I said that's enough! Now, cut it out."

Clark planted a hand against Gator's shoulder as if to force him aside, but the new guy swept Clark's hand away and stepped to within an inch of my handler's face. "That's enough. Knock it off."

Clark tried to hide his crooked smile and stepped away.

Gator turned to Brewer and surveyed every inch of his body. The wounds Clark had inflicted were superficial but looked extremely painful. Nothing appeared to be broken, but blood, saliva, and sweat dripped from Brewer's flesh.

"Are you ready to cooperate?"

Brewer raised his head and appraised Gator. "I'm an American. I have rights."

Gator scoffed. "Rights? What kind of rights do you think you have in international waters?"

"You can't do this to me."

Gator thrust a claw beneath Brewer's chin and dug his fingertips into the flesh of his neck. "Let's talk about rights. You've got the right to remain silent, but doing so will result in more pain than you're capable of enduring. If you give up this right and tell us everything you know, anything you say may save your miserable life. You've got the right to an attorney, if you can find one. Unfortunately, our phone lines are down, and there aren't any barristers on board. If you can't afford an attorney, that's too bad because nobody will ever find your body. Do you understand these rights as I've explained them to you?"

Brewer caught his breath. "You're going down for this. You're going down."

Gator tugged at his shirt and seemed to examine his body. "I'm not sure you understand the gravity of your situation. I'm not bleeding, sweating, or tied up. I don't think I'm the one who's going down. From my perspective, you're the one who needs to reconsider his position here."

Brewer muttered a string of obscenities at Gator, and that seemed only to encourage our new recruit.

He shrugged. "I gave you an opportunity. That's all I can do. I guess it's time to bring in the relief pitcher to throw a few fastballs."

Brewer kicked and twisted in his bindings, doing his best to turn away from Gator, but the kid sidestepped, matching his every move. "One last chance. Are you ready to talk?"

The profanity that escaped Brewer's mouth was met with a thundering elbow shot from Gator, who growled. "It's time for you to grow some respect."

Gator pushed his way back through the door and into the observation room. "Sorry. I got carried away. I shouldn't have hit him."

Singer said, "Don't be sorry. You did exactly what you should've done. We're a long way from him giving in. He won't remember your short little visit when all of this is over."

Gator looked at me as if asking for approval, and I said, "Nice job, kid. Have a seat. It's Hunter's turn."

The cycle continued through the night as the abuse grew more aggressive and painful, with every passing hour, until I pulled Kodiak, the fourth punisher, off Brewer.

"Take a break," I said. "I'll finish this."

Kodiak shoved past me and stuck a finger in Brewer's face. "You're going to wish I had killed you."

I made a show of shoving Kodiak away, and he disappeared through the door.

Brewer's face looked like a purple sack of flesh when I stepped to within an inch of his eyes. Instead of threatening him or inflicting more pain, I simply stared into his eyes with expectation in my gaze. His body rose and fell with every labored breath, and his breath smelled of iron and vomit.

I stood in stalwart determination to outstare the man. Everything inside of me wanted to cut his heart from his chest and watch him die in front of me, but I wouldn't. A great good lay just beyond Brewer's resolution to hide behind his defiance, and I was determined to find it by any means necessary.

He caught his breath. "What? What do you want?"

I didn't say a word and continued staring. To my surprise, his eyes fell.

There are unforgettable experiences in life: the first time the head cheerleader leans in for that first kiss, the first time you look into the eyes of your newborn child, and the moment a prisoner breaks instead of dying.

I whispered, "It's over, Evan. No more. Just tell me what's going to happen, and I'll make the pain stop."

He spoke through an exhausted breath. "You can't stop them."

He wanted me to ask a question, but I wouldn't. I waited in silence until he said, "They're just going to blow up the Statue of Liberty. No one will be there. They're not going to hurt anyone."

"When are they going to do it?"

He gagged and coughed. "They'll do it without me. They can't be stopped."

"When, Evan? *When* are they going to do it?"

"Sunday . . . Sunday afternoon. What day is it?"

I showed no reaction to the revelation, but I had little doubt that everyone on the other side of the two-way mirror bolted into action.

Feigning disinterest, I said, "What about the second boat, the *Scimitar*?"

"What about it?" Brewer labored through the question, but I didn't relent.

"Where is it going, and what is their mission?"

He drew a rattling breath. "It doesn't matter. You can't stop them, either."

"What we do with the information doesn't concern you. Just tell me when and where, and I'll make all of this stop."

He slowly shook his head in forced arcs. "The cruise terminal in Miami."

I lifted his chin with a finger. "Listen to me, Evan. You're going to prison for the rest of your life, and there's nothing I can do about that, but . . . ."

He raised his eyes to meet mine again. "Please kill me."

"No, Evan. That's not what we do. We were never going to kill you, and I won't apologize for what happened to you today. Everything that happens in our lives is the direct result of our decisions. You chose to turn your back on our country, and what you're experiencing is the price for that decision."

"Just kill me."

"No. I won't kill you, but I will stop the pain."

He sighed. "You don't understand. It was too much."

"I know. What we do is extreme, but—"

"No," he hissed. "Not this. Everything before this. It was all too much. I couldn't . . ." His breath heaved, and his body shuddered. "They gave me a way out of it all. It was going to be—"

"Listen to me, Evan. They would've killed you. They weren't offering a way out. They were offering you a death sentence, and you accepted their offer. That makes you a traitor—an enemy of everything I love and everything you swore to defend."

"What are you going to do with me?"

"I'm going to surrender what's left of you to the men and women at Guantanamo Bay. What happens to you after that is none of my concern. My team and I will move on and forget you ever existed. That's the legacy you've chosen to leave behind—a forgotten traitor who failed his country, his family, and most of all, himself. I'm a compassionate man, Evan, but there are sins I cannot forgive, and yours are among those. You're the reason men like me are necessary, and for that, you must pay a price that cannot be taken away."

Tears flowed like rivers from his face, and I had no pity to give.

"I'll pray for you, Evan, for God is the only force in existence that can forgive you."

I cut the rope holding the shell of the man to the ceiling of the interrogation cell, and he fell to the deck in a wilted, lifeless heap. The medical team lifted him on the waiting gurney, administered the morphine his body longed to taste, and cuffed his wrists to the rails. His body would be kept alive, and his wounds would be mended, but the man's soul remained in dire peril that Doctor Shadrack couldn't heal, and despite my claims to the contrary, my team and I would never forget the hours we spent drawing the truth from deep within the tortured mind of a man who mocked the truth we clung to.

Chapter 31
Another Heart-to-Heart

There was only one place for me following the conclusion of Evan Brewer's interrogation, and I pushed into the CIC to find my team, the weapons officer, and Captain Sprayberry. "Is everyone up to speed?"

Skipper said, "We got it all, and I'm putting together a call with the Board."

I said, "Captain Sprayberry, put us in New York Harbor at full speed. I don't care who sees us running on the foils."

With a nod, he was on his feet and out the door, and I took a seat next to our analyst. "Have you sent the briefing package to the Board?"

"No, I thought it would be better to do this one live. Here they are."

I rolled back to see the monitors from a better angle, and soon, the screens filled with the images of our oracles.

The man said, "Good evening. I understand you have an update."

I glanced at Clark, and he said, "It's your show," so I faced the camera. "Yes, sir. We do. I apologize for the hour, but we just wrapped up the interrogation of Evan Brewer."

He said, "I trust it was productive?"

"It was. He confirmed the target we already knew, but he also divulged the time of the strike. They're planning to hit the Statue on Sunday afternoon. We're steaming north now."

"And Brewer's status?"

I considered my response before opening my mouth. "Moderate, non-life-threatening injuries, exhaustion, and some blood loss. He's in medical now. We'll have an update on his condition in the morning. May I assume he's bound for Gitmo?"

"You may," he said. "But we'll arrange a rendezvous to take him off your hands. Are you sure you've gotten everything out of him?"

"I believe so, but the boys at Gitmo may be able to shake his tree hard enough to make a little more fruit fall out. We have everything we need from him. He is suicidal, but that's to be expected. We won't leave him alone as long as he's in our custody."

"Very well," the man said. "What else do you have?"

I resituated myself in the chair. "We're tracking the original boat, the *Scimitar*, out of Havana. According to Brewer, it's bound for the Miami cruise ship port. We don't have a specific target beyond that. Our analyst in Silver Spring is tracking her, and we have the capability of crippling the vessel at will."

The man shared a glance with several other Board members and said, "Chase, we trust your judgment on this one, but in a perfect world, we'd like to make the apprehension or elimination as quiet as possible. We want Congressman Claven to believe the extremists failed. When men like him get desperate, they do foolish things, and we believe that'll open the door for us to step in and remove him from the scene."

"As you wish," I said. "But I can't promise an outside source won't pick up on the story and break it."

"We'll deal with that if and when it happens, but for now, proceed with the mindset of secrecy."

I nodded. "Wilco."

He continued. "I realize I don't have to reiterate this, but we want the terrorists alive, if possible."

"Yes, sir. I understand. But again, I can't make that promise. If they resist with extreme aggression, we'll have no choice other than protecting ourselves."

"Understood. Do you need anything from us?"

"Negative, sir. Just let Skipper know where to rendezvous with Brewer's pickup team."

"Plan for a rendezvous near Virginia Beach."

"SEALs?" I asked.

"Operators," was his only response.

"If there's nothing else, sir, my team needs some sleep."

"That's all we have, Chase. We're pleased with what you've done so far. Keep us in the loop, and keep up the good work."

Skipper closed the connection and spun in her seat. "There's one more thing." With the team hanging on her every word, she said, "I gained access to Claven's calendar, and he's scheduled for a press conference on Sunday evening at seven in Manhattan."

"That's convenient," I said. "How could he know something warranting a press conference is coming on Sunday afternoon?"

Clark said, "He must be one of those clair-a-vonts or something."

I palmed my forehead. "It never ends with you, does it?"

"Nope. I'm like a pomp-a-tential motion machine of wisdom."

"That's exactly what I was thinking. You're practically a modern-day Confucious."

* * *

With the *Lori Danielle* cruising at top speed high on her hydrofoils, the ride was smooth, and the ship emitted a hum that made for perfect sleeping conditions. When coming down from an adrenaline-charged operation, sleep typically comes as punctuation to sheer exhaustion, both mental and physical. That night, though, my mind and body succumbed to the relative peace of the ship's decks and bulkheads, and as Clark would say, I slept like something that sleeps a lot.

As if an explosion went off in my head, I sat bolt upright in my bed, looked down to see my prosthetic still in place at the end of my leg, and sprinted for the CIC. Thundering through the hatch, I caught Skipper completely off guard, and she nearly leapt from her skin.

"Jeez, Chase. What are you doing, and why don't you have any clothes on?"

There are people on Earth, like Skipper, who have the impressive capacity to store, process, and recall massive volumes of information in their heads. I've never been one of those people. I'm barely smart enough to remember to feed myself on a regular basis, and that morning, my knuckle-dragging brain apparently decided a pair of boxer shorts and a prosthetic leg were all the accessories I needed.

"Sorry, but this can't wait. Where's the *Scimitar*?"

She threw up her hands. "How would I know? You ordered to me to focus on our prey and hand the *Scimitar* off to Ginger."

"Get her on the phone!"

"Wow! Bossy much?"

"Just do it," I ordered, and the analyst's voice filled the space seconds later.

"Good morning. Let me guess. You're looking for a position update on the *Scimitar*."

"Exactly. Where is she?"

Ginger said, "She's a hundred twenty miles south-southeast of Miami, and if that's her target, she's got a terrible navigator on board."

"What do you mean?" I asked.

"They could've made Miami an hour ago with a direct route, but they're laying well offshore. I can't figure it out. Oh, and Chase, not that I mind the scenery, but why aren't you wearing any clothes?"

I shot a look up at the monitor to see Ginger's smiling face staring back at me, and for some reason, I was suddenly more self-conscious than I'd been thirty seconds earlier.

"I haven't picked up my laundry in a few days."

"It's a good look for you," she said. "If Penny ever decides she wants a two-legged man instead of"—she waved her finger at the camera—"that, there's room in my closet for a boot."

I shook my head. "I'll keep that in mind if Penny ever comes to her senses, but let's talk about the *Scimitar*. If she's not heading for Miami, where's she going?"

Ginger said, "It doesn't look like she's going anywhere. There's no rhyme or reason to her course."

I pictured the water 120 miles south-southeast of Miami. "How far is she from the nearest dry land?"

Ginger said, "Give me a second."

In little more than a second, the answer came. "She's sixty-five miles to the nearest piece of ground, but that's the West Side National Park on Andros Island in The Bahamas. The closest civilization is a hundred miles northeast at Red Bay, and that barely qualifies as civilization. There's no port and only a handful of residents."

"How fast are they moving?"

"Eleven knots for the last three hours."

I closed my eyes and studied every detail of our situation. When I had a reasonably well-devised plan, I said, "They're delaying, waiting for the prearranged time to hit a cruise ship in Miami."

Ginger said, "Hitting a cruise ship in Miami isn't an easy task. There's always a dozen Border Patrol and Miami Police boats around every ship leaving the fairway. I can't imagine them letting anybody get close enough to harm one of those ships."

I added Ginger's input to every other fact, opinion, and morsel of intel I had bouncing around in my head.

If I wanted to hit a cruise ship with a couple tons of explosives on board, when and where would I do it?

I said, "They're going to hit the ship when it slows down to drop off the harbor pilot outside the port."

"What makes you so sure?" Ginger asked.

"Because that's where I would do it. It's outside the protection of CBP and the Miami Marine police. It's a point at which the ship would be slow and un-maneuverable because of the proximity to the pilot boat. On top of that, it's close enough to land to get plenty of news coverage and inflict optimum fear. It would shut down the cruise industry for weeks, at least, and leave a lingering fear in the populous for years to come."

"Okay, I'll buy that, but how will they escape?"

I stared up at the camera. "When was the last time a true believer planned a post-bombing escape?"

Her expression fell, and words weren't necessary.

Skipper bit her bottom lip. "So, what are we going to do?"

I stood. "The first thing we'll do is have another talk with Brewer."

Hunter had been the most convincing interrogator, so I plucked him from his cabin and headed for sick bay. We found Brewer still cuffed to his gurney behind a double wall of curtains.

Hunter said, "Aww, doesn't he look peaceful?" He clamped down on Brewer's exposed toe with his viselike thumb and forefinger. "Wakey, wakey, Sleeping Beauty. You have some more to tell us."

Brewer yanked his foot from Hunter's grasp and jerked against his restraints. "What do you want? I told you everything I know."

Hunter leaned in as if examining the wounds on the traitor's face. "I need a little more convincing. You see, I think you left out a couple of key details, like when the *Scimitar* is going to hit its target."

Brewer made himself as small as possible on the gurney. "I told you what I know. They're going to hit a cruise ship in Miami."

"Yeah, we got that part," Hunter said, "but we'd like to narrow down a window of time for that little event."

"I don't know! I swear!"

Hunter grinned and giggled like a schoolgirl. "Oh, goody. He wants to come out and play some more."

He pulled the handcuff key from his pocket and unlocked both sets, where they were connected to the bedrails. With no concern for Brewer's personal space, my partner roughly rolled the man onto his side and linked the handcuffs together between Brewer's legs. With one motion, he lowered the bedrail and yanked him off the gurney. Brewer landed with a thud on the deck, and Hunter planted a boot on the inside of our prisoner's knee. With a few pounds of pressure, our friend developed an attitude of cooperation.

"Wait! Wait! All I know is—"

Before he could finish, Dr. Shadrack threw back the curtain. "What's going on in here?"

I said, "We're asking a couple of follow-up questions and encouraging our guest to provide the right answers."

"Not in here, you're not. I won't have this in my sick bay. You can take it somewhere else, but you're not doing it here."

Hunter put on his giddy expression again and yanked his belt from his pants. As if tying a steer's feet together in the rodeo, he wrapped the belt twice around Brewer's ankles and laced his hand through the loops. "This day just keeps getting better. Now I get to drag your treasonous ass all the way down to the interrogation cell and start our little dance party all over again."

Brewer bucked and pulled against his restraints and Hunter's strength, but he was no match for the cuffs, belt, and my partner's relentless determination. "Wait! It's the same time! I swear!"

That stopped Hunter in his tracks several strides from Brewer's bed. "The same time as what?"

"As the attack in New York. That's what they were doing in Havana . . . taking on explosives."

I planted my knee inside the man's thigh and pressed all my weight into the long muscles of his leg. "Which ship?"

"I don't know. I swear! If I knew, I'd tell—"

With a slight twist of my leg, I ground my kneecap further into his thigh. "Which ship, Evan? Either you tell me, or I'll walk away, and you and my friend can spend some quality time together back down in your favorite spot."

"I'm telling you, I don't know which ship, but they said something about making it the second or third outbound ship. That's all I know."

I could almost read the dread and fear on his face over what Hunter would do to him back inside the interrogation cell.

I lifted my knee about an inch and drove it back into his thigh. "If you know anything else that you haven't told us, and we find out . . . Well, Brewer, let's just say I wouldn't want to be in your shoes."

"I know the mastermind," he blurted out.

I increased the pressure on his thigh. "I think we've got those bases covered, but if you think of anything else, be sure to let us know."

"No, I mean the real mastermind. Not Hamza al Kassis."

Although I couldn't let him see my reaction, I lifted my knee. "If al Kassis isn't behind this, who is?"

"No, al Kassis is way up the chain, but it was the American who came up with the whole idea. He's the one who recruited me and the others."

"What others?"

"Kennedy's team."

I said, "What's the guy's name? The mastermind?"

Brewer groaned. "I don't know his name, but he goes by Plymouth. He's a little guy, maybe five-eight and a buck eighty. Black hair and eyes, maybe fifty or a little younger. It was hard to tell."

I buzzed Skipper. "Hey, look for a high-level guy who goes by the name Plymouth. Dark hair and eyes, five-eight, one-eighty. Brewer says he's an American and the mastermind."

"I've already got him," Skipper said. "I didn't know how he fit in, but I'll tell you everything when you get back up to the CIC."

Chapter 32
Plymouth Rock

There were no pleasantries when I stepped through the hatch and into the combat information center.

Skipper hooked the leg of a chair and dragged it beside her workstation. "Sit down. You're not going to believe this."

I obeyed and slid onto the chair.

Skipper said, "What do you know about the structure of Homeland Security?" I stammered, and she said, "It doesn't matter. There's a guy named Alexander Rutledge, and he's the assistant secretary for Counterterrorism and Threat Prevention and Law Enforcement. He works for the undersecretary of the Office of Strategy, Policy, and Plans, who works directly for the secretary. None of that matters except for the fact that Rutledge is like third from the top at Homeland."

I said, "I'm listening."

She shuffled through some handwritten notes. "Okay, so any officer like Rutledge qualifies for executive protection on trips where security is likely to be an issue. Everybody who falls into that category has a code name assigned by the Secret Service, even when the Secret Service isn't providing the protection. Rutledge is Plymouth Rock."

"Okay, I get that, but that doesn't mean he's the Plymouth that Brewer was talking about."

She said, "You're right, it doesn't, but I'm not finished. Rutledge's wife, Gloria Swain Downing, is listed as one of the members of a Delaware corporation that—among three others—owns Analytical Systems, Incorporated, Jack Flannery's company that stands to benefit in the hundreds of millions when Congressman Claven's bill becomes law."

I leaned back in my chair, stared at the ceiling, and unconsciously hummed. "I'm just a bill . . . sitting here on Capitol Hill . . ."

"Chase, this is no time for Schoolhouse Rock. Get it together."

"Print out a picture of Rutledge." The sheet of paper was soon in my hand, and I said, "I'll be right back."

My next stop was sick bay, but I made the trip alone. Brewer was back on his gurney with his cuffs back in their correct configuration.

I held up the picture in front of his face. "Don't make this harder than it has to be. Who is this guy?"

Brewer squinted and then widened his eyes. "That's Plymouth."

"You met him?"

"Yeah, he came to my house."

I shoved the paper in my pocket. "Are you willing to testify to that?"

He screwed up his face. "Testify? Yeah, right. Like this thing will ever go to court. But sure, I'll testify if get an immunity deal."

I wanted to tie the knot they'd use to hang Brewer from the gallows, but what happened to him was so far out of my hands that I could make any promises he wanted to hear and they'd never have any value beyond convincing him to cooperate without ripping out any more of his fingernails.

I said, "I can't make any promises, but I can lobby for a reduced sentence."

He mumbled something, but I'd long since stopped listening.

Back in the CIC, I handed the picture back to Skipper. "That's Plymouth, all right. I want a tail on him, Flannery, and both Clavens until we wrap this thing up."

"Overt or covert?"

"If we go overt," I said, "they might run."

"Yeah, or they might get nervous and make a mistake."

"They've already made all the mistakes we need for now. Make the tails covert for now."

"Consider it done," she said. "I'll also put together a brief for the Board."

"Good. How far are we from New York, and how far behind us are the bad guys?"

"We're six hours out, and they're twelve hours behind us."

I checked my watch. "And today is Saturday, right?"

"That's right."

I left Skipper to her toils and headed for the aft deck. Along the way, I texted the team and gave the order to huddle up. We gathered on the deck, and I caught everyone up on the recent intel.

Hunter said, "This thing is getting outside of our world. It's starting to sound like a game for the lawyers."

"That's about to change," I said. "We'll be in New York in less than six hours, and our playmates will be twelve hours behind. It's time for us to do what we do best."

"Kill bad guys and break things?" Clark said.

"Something like that. Get your kits together. We're digging in at the Statue of Liberty, and we're going to keep the old girl on her feet."

Hunter clapped. "Now, that's what I'm talking about."

I said, "We've still got one decision to make before we strap on our battle rattle. All of you know about the *Scimitar* laying off Miami so it can hit a cruise ship simultaneously with the attack on the statue." Heads nodded, and I said, "I want to blow their rudder away and leave them adrift and taking on water. The wind and Gulf Stream would likely put them aground on Andros within half a day. That'll buy us—or somebody—the time to roll them up."

Singer held up a finger. "There's something you're not considering. There's no way they're going to let themselves be taken. If we blow the rudders away, they'll assess the damage to figure out if they can make Miami and steer on differential power. If the hole we make is too big for their bilge pumps, they'll roll out their prayer mats and set off the explosives meant for the cruise ship so they can pick out their seventy-two virgins."

I turned to our big-brained giant. "Do some math, big man. What do you think?"

He and Hunter talked through the explosive charges and their exact placement on the yacht.

Gator confirmed Hunter's recollection of the positions and quantities, and Mongo said, "That'll blow more than just the rudders, and I doubt they'll have the onboard pumps to manage that much water. When we came up with that plan, we wanted to be able to make them run twenty miles—not a hundred miles—into shallow water."

"Is there a way to blow only part of the charges?" I asked.

Hunter laughed. "Not hardly. That's not how we rig underwater charges. When I set them, I make sure that every ounce will go boom."

"In that case," I said, "I'm open for suggestions. If I make the call, I'm going to sink them where they sit."

My team was rarely short on opinions or ideas, but at that moment, no one made a sound. I could've taken their silence as support and approval for my desire to sink the *Scimitar* and leave her in the depths of the turbulent Florida Straits, but an unease behind Singer's eyes drew me from my confidence and left me desperate to know what was happening inside his head. Was he processing the decision with the eye of one of the world's deadliest snipers or with the heart of the godliest man I'd ever know?

"Let's have it, Singer."

Our sniper was a man of few words, but when he spoke, the wisdom that poured from his mouth was undeniable. I learned how to stay alive from Clark Johnson. I learned how to truly fly with precision from Disco. I learned how to love from Penny. But every time Singer sat beside me and spoke in his soft, confident tone, I learned humility and peace.

He bowed his head and appeared to replay a distant memory. "A long time ago, before I met most of you, I crawled on my belly for half a mile through a landscape that could've been the moon— if the moon were populated by snakes, spiders, scorpions, and countersnipers."

A brief pause seemed to freshen the memory even more. "It took eleven hours to reach my objective and two more to construct my hide. I was alone with enough water to last three days, if I rationed it properly, and enough protein bars to keep me alive for those scorching days and endless shivering nights. I was on the side of a mountain that didn't have a name, overlooking a valley that seemed to be Hell's turnpike. The next forty-four hours were spent with one eye focused through one of the best scopes that has ever been put on a rifle."

The longer Singer spoke, the closer each of us was drawn to him, and the softer his tone became.

"My target was a bombmaker named Muhammad Zalmai. He was elusive and terrifying. Zalmai killed more Americans in the twelve months prior to my mission than all other Al Qaeda bombmakers combined. This man had to be eliminated."

He paused and drew a mouthful of water from his CamelBak. "I watched him through that scope for nearly two full days and nights as he constructed a device with such precision and care that I became fascinated with every drop of solder and every connection of wire to a component. But that wasn't the most fascinating part of those two days. Zalmai wasn't alone. He was demonstrating and teaching his skill to a young boy of maybe ten. Occasionally, he would allow the boy to make a connection or place a component into the collection of electronics that would, no doubt, become the brain of his next weapon. I had no hesitation about my mission. It was well justified, necessary, and it would save American lives in the years to come. I was the first sniper to lay a reticle across Zalmai's chest, and I would be the last."

Singer wiped the sweat from his brow with the sleeve of his shirt, took another drink, and continued. "I wanted to stay where I was and continue watching until the buyer arrived to collect and pay for the deadly implement Zalmai and the boy had created, but I was down to a pint of water and two protein bars. It was time to fulfill my purpose, so I raised my head from the scope, stretched my neck, and pressed my cheek back to the stock of the rifle. My crosshairs were crisp and clear, hovering like a ghost over Zalmai's chest. I felt the flesh of my finger flatten against the face of the trigger as I applied pressure. The range was precisely measured, the wind was estimated with every ounce of skill I possessed, and the elevation was applied perfectly. The trigger broke identically as it had every time I'd fired that weapon. The round left the muzzle and far outran the echoing report of the rifle across the valley. Zalmai would never hear the shot, but his student would. I counted the tenths of seconds and watched Muhammad Zalmai's torso turn to pink mist a full two seconds before the boy would hear the thunder."

He took a long, deep breath and stared down at the deck. "I cleaned up my hide and crawled back out, but not on the same path I'd used three days before. When I was picked up by my team a mile from where I'd taken the shot, I was out of food, water, energy, and the ability to stay awake. I poured a quart of water down my throat, and the medic stuck an IV in my arm before I collapsed with exhaustion."

Our sniper took another long swallow of water and sat in silence until I said, "Is that story supposed to teach me patience?"

He slowly shook his head. "When I woke up, there was an old, crusty SF guy standing beside my bunk, and I knew he was standing there to deliver a message I didn't want to hear. He'd said, 'That was a hell of a shot you made on Zalmai, but the man you killed wasn't Muhammad. He was Nassar, Zalmai's brother, and he was teaching his son to build a transistor radio for the boy's tenth birthday.' So, no, Chase. This story isn't supposed to teach you patience. It's supposed to teach you prudence. We know the *Scimitar* was in Havana, and now we know she's south of Miami. Everything else we think we know about her came from the mouth of a traitor. If you sink her, we'll never know if Brewer is telling the truth. We're not out of water or protein bars, and we've got plenty of time to watch, identify, and act."

I let the *Scimitar* live for the time being, but we wouldn't take our eyes off her.

Chapter 33
Damsel in Distress

The six-hour run to New York City passed in fast-forward, and the Board paved the way for us through cooperation with the U.S. Park Police. The commander of the Statue of Liberty protection detachment agreed to stand down and allow his little island to temporarily fall into our more-than-capable hands, with one caveat. The full force of the assigned Park Police would stand by, aboard three vessels, within two minutes of the island, just in case we weren't as good as advertised and the terrorists overran both us and the island. No such concern found purchase in my mind, but I agreed to the placement of the small force in an effort to keep the peace between our operation and the National Park Service.

We passed beneath the Verrazzano-Narrows Bridge and mounted the RHIB for the first of our two runs to Liberty Island. We'd put the boots of our full team on the ground before delivering our gear and equipment on the second run.

Just as the Park Police promised, the island was completely abandoned, and everything about it felt wrong. The place should've been crawling with tourists, National Park Service employees, tour guides, and school children on field trips, but instead, an ominous tone seemed to ring from the hallowed ground on which Lady Liberty—and now my team—stood.

The second RHIB run delivered our gear, and we humped every piece of equipment we might need to our rapidly approaching rendezvous with Burj Aldam, the terrorist group working in alliance with honorless men—traitorous Americans bent on selling fear to the highest bidder to enrichen themselves and enslave the populous.

With our equipment staged, I took Singer by the shoulder and motioned toward Lady Liberty's crown. "Are you thinking what I'm thinking?"

"Great minds," he said, and trotted toward the base of the statue with a pair of rifles slung over his shoulders and the tools he'd need to provide the God's-eye overwatch we'd come to trust like a child's security blanket. With Singer's eyes and his flawless craft behind a rifle, nothing in the environment would surprise those of us anchored to the ground. No one on the team, including Singer, wanted his rifle to thunder, but should the necessity arise, there was no one on Earth we'd rather have on that weapon.

The eleven points of the star-shaped rampart surrounding the base of the statue made for easily defendable high cover and concealment. The seven remaining shooters, including me, would dig in behind the protection of those walls and prepare for the coming engagement.

Having hours to prepare a fighting position was a luxury we rarely experienced. Walking or running into a gunfight was our typical operational style, but not on that night. Everything about the mission up to that point felt rushed and reactionary, but creating nests from which we'd both start and end the fight gave us the confidence everyone needed. For the first time in the operation, we were out front and waiting for our foe to walk into our web instead of chasing them across the water.

Each of us built our fighting positions under the same basic premise of creating a defendable, concealed nest from which to fight aggressively without giving the enemy any unnecessary advantage, but each of us also built our own comforts and peculiarities into our nests to give us any additional advantage—even if that advantage were only psychological. I had every faith Singer was doing exactly the same nearly two hundred feet above our heads in the crown.

When everyone reported they'd finished constructing their fighting positions, I called everyone to my nest. "I want each of us to study everyone else's position in case we have to consolidate and fight from another perspective."

Nods and grunts of agreement rose, and we spent an hour studying and improving each other's hidey-holes.

Singer descended from his high perch and briefed the team on his perspective from above. "I've got excellent visibility in nearly three hundred sixty degrees. The arm blocks about ten degrees of visibility, but there's enough room to maneuver in the crown to overcome that obstacle. As long as the weather is good, I'll have unlimited visibility, but I need a few hours to watch the typical traffic on the water."

Gator cocked his head. "What does that mean?"

Singer said, "It's impossible to know what's out of place if you don't know what's typical. After I watch the boat traffic for a few hours, I'll pick up patterns of operation. That'll give me the ability to recognize when someone isn't following the patterns I expect."

Gator shook his head. "I've got so much to learn."

I threw an arm across his shoulder. "We all do, kid, but look around. You won't find a finer staff of teachers than these anywhere in the world."

Singer leaned toward me. "Let me borrow him for a couple hours."

I checked my watch. "Teach well, Professor."

The sniper gave his understudy a shove. "Last one to the crown buys the first round."

Gator said, "First round of what? You don't drink."

Those seven words out of Gator's mouth gave Singer the only head start he'd need to outclimb the decade-and-a-half younger warrior. I never remember either man gloating or groaning over the results of the race, but I'm confident Singer turned it into a lesson.

While Gator was being taught how to understand the world from three hundred feet above the water, the rest of the team and I scoured the statue for pre-set explosives just in case the terrorist's plans ran deeper than we suspected. After two hours of acquainting ourselves with every inch of the interior of the statue, we were satisfied the damsel was not in distress, and like courtly knights of old, we were determined to defend not only her moral chastity and virtue, but also her very existence.

With the full team reassembled at the base of the grand old girl, celestial noon arrived, and like the navigators who once stood on the decks of tall ships in search of the freedom for which Lady Liberty stood, I made the observation with my gaze cast into the heavens and confirmed the clock of my eye with the one on my wrist.

"CIC, Alpha One."

Skipper answered. "Go for CIC."

"How long do we have to wait for the guests of honor to arrive?"

"I was seconds away from calling you. They're less than an hour southeast, but they've reduced speed considerably."

Hunter said, "That prop shaft bearing finally gave up the ghost."

"That's good news," I said. "That way, we won't have any trouble catching them if they turn tail and run."

Skipper said, "I don't think they have any plan of doing any running, no matter what resistance they face on that island."

"We're going to give them all the resistance they can stand, and then some."

As the words left my lips, a sense of impending dread came over me, and I ran through every detail of the plan to defend the island and statue and played those plans against the determination and capabilities of the approaching enemies of freedom. Nothing about the terrorists frightened me. We had them outnumbered, outgunned, and out-positioned. Unless they ran a recruiting drive on their way up the eastern seaboard, we were a superior force in every way.

"Just don't get overconfident," Skipper said as if feeling the same sense that had overtaken me in the moment.

I said, "When they approach the Verrazzano-Narrows, put a pair of drones on the boat and at least four in the air above the island."

"Roger. The drones are standing by with a full complement of replacements should anything happen to the first flight."

It was time to change focus momentarily. "Where's the *Scimitar*?"

Ginger's voice sounded inside my head. "She's two and a half hours from the port of Miami and bearing on the port at twenty knots."

I glanced up at Singer as if asking permission to cash in my voucher of prudence for a writ of destruction, and he gave me the nod I both expected and desired.

"Dispatch the Coast Guard—or whoever you've got lined up —and put the *Scimitar* adrift."

I could almost hear the satisfaction in her tone when Ginger said, "We've got a few former frogmen who needed a little extra spending money, so we told them you'd write a nice check if they helped us out."

I said, "Tell them I'll write an even bigger check if they can pluck those guys off that boat while they're still breathing."

"Frogmen always love a challenge, especially when it comes with a bonus."

"How long will it take for them to intercept the *Scimitar*?"

She said, "They're just over the horizon, so they can close the distance in twenty minutes."

"Twenty minutes?" I asked.

Ginger said, "Yeah, Chase. Twenty minutes. You're not the only person on Earth with a Mark Five patrol boat."

"What would I ever do without the two best analysts on Earth?"

Skipper said, "Our status extends beyond the limits of just this planet, so we'd appreciate some galactic praise if you wouldn't mind."

"The finest in all creation," I said. "Have the squids initiate their approach and blow the charge."

In a foolish effort, I turned an ear toward the coast of South Florida as if I could hear the explosion from a thousand miles away.

Skipper said, "Fire in the hole."

I almost held my breath until she said, "The *Scimitar* has slowed to six knots and turned northeast."

Hunter gave me a wink and shrugged. "Sorry. I may have gotten a little carried away."

I said, "They didn't slow. They stopped, and those northeast-bound six knots are the handiwork of the Gulfstream."

Ginger said, "SEALs are in visual range and requesting permission to sink the vessel to force them to abandon ship."

I turned to Mongo, and he said, "They're worried about boarding the yacht and having the terrorist blow the thing to Valhalla."

I said, "Surrender the operation to the SEALs, and tell them to make the call that keeps them alive and puts the bad guys in their net."

Ginger said, "I'll keep you posted on their progress."

Skipper said, "Our target is approaching the Narrows. Drones away."

I met the eyes of every man. "Am I missing anything?"

Clark put on that crooked grin that foretold of the demise of many a fair maiden across the globe and devastation for countless enemies. The tide of battle was fast approaching, and not only would we meet that tide with determination in the name of everything we loved and held dear, but we'd also beat back that rising tide of war until it ebbed in a crimson flow, with the blood of the vanquished being devoured by the sea around us, until their purpose was nothing more than a forgotten battle cry in the depths of the boundless abyss.

Chapter 34
Party Crashers

I gave the order to disperse and man our fighting positions. Singer disappeared into the depths of the statue on his way to the perch, high above, where he would direct the battle and silence any gun we couldn't defeat from the ground. The rest of the team sprinted to their chosen nests with their eyes and barrels trained on the five miles of open water that lay between Liberty Island and the Verrazzano-Narrows Bridge.

I changed radio frequencies and called the National Park Police, who were poised for action in their patrol boats barely two minutes away. "Police One, Alpha One."

"Go, Alpha One."

"We're in position, and the target vessel is inside five miles. Stand by for the QRF call from any member of Alpha Team or CIC."

The commander said, "Roger. Quick Reaction Force is standing by."

Back on our discrete frequency, I conducted a radio check with every firing position. We were ready, but in my mind, our foe was not.

Singer announced, "Alpha Six has target vessel in sight and approaching on plane."

"Roger."

288 · CAP DANIELS

Gator said, "Alpha Eight has vessel in sight approximately thirty-seconds out."

I raised my head to add my eyes to the others on the island peering seaward until I had the boat in sight. As it grew nearer, six men appeared in the bow of the vessel with bulging backpacks strapped to their shoulders. The speed and direction of the vessel looked as if they were planning to run her aground at the southeastern tip of the island, but if they didn't reduce speed, the men in the bow would be ejected from the boat and likely wounded or killed in the collision with the jagged rocks lining the protective seawall around the shore.

At the last possible moment, the bow of the boat dipped as the helmsman applied full reverse thrust to avoid the collision I predicted. The man at the helm made seven, and I was baffled by the head count. Where had the extra personnel come from? The team preparing to take Liberty Island had grown to at least seven men, and the aggressors aboard the *Scimitar* all added up to a number that none of us expected. At that moment, though, no count could change our mission objective. We would defeat the force with which we were presented, regardless of their might and number.

I lost sight of the boat as it passed beneath the edge of the parapet, but from his lofty perch, Singer had no such limitations.

"Alpha Six has seven . . . Stand by . . . Make that eight combatants on the rocks, and the boat is turning away to the south."

"Is the boat adrift?" I asked.

Singer said, "Negative. It is underway, making way and under command."

That's nine bodies, at least. How many more uninvited guests are going to crash our party?

"Let them come," I said. "We want 'em up here with us. We'll pin them down at the base of the statue and restrict our fire toward the base instead of onto the water. They don't appear to be armed. Do you agree, Alpha Six?"

"No arms visible," came Singer's answer, and six more clicks came as acknowledgment of my order.

Skipper said, "Drone footage confirms Alpha Six's count, and no weapons visible."

"Roger."

The unique configuration of the bulwarks gave each of us an angle of fire on the base of the statue that put no one else in the line of fire. If the terrorists emerged en masse, we could pin them to the walls without risking the lives of any noncombatant in the area. As badly as I wanted the Arabs in my trap, I would go to great extremes to avoid involving innocent bystanders.

As we waited for them to emerge, I counted the thundering heartbeats inside my head. Sufficient time passed for the men to have climbed the stairs, even at a moderate pace, and step into the open.

Where are they? What's happening?

"CIC, Alpha One. Do you see our targets?"

Skipper said, "Negative, Alpha One. I started the clock when they stepped through the doorway. That was eighty seconds ago."

I said, "Alpha Six, do you have eyes on our prey?"

Singer said, "Negative. I'm blind straight down."

A gunfight in a stairwell is almost as deadly as a knife fight with Anya, but if the terrorists were truly unarmed, it would be like shooting fish in a barrel.

I closed my eyes and willed my mind to make a decision. "Alpha Two, Three, and Four, clear that stairwell."

I neither expected nor heard a response. Instead, Clark, Hunter, and Mongo exploded from their fighting positions and closed on the upper opening of the only stairwell the terrorists could be using.

If the extremists were planting massive charges in the stairwell, I may have just ordered three men to their deaths, but if they were stalling for some other reason, having them caught in a fatal funnel was a gift from above.

Skipper's uncertain tone rang in my head. "Uh, Alpha One, the Park Police are moving in."

"Say again," I demanded, certain I hadn't heard her correctly.

She said, "The Park Police boats are moving in from the west and north. What's going on down there?"

I thumbed my radio to change to the police frequency. "QRF, stand down!"

No answer came, so I grabbed my radio to double-check the frequency. "National Park Police, Alpha One. Stand down. Stand down. Stand down. Do not approach. Acknowledge immediately!"

Nothing.

What's happening? Why is none of this making sense? What have I missed?

My answer came amid the pulsing echoes of 30-caliber automatic rifle fire.

I yelled, "Down! Down! Down!"

When I was certain my team was either in the prone position in open ground or well covered in their nests, I said, "The Park Police have opened up on the targets. They must be exposed below."

Skipper said, "Negative, Alpha One. There are no targets exposed on the level below. The cops are firing at nothing."

I growled at myself for agreeing to let the National Park Police play any role. The gig was up, and there would be no way to keep the incident off every television station in the English-speaking world. The cops had blown our operation. All we could do was apprehend the terrorists, dismantle their explosives, and deal with the fallout.

As my anger became rage, the unmistakable pop, whistle, and hum of supersonic rounds cracked around my head.

In that instant, I gave an order I never thought I'd issue. "Singer, they're not firing at the terrorists. They're firing on us. Silence those guns and kill the boats."

Our sniper's calm baritone rang, "Roger."

I continued issuing instructions. "All Alpha ground elements, remain under cover. Do not engage!"

Six clicks answered, and Singer's rifle sounded like the rolling thunder from the heavens. Four rounds broke the early afternoon air, and the incoming fire was reduced considerably. Heavy fire continued to pour in from the west, and Clark, Hunter, and Mongo low-crawled to the western wall.

Singer reported, "They're in the shadow of the arm. I can't get an angle."

I was on the verge of ordering my team to open fire on U.S. federal law enforcement officers in New York City, but before I could give the order, Skipper said, "Little Bird is airborne and inbound."

A thousand conflicting decisions pranged together in my skull as I tried to develop a plan to neutralize the short-term problem of the Park Police and still deal with the long-term issue of the explosives strapped to the backs of seven Arabs in the stairwell a hundred feet away.

The buzz of the Little Bird thrummed overhead as Gun Bunny crossed the torch of the statue by inches and banked hard to the southwest. Ronda No-H hung from her harness behind the GE Minigun and laced a 6,000-round-per-minute line of 7.66 x 51 across the water, just in front of the bow of the still-racing police boat.

The helmsman reacted and broke north back toward Manhattan, and Gun Bunny mirrored his turn and gave chase. The skilled helmsman executed high-speed S-turns in an effort to evade

Ronda's fire from above, but the Minigun was silent for the moment. She wouldn't fire on a fleeing enemy, especially an enemy wearing the uniforms of our nation.

Skipper said, "The boat to the northeast is making way again."

Singer said, "I'm on it." Seconds later, he said, "I took out the steering, but they're motoring inbound and steering by two officers wrestling the outboard. I can't take out the engine without putting the officers down. Make the call, Alpha One."

I didn't hesitate. "Sink the boat, Alpha Six."

Five thunderous rounds echoed from Singer's 50-cal, and he said, "They're on the way to the bottom."

The weight of command is a burden few men can truly bear, but making the call to fire on Americans was too heavy for anyone. I wouldn't give the order to kill the police officers, but I would destroy their machines and their will to continue the fight.

"Little Bird, Alpha One. Keep that boat off the island, but do not engage personnel."

Gun Bunny said, "Roger. We'll hold them off."

"Push them to the east if you can so Alpha One can put them on the bottom."

She said, "We'll push them if that's what you want, but we can sink them in ten seconds."

"Keep pushing them east for now." I called Skipper. "Get the Board on the phone, and get a directive. I don't want to shoot those cops."

"I'm on it," she said in the same instant my trainwreck became a head-on collision.

I yelled, "All Alpha elements, our primary targets are on the move. Pin them down!"

Every gun on the ground turned toward the base of the statue as the terrorists with their heavily laden packs exited the stairwell opening. Hunter, Mongo, and Clark resumed their rush toward the base of the statue with M4s shouldered and trained on the would-be human bombs.

My three commandos froze in their tracks and dived into the prone position.

Clark said, "They've all got dead man's switches."

I broke from cover to visually confirm Clark's report, and my heart sank. He was right. Each of the terrorists carried an activated switch in his right hand with the trigger depressed. The instant any one of them released the trigger, his pack would turn into a concussive blast big enough to decapitate anyone closer than fifty feet.

I was in a gunfight and airborne assault with the National Park Service police and facing seven maniacs who couldn't wait to blow themselves to the promised land. There was no good decision to be made. My superior position had been reduced to a suicide stand from which we may never escape, and I had made every decision that put us in the middle of the chaos. Anything I did next would only worsen our situation, but doing nothing meant losing Lady Liberty, and our lives, in the coming seconds. If desperation had a face, my situation would be its countenance.

Chapter 35
The Cavalry

The only possible good news came from the voice of an angel. Skipper said, "The NYPD Marine Unit is responding, and deadly force is authorized against all aggressors."

I closed my eyes and sent up a prayer of thanks and a cry for absolution from what I would do next.

"Little Bird, Alpha One. Sink all Park Service Police vessels by any necessary means."

Just as any responsible operator would do, Gun Bunny questioned my command. "Verify open fire on the boats, Alpha One?"

"Affirmative! Sink all three boats, but do not fire on the NYPD."

Ronda's Minigun drummed its deadly song as she poured hundreds of rounds into the remaining operable boat. I still didn't like the feeling in my gut, but the traitors on those boats were no better than Evan Brewer or any of the men with a handful of dead man's triggers.

The second morsel of positive information rang in my head when Skipper said, "FDNY is responding with six firefighting vessels. They'll be on the scene in minutes."

The battlefield roar filled my head as the Little Bird hummed overhead, Ronda's Minigun belched fire, and the sirens of the NYPD vessels approached from every direction.

Amidst the chaos, clarity fell upon me, and I asked, "CIC, do you have comms with the fireboats?"

"Affirmative."

"How far out are they?"

A beat later, she said, "The first two are on the scene, and the rest are only seconds behind."

"Have them pour every ounce of water they can pump onto the base of the statue, and don't stop until their pumps melt through the decks."

"Roger, Alpha One. Stand by for water."

I didn't have to wait long. The first stream came across the parapet directly above my head, followed an instant later by a massive steam from the north.

Bullets in the brains of the terrorists would release the triggers, and we would fail. We had only one shot of saving ourselves and the statue. Without a moment's hesitation, I ordered, "Take them, hand to hand."

None of my men faltered, delayed, or questioned my command. Their boots pounded the ground growing wetter by the second, and they collided with the bombers like linebackers on an errant quarterback. Every one of us had to succeed, or we would all die in the resulting explosion. I had no idea if the water pouring down from the cannons aboard the fireboats would do anything to dampen the explosions if they came, but it was too late to worry about such a trivial concern. We had our very lives and the lives of the team in our hands.

My shoulder hit my bomber just below his chin, and my right hand gripped his left where he held the trigger. I crushed his thumb against the plastic loop and pinned it between our bodies, desperately working to keep him from releasing his grip. I threw a powerful knee-strike to his midsection, bending him at the waist and sending a rush of air from his lungs as he collapsed against me.

I rechecked our grip on the trigger and followed him to the ground. With his lungs empty and mine full, I was in command of the fight until a massive wall of water poured down on us, forcing me from on top of the bomber and onto the muddy ground. Nothing mattered except containing the trigger, so I let the fall happen and reached for my right hand with my left. That momentary lapse of defensive judgment cost me a right cross from the terrorist to my jaw, and I saw watery stars encircle my head.

Maintain the trigger, Chase. Maintain!

As I regained the wherewithal to continue the fight, I abandoned the hand-to-hand battle and drew my pistol with my left hand. As the weapon cleared the top of my holster, I tried to spin it into the palm of my left hand to end the fight with the press of the Glock's trigger, but my opponent wasn't ready to surrender.

He threw an elbow to my face just as the pistol spun in my hand and a second blast of water hit us like a freight train. We rolled across the sodden ground with my hand still clenched over his, and the undeniable report of a pistol sounded somewhere to my right. If one of the bombs went off, I'd be reduced to mist before the sound could make its way into my skull, so the pistol shot served only to strengthen my resolve. One of the bombers was likely standing in line to meet his maker.

As I pulled myself from my momentary celebration, the realization of my pistol slipping from my palm exploded in my psyche, and the battle raged on. My target fought like an animal with his right hand and both feet while he yanked his left in a relentless effort to free the trigger from my grasp. It wouldn't happen. I'd die fighting the man before I'd allow him the precious prize of the explosion he so desperately wanted.

I absorbed blow after blow and retaliated after every shot with a counterstrike of my own. The man was a worthy opponent and a more-than-capable fighter.

His demise came when he leaned back in preparation to deliver a forehead strike to my nose. He telegraphed the coming attack as if he'd switched on a flashing neon sign, and I took full advantage of his foolish error. I drove my shoulder into his presented throat and forced him backward until we collided with the base of the statue's pedestal.

Water still rained down on us in sheets, and a second pistol shot cracked the roar of the falling water. I couldn't see any of my brothers or any of my opponents, but I had no other choice than to trust my team to complete the mission, stay alive, and keep the rest of us breathing in the land of the living.

If there was any radio chatter, I couldn't hear it. I had no way to know if my radio still worked in the deluge of crashing water. Comms, in that moment, would be nothing more than a wasted distraction, so I seized the brief instant of advantage I had and drew my knife. That weapon didn't care which hand it was in. It knew only one thing—kill on command. And kill, it did.

The upward strike landed beneath the bomber's ribcage, and I twisted the blade with all my might. The diaphragm, heart, and lungs were my targets. Any or all of them would be sufficient to destroy my enemy's ability to carry on, and his soul left this world before his mortal body wilted to the ground.

I followed him down and forced the trigger from his hand. A pair of zip-ties temporarily secured the trigger, and two more pistol shots split the liquid air.

I lost count of the shots fired as I caught my breath and battled my way against the onslaught of high-pressure water until I fell across a dead body with his two thumbs forced through the body of the trigger, holding the device in place. The man had no face after the 9mm round made its way on its deadly course through his skull.

The next body I encountered was still breathing, and from his monstrous size, I had no question who I'd found.

"Are you all right?" I yelled.

"Yeah, I'm good," Mongo answered. "You?"

"Have you still got comms?"

"I don't know. Maybe."

At his feet lay a corpse with zip-ties circling his left thumb and the plastic body of the trigger.

I stayed on Mongo's hip, and we backed away from the base of the statue to escape the monsoon. As we cleared the wall of water, I collided with another pair of bodies. To my delight, I wiped the water from my face to see Gator lying on his back with his legs wrapped around the waist of one of the bombers and his arm wrapped tightly around the man's neck. The bomber's left arm lay in a twisted, broken angle with the new guy's thumb pinning the trigger to its stop.

I stared down at him, and Gator said, "You wanted one of them alive, right?"

I nodded, and he said, "Well, here you go. Take this one. I'm going back in."

He shoved the still-breathing but badly wounded bomber into my arms, and I replaced his thumb with mine.

Another zip-tie job secured the trigger, and Mongo planted a massive boot in the center of the man's chest. "You just stay down, and I won't have to crush you."

I fumbled for my radio and found the green light still illuminated. With exhaustion pouring from my lips, I said, "CIC, Alpha One. Stop the water."

I didn't hear Skipper's reply, but I suddenly knew how Noah felt on that 41st day when the rain stopped. My team was scattered about the base of the very symbol of why we were on the Earth, the essence of our necessity. And at the feet of each of my men lay the bodies—some still breathing—of would-be martyrs of the jihad being waged by Burj Aldam, Hamza al Kassis, Jack Flannery, and Congressman Richard Claven.

As if on cue, each of us fell to our knees, and I made the last meaningful transmission of the operation. "Mission complete, but we're going to need a few bomb techs up here."

The next sound I heard was a commanding voice over a bull-horn. "Hold your fire! NYPD! Hold your fire!"

Seven voices, including mine, answered in succession. "Clear . . . clear . . . clear . . ."

A column of men in black SWAT uniforms and full combat kits emerged from the same stairwell the bombers utilized what seemed like hours before.

The same authoritative voice—this time without the bullhorn —asked, "Who's in command?"

I held up a hand, and the man stepped beside me. "Is that your chopper with the Minigun?"

I gave him a nod, and he said, "I recommend getting that thing down here and getting your asses off my island. I never saw you, and you were never here."

It took two trips, but before the television cameras arrived, eight pairs of muddy boots stood on the deck of the Research Vessel *Lori Danielle* as it steamed eastward into international waters of the North Atlantic.

Epilogue

In the days that followed, as my team and I recuperated on the island of Bermuda, officers of the U.S. Department of Homeland Security and the FBI apprehended Alexander Rutledge, the assistant secretary for Counterterrorism at Homeland, CIA Case Officer Richard Andrew Claven III, American businessman Jack Flannery, twelve officers of the National Park Service police, Retired CIA Case Officer Quentin Palmer, and Congressman Richard Andrew Claven II, following testimony by Evan Brewer and three failed suicide bombers of Burj Aldam.

The NYPD earned the credit they deserved for capturing or killing all of the potential attackers of the mighty Lady Liberty that would continue to stand vigil off the tip of Manhattan, thumbing her nose at any enemy who dared try to bring her down.

We gathered as a team on the stern deck of our ship, and I thanked every man and woman who contributed to the success of our mission. Four of the men I thanked wore faces none of us had ever seen, but I had a feeling they'd become familiar in years to come.

I presented each of those four men with a zipped pouch of hundred-dollar bills for their work in delivering the six jihadists from the motor yacht *Scimitar* and into the waiting hands at Guantanamo Bay.

One of the former SEALs unzipped his bag and peered inside. He coughed and let out a low whistle. "There's enough cash in here to burn a wet mule."

Mongo punched Clark. "With wisdom like that, he must be kin to you."

The frogmen made their exit, and my team began an age-old ritual that Clint "Gator" Barrow had never witnessed. One by one, every member of the team, from Ronda No-H all the way to me, raised their right hand into the air.

I took Gator by the shoulder and turned him around to face the crowd of raised right hands. "Do you know what all those hands mean?"

"No, sir."

"It means every one of those brave men and women would gladly put their lives in your hands and proudly hold yours in theirs. Welcome aboard Tactical Team Twenty-One."

The young warrior either couldn't or chose not to speak. He just watched the hands slowly fall and reach for his to welcome him to the team.

When Kodiak made it to the front of the line, he said, "I can't tell you how much I appreciate what you've done for me."

Gator cocked his head. "What do you mean?"

Kodiak grinned. "This means it's official. I'm no longer the new guy."

When the revelry ended, Gator took my arm. "Can we talk?"

What I expected was for him to tell me how he didn't feel ready to be a full member of the team because he still had so much to learn, but that's not what came out of his mouth.

We found a quiet corner of the ship, and he took a long swallow of water. "I was going to be a safety in the NFL. I was one of the best in the country, and I was already getting nudges from recruiters. I'd made the decision to declare myself eligible for the draft when I returned back to school after visiting my mom and dad."

He paused, stared into the sky for a moment, and continued. "My dad and I spent the afternoon shooting targets on their property in Kansas. It was one of my favorite things to do with him. Anyway, we hadn't cleaned the guns when we came inside because Mom had supper ready, and we sat down to eat. When we finished, Mom got up to bring dessert in from the kitchen, but I told her I'd get it." He took another longer pause and bit his lip. "What happened next is hard to talk about."

I listened and didn't interrupt.

"While I was getting the dessert from the kitchen, four guys came through the front door like some crazed animals. They were waving guns and yelling. The guns my dad and I shot that afternoon were still in the mudroom, but there wasn't any ammunition left. I took a chance and tried to bluff the guys with an empty shotgun. It didn't work. They started shooting, and I ran back into the kitchen like a coward."

His eyes fell to the deck, and he went silent. He needed to talk, and I needed to hear him let it out, so in my softest tone, I said, "Go on."

"Well, the way our house was laid out, it had two entrances into the kitchen. One of them went into the dining room where my folks were, and the other one went into the living room. One of the guys with guns chased me through the kitchen and into the living room. That's when I saw the fireplace poker. It was like I was meant to run straight toward it. I can't explain it, but it practically jumped into my hand. The next thing I knew, the guy who'd chased me in there was dead on the floor with blood pouring from his head. Looking back now, I should've picked up his gun, but I was in some kind of trance or something, and that poker felt like an extension of my arm. All of a sudden, I wasn't afraid anymore. The coward who'd run back into the kitchen turned into something else, like I was on the football field. In what felt like the next second, I killed another guy with the poker and fought the two remaining guys with my bare hands until I broke one of their backs and almost beat the last one to death with my fists."

He took another drink of water. "When it was all over, my mom and dad were dead—shot a dozen times—and I was the only one left standing. I couldn't go back. You know . . . to school. I couldn't face it all. I knew I wouldn't be able to hear a thousand people asking me if there was anything they could do and how sorry they were. I just couldn't hear it."

His tone was rising, so I leaned in closer and just listened.

"I thought I'd lost it all—my family at home and my family on the football team. They were all gone, and I was alone. I never . . ." He waved a hand at our ship. "I never knew all of this existed . . . all of you. I never knew. What I've been through over the past two years has been . . . I don't know how to put it into words, and it's going to sound stupid, but I didn't know there was another family out here for me."

A tear escaped his eye, and he quickly wiped it away. "I know it sounds dumb, but that's what it feels like . . . a whole new family, just for me. You know?"

I'd listened to countless stories from more patients than I could name, but I'd never been moved like Clint Barrow touched my soul. I slid close to him, laid an arm across his shoulder, and spoke barely above a whisper. "The blood of sacrifice is stronger than the water of the womb. Every man you fought beside a few days ago has a story, just like yours. Just wait until Singer tells you his story. Mine wasn't a home invasion, but the family I have in this world is all aboard this ship, and I wouldn't have it any other way. You were born to play football, just like I was born to play baseball, but fate or God handed us a different future. Doing what we do will never put us inside a stadium full of cheering fans, but I promise you one thing. When we reach the end, however that end comes, we'll be able to look back, hold our heads high, and say we gave everything in defense of everything that matters."

Author's Note

As I do every time I speak directly with this group of amazing readers, I must thank you from the depths of my heart for making my dream of becoming a professional novelist come true. My editor will probably make a note in the margin to remind me that I've written that before, and she'll be right, but no matter how many times she reminds me, I'll never stop thanking you. I truly love being your personal storyteller, and I can't imagine doing anything else.

I like to start at the front, so let's talk about the cover. As many of you already know, I'm not the typical writer who plans how his stories will grow, rise and fall, twist and turn, and finally end. No, I don't do any of that. I just sit down and write a story for you as it falls out of my head. One of the weirdest parts of writing the way I do is the cover art for the next book. If you haven't already, you'll soon see the cover of *The Silent Chase*, and at the time of the writing of this author's note, I've not written a single word of that story. I don't know what it's about, how it will flow, or especially how it will end, but it already has a cover with a cool picture that is somehow tied to the plot.

The same thing happened with this book. I sent a picture of the Statue of Liberty to our wonderful cover designer, and, as she always does, she sent back another brilliant cover that I love.

Back then, I didn't know how the Statue of Liberty would play into the story, and just like the hot air balloon on *The Phantom Chase*, the book before this one, the new cover finally made sense. It took a while, but it worked itself out, and I love how it came together. There may come a day when it doesn't work, but for now, I'm having a blast playing Russian roulette with my covers. So, stick around, if for no other reason than to see if I can keep making it work.

How about Gator? I never know when a new character will show up. Prior to this book, Kodiak was the new guy, and I'm so glad he arrived on the scene. He adds an element to the team that was missing, and I'm having a great time writing him. Ultimately, Clark Johnson is going to get too old to stay in the fight, and I'll have to slip someone into his boots on the battlefield while Chase's beloved handler stays behind in the ops center. Maybe Clark's boots will fit Kodiak's feet. We'll see. Regardless of Clark's future, Gator is one of my new favorite characters. I love his willingness to do absolutely anything that needs to be done without question. He's brave, smart, strong, and he reminds me a lot of a young Chase Fulton. He is, in my opinion, an excellent addition to the team, and I hope you feel the same. I'm always open to talking about characters with readers, so please feel free to email any time if you love, hate, like, trust, fear, whatever one of my characters. I want your input. I want your opinions. Most of all, though, I want to create characters you enjoy.

The terrorist group, Burj Aldam, literally translates to Tower of Blood in English, but I made it up. To my knowledge, there is no such organization. It is purely a figment of my imagination, but I believe it to be a plausible possibility. I only try to write things that are possible, even if they aren't plausible. Likewise, Hamza al Kassis is based on no one and is entirely fictional. There may be a man with that name, but I don't know him, and

I hope he's a nicer guy than my fictional version. I'm also not picking on the Middle Easterners in general. I'm merely playing the odds. I have absolutely nothing against any race of people. I'll never judge a person based on an attribute he/she didn't choose. None of us chooses where or how we are born, our parents, or the economic conditions into which we are born. I base my judgments of a person's character on how he/she treats other people. Regardless of heritage, I have deep-seated ire for enemies of freedom, and that will never change.

Now it's time to talk about Liberty Island, the Statue of Liberty, and the National Parks Service Police. Although the geography of the island is accurate, everything else is completely made up. The brave men and women of the National Park Service police are great Americans . . . I assume. I don't know any of them, but I have no reason to believe any of them would become a co-conspirator in a plot to destroy the beautiful statue they're charged with protecting. As far as I know, there is no circumstance that would cause the police force to abandon the island, but I needed it to be empty for my storyline to work, so, once again, I made it up.

I have no idea if spraying massive amounts of water from FDNY fireboats would do anything to stop or even soften conventional explosions. I needed to cause chaos, confusion, and melee, so I used water. A lot of water. I suppose we can consider it one of Clark's tactical baptisms on a massive scale.

I was pleased and proud to use the NYPD in a noble and highly positive way in this story. They, along with their brothers and sisters of the FDNY, are heroes, and the people of New York City are fortunate to have such individuals serving and protecting them.

Since we've never talked about it before, let's have a chat about Guantanamo Bay. The base has a long and storied history that I won't retell here, but when you run out of cat videos to watch, I recommend having a look at the history of that installation. It's quite fascinating, and there's a strong probability that you hold opinions of the facility and what you believe happens there that are based solely on rumor, conjecture, and misinformation.

Here's my opinion of Gitmo: I believe America is worthy of protection and is the last true bastion of freedom on the planet. I believe we're a great nation with a great future, and that future should be guarded and given the opportunity to flourish. Sometimes, in the protection of freedom, it becomes necessary for men and women of valor and great fortitude to do things most of polite society cannot stomach or understand. These things are tragic and unfortunate, but as the worn-out cliché goes, freedom is never free. It comes at an enormous cost, and that cost is never pretty and is always eternal. Instead of lamenting the cost, I choose to celebrate the exceptional men and women who devote their lives to paying those prices on our behalf so we can sleep in peace instead of fearing the ever-present demons at our doorsteps. I hope for the day when such payment is no longer required, but until that day comes, I will continue to give thanks and pray for the men and women who stand between me and enemies at the gates.

Let's change gears and chat about something positive. You asked for longer books, so I delivered. This one is almost 15% longer than the typical Chase Fulton Novel. I didn't really do it on purpose. It just took me longer to tell this story than some earlier ones. I'll do my best to continue that trend, but as you know, I'm little more than a typist when the stories come rolling out of my head. You've also asked for more accompanying stories giving the details of individual characters' lives like I did with *Singer — Memoir of a Christian Sniper*. I'm kicking that idea around in my head, and we'll see if I can put something together.

Right now, though, Chase's stories are coming to my mind very quickly, and I'm smart enough not to squander them. Chase will remain my first priority, but as time and inspiration permits, I may create some more backstories for you.

After the release of *The Phantom Chase*, one of the most common email questions has been why Penny and Anya didn't share a scene to highlight the gift Anya gave to Penny. There are two answers to that question. The first one is a boring explanation of point of view, so we'll get that one out of the way first. I write the Chase Fulton Novels in first person limited point of view. That means everything that happens in the stories has to be seen, heard, or experienced by Chase; otherwise, it can't show up in narration or dialogue. That is one of the major weaknesses of writing in that point of view. I wasn't smart enough to understand that limitation when I wrote *The Opening Chase* so long ago and established the perspective for the series. I didn't feel I could write a scene between Anya and Penny and give it the weight it deserves with Chase eavesdropping. That just wouldn't be cool. The second reason it didn't happen is less boring and far less technical. It simply didn't come to me. I write what shows up in my head, and for some reason, the muse didn't deliver that scene . . . yet. Perhaps it'll show up in *The Silent Chase*.

Finally, I must remind you how precious and treasured the gift you've given me is. I love being your personal storyteller, and I have no plan to ever stop. I will continue to do everything in my power to create the best stories I'm capable of putting onto paper and getting them into your hands as quickly as possible. I have an outrageous goal for 2024 in terms of the number of words I will write and the number of books I will publish. I'm not willing to tell you the goal, but when 2025 arrives, I'll let you know if I hit the number. Until then, I hope you love every book you pick up, regardless of whose name is on the cover, and I look forward to hearing from all of you who take the time to email in the future. I love corresponding with readers, so please don't hesitate to drop a line. James Patterson and Stephen King probably won't write you back, but if you email me, I will. I promise.

—Cap
Cap@CapDaniels.com

About the Author

Cap Daniels

Cap Daniels is a former sailing charter captain, scuba and sailing instructor, pilot, Air Force combat veteran, and civil servant of the U.S. Department of Defense. Raised far from the ocean in rural East Tennessee, his early infatuation with salt water was sparked by the fascinating, and sometimes true, sea stories told by his father, a retired Navy Chief Petty Officer. Those stories of adventure on the high seas sent Cap in search of adventure of his own, which eventually landed him on Florida's Gulf Coast where he spends as much time as possible on, in, and under the waters of the Emerald Coast.

With a headful of larger-than-life characters and their thrilling exploits, Cap pours his love of adventure and passion for the ocean onto the pages of the Chase Fulton Novels and the Avenging Angel - Seven Deadly Sins series.

Visit www.CapDaniels.com to join the mailing list to receive newsletter and release updates.

Connect with Cap Daniels:

Facebook: www.Facebook.com/WriterCapDaniels
Instagram: https://www.instagram.com/authorcapdaniels/
BookBub: https://www.bookbub.com/profile/cap-daniels

Also by Cap Daniels

The Chase Fulton Novels Series
Book One: *The Opening Chase*
Book Two: *The Broken Chase*
Book Three: *The Stronger Chase*
Book Four: *The Unending Chase*
Book Five: *The Distant Chase*
Book Six: *The Entangled Chase*
Book Seven: *The Devil's Chase*
Book Eight: *The Angel's Chase*
Book Nine: *The Forgotten Chase*
Book Ten: *The Emerald Chase*
Book Eleven: *The Polar Chase*
Book Twelve: *The Burning Chase*
Book Thirteen: *The Poison Chase*
Book Fourteen: *The Bitter Chase*
Book Fifteen: *The Blind Chase*
Book Sixteen: *The Smuggler's Chase*
Book Seventeen: *The Hollow Chase*
Book Eighteen: *The Sunken Chase*
Book Nineteen: *The Darker Chase*
Book Twenty: *The Abandoned Chase*
Book Twenty-One: *The Gambler's Chase*
Book Twenty-Two: *The Arctic Chase*
Book Twenty-Three: *The Diamond Chase*
Book Twenty-Four: *The Phantom Chase*
Book Twenty-Five: *The Crimson Chase*
Book Twenty-Six: *The Silent Chase*

The Avenging Angel – Seven Deadly Sins Series
Book One: *The Russian's Pride*
Book Two: *The Russian's Greed*
Book Three: *The Russian's Gluttony*
Book Four: *The Russian's Lust*
Book Five: *The Russian's Sloth*
Book Six: *The Russian's Envy* (2024)
Book Seven: *The Russian's Wrath* (TBA)

Stand-Alone Novels
We Were Brave
Singer – Memoir of a Christian Sniper

Novellas
The Chase Is On
I Am Gypsy